William Osborn Stoddard

Grover Cleveland

William Osborn Stoddard

Grover Cleveland

ISBN/EAN: 9783337427139

Printed in Europe, USA, Canada, Australia, Japan

Cover: Foto ©Andreas Hilbeck / pixelio.de

More available books at **www.hansebooks.com**

THE LIVES OF THE PRESIDENTS

GROVER CLEVELAND

BY

WILLIAM O. STODDARD

*Author of "George Washington," "John Adams and Thomas Jefferson,"
"Madison, Monroe and John Quincy Adams," "Jackson and Van
Buren," "Harrison, Tyler and Polk," "Taylor,
Fillmore, Pierce and Buchanan," "Lincoln
and Johnson," "Ulysses S.
Grant," etc.*

NEW YORK
FREDERICK A. STOKES & BROTHER
1888

CONTENTS.

GROVER CLEVELAND.

CHAPTER XIII.

CHAPTER XIV.

CHAPTER XV.

CHAPTER XVI.

CHAPTER XVII.

CHAPTER XVIII.

CHAPTER XIX.

GROVER CLEVELAND.

TWENTY-SECOND PRESIDENT.

By WILLIAM O. STODDARD.

CHAPTER I.

The Cleveland Family—A Spreading Tree—The Eighth Generation—The Young Minister's Romance—A Country Parsonage—Birth of Grover Cleveland.

ABOUT a quarter of a century before the Washington family settled in Virginia, there arrived in the colony of Massachusetts Bay a man named Moses Cleveland.

In the year 1635 only a few scattered settlements along the Atlantic coast were held by the English pioneers. Only a very few clearings had been made above tide water on the bank of any river. The Canadas were held by the French, and they claimed also the vast interior, the lake country, and the valley of the Mississippi and its tributaries. The Spaniards had as yet no thought of ever losing any part of their possessions on the continent or among the islands. Great Britain herself was in the early dawn of her present greatness, and her American colonies had before them a century and a half of unceasing struggle with adverse circumstances ere they would be ready to set up for themselves. There was no man in that day so stark mad as to assert that they would ever do so, much less that they would yet own tenfold more American land than the King of England then asserted a right to govern. His government of the colonial patches was, indeed, undisputed by the colonists, but it was altogether unrecognized by the powerful tribes of red men, who resisted every advance of the white man's frontier as an invasion.

The colonists, as a whole, had come to the New World to found an empire of whose extent and character and power they could form only vague, indefinite imaginations.

Each particular colony had undertaken to found a State, a new province of Great Britain, quickly developing a sensitive jealousy concerning its char-tered rights, as against any usurpation by the mother country or any encroachment on the part of any other colony. Then and afterward there was no other political element more important or a root of greater events than that historic jealousy.

Each individual colonist, if a man of character and worth, like Moses Cleveland, came to the col-ony of his choice to found a family, and the history of this Republic groups itself very readily among the roots and the widely spreading branches of these old family trees.

Moses Cleveland came from the town of Ipswich,

Suffolk County, England, which had already sent out so many emigrants that one New England town had borrowed its name. He did not at once become a citizen, but deferred taking the '' freeman's oath'' required by colonial law until 1643. He married, September 26th, 1648, Ann Winn, daughter of Edward and Joanna Winn, of Woburn, where he made his home, and where he died, January 9th, 1701. The Cleveland family in America was founded, for seven sons and four daughters came to the Woburn homestead. Among their descendants there have been many good men and noble women ; citizens of every reputable occupation and profession ; farmers, mechanics, lawyers, and physicians ; sailors and ship captains ; soldiers and army officers up to the grade of major-general ; ministers of the Gospel and missionaries to foreign lands. Through generation after generation, among the older colonies and States, and as pioneers of new States that they helped to found and form, the descendants of the sons and daughters of Moses Cleveland were scattered far and wide, until the most distinguished of them all grew to manhood in a region which, in 1635, was held by a nation of red warriors strong enough to have swept away the infant colony of Massachusetts Bay.

The second son, Aaron, became a farmer, a house carpenter, and a man of property. The assessors valued his taxable estate at two hundred and twenty-one pounds, eight shillings, threepence, and that was almost wealth in those hard old days. He continued to reside at Woburn, as is testified by his

gravestone in the cemetery. The only clear glimpse
of his personal character is gathered from the tradition that Dorcas Wilson, whom he married, was
considered the belle of Woburn. Once more the
family tree flourished notably, for ten children came
to this one branch, without mentioning the fruitful-
ness of any other.

The eldest son in this third generation, Captain
Aaron Cleveland, made a home for himself at East
Haddam, in the Connecticut colony, in 1738, and
he was then already a man of wealth and family.
He had married, in 1702, a lady named Abigail
Waters, of Irish descent, whose personal charms
and accomplishments became one of the traditions
of the family. The captain is said to have made his
fortune mostly in land speculations. It was esti-
mated at his death at three thousand pounds, and
the fact that his income rendered any trade or. business unnecessary is indicated in the Haddam records,
which describe him as a " gentleman." Once more
the tree had many branches, for ten children gathered around the table of Captain Aaron Cleveland,
and most of these became pioneers, like their an-
cestors.

The seventh child in this fourth generation was
named Aaron, after his father and grandfather, and
he also grew to manhood as an Englishman. He
entered Harvard College at sixteen, was graduated
in 1735, studied theology, and became a minister of
the Presbyterian Church. After a useful pastorate
at Haddam, Conn., and another at Malden, Mass.,
a change of views led him to enter the ministry of

the Church of England. He crossed the Atlantic Ocean to be ordained in London, and returned to take charge of a parish at Halifax, N. S. He married, in 1702, Susannah Porter, herself the daughter of a clergyman of an old Massachusetts stock. Once more the olive branches were ten in number, and the country was in need of as many men and women of that kind as it could possibly be blessed with. Clearly and unmistakably is its patriotic tone and tendency indicated in the fact that its elder son, Stephen, was the first naval officer commissioned by the Continental Congress, and that its head was the warm personal friend of Benjamin Franklin. At the close of his charge at Halifax, Mr. Cleveland was appointed to the parish of Newcastle, Pa. On his way he made a visit to Dr. Franklin, at whose house he was taken ill and died. The obituary notice written and printed by the doctor himself, then editor of the Pennsylvania *Gazette*, testifies to the esteem with which he regarded his friend.

Like many another minister of the Gospel, Aaron Cleveland died poor. His widow returned to Massachusetts and, with the aid of friends, set up a small "store" at Salem. She managed to make a respectable living for her family, but as fast as they grew old enough they each in turn began to care for themselves. The second son, Aaron, was apprenticed to a hat maker. He served his full time, and then became clerk and general helper for a hatter at Norwich. He worked his way into a partnership, and then set up in business on his own account. His wife's maiden name was Alice Hyde, and thir-

teen children came to them. The young hatter was
an exceedingly energetic and capable business man.
At the age of thirty years he had acquired an independence. He also stood so well in the opinion of
his neighbors that they sent him to the Legislature.
He was one of the earliest of abolitionists, and emphasized his radicalism by introducing a bill for the
immediate abolition of slavery in the State of Connecticut. After taking an active part in politics,
this Aaron Cleveland also entered the ministry and
became well and widely known not only for his
usefulness, but for a vein of dry fun which made
him unpleasant company for scoffers. He died at a
good old age, in the year 1815.

A son of the abolitionist clergyman, receiving
the name of Charles, born in 1772, became a clergyman, and was during many years a city missionary
in Boston. He was widely known and honored as
" Father Cleveland." The next older brother of
the city missionary was named William. He was
the second in the long row of children, and was born
in 1770. He was, therefore, but six years old when,
in 1776, he ceased to be an English boy, and became
an American by the Declaration of Independence.
As he grew up he developed uncommonly good
mechanical capacity, and became an expert silversmith and watch maker. Many a long year afterward a grandson of his was assured by men who had
carried watches made by William Cleveland that a
Governor of New York would be a complete success if he could make the State run as well as one of
his grandfather's timepieces. They should, per-

haps, have noted that the governor did not make the State, nor could he take it in pieces and clean it and put it together again.

The silversmith married at the age of twenty-three, for his wedding with Margaret Falley took place in the week before Christmas, 1793. The greater part of his life was spent in Connecticut, but he finally removed to Black Rock, near Buffalo, N. Y., where he died in the year 1837. He was a man of high character, and was during twenty-five years a deacon of the Congregational Church. His first-born son died early, but his second grew to manhood. He was born June 19th, 1805, and was named Richard Falley Cleveland, and with him the history and tendencies and traditions of the Cleveland family became of special interest to all the people of the United States. He was a scholarly and thoughtful boy, taking such advantage of the schools provided for him that he was prepared to enter Yale College in 1820, although he had already been compelled to earn a part of his own support. He was graduated, with honors, in 1824, and had long since determined to become a minister of his own denomination.

In order to obtain an addition to his means of support during a three-years' course at the Princeton Theological Seminary, he obtained employment as a tutor in the city of Baltimore. He was only nineteen, too young to think of marriage, but not at all too young to be fascinated by the beauty and the many excellent qualities of Miss Ann Neale. Her ather was a gentleman of Irish descent, and held a

good social position.   He was a law-book publisher
and had other business affairs, but was not wealthy.
Nobody knows precisely how much or what was
said by Richard or by Ann or by her father during
that year of tutorship work in Baltimore, nor is
there any record of the use made of the vacations
in the three years' theological course at Princeton
which followed.   The days of probation came to an
end, however, and the scholarly young graduate of
the Theological Seminary received at once a call to
the pastorate of the Presbyterian Church at Windham, Conn.   It was true that the salary offered was
small, but then it was a beginning, and it was accepted.   Richard's pulpit work began, and ·after
only a few months of it he was ready for another
visit to Baltimore, in the Autumn of 1829.   Ann
Neale had loyally waited for him, and the long-
promised wedding took place.   It was a bright day,
full of promise, but not prophetic of this world's
wealth or honor.   The great, bright hope before
the young people was wonderfully pure and unsel-
fish, and it was realized, usefulness, happiness, trials,
and all.   As the years went by, no less than nine
young faces gathered around the minister's table
and fireside.   Five were girls, of whom four in due
time were married, and of these one went as a missionary to Ceylon.   Four were boys, and of these
one became a Presbyterian clergyman, two were
Union soldiers in the Civil War, and were afterward, in 1872, lost at sea ; while the other, fifth
child and third son, became President of the United
States.

The first pastorate at Windham, Conn., and a second at Portsmouth, Va., were followed in 1834 by a call to the Presbyterian Church at Caldwell, N. J., not far from the city of Newark. Mr. Cleveland was installed in December of that year with a salary of about five hundred dollars. The parish had long been under the care of Rev. Stephen Grover. He had even been the first occupant of the "manse," as people called the parsonage, into which his young successor now entered. It was a very comfortable home for a rural minister—a plain, old-fashioned two-story house, with tall trees in front and with about two acres of land belonging to it.

In this house, on March 18th, 1837, Stephen Grover Cleveland was born. He was named after the honored old pastor of the Caldwell church, as is testified by the parish record of births and baptisms, but he was never called Stephen. When he grew older, the one name by which he had been known from infancy seemed to him to be all that he required, and the other boys found "Grove" as good a nickname as "Steve" could have been. There was nothing whatever remarkable about the new baby, for he was even considered slight and small at first, although vigorously healthy. It must be said, however, that he came into the world surrounded by every necessary care and comfort, and with every advantage except wealth. His first three years were passed at the Caldwell parsonage, and then that home was exchanged for another every way as quiet and as rural.

CHAPTER II.

Central New York—Early Political Training—Going
to the Academy—A Noisy Bell—A Clerk at Twelve
—Habits of Study—More Schooling—Two Years
in a Country Store—Death of Rev. Mr. Cleveland.

IN the year 1841 Mr. Cleveland accepted a call to
the pastorate of the Presbyterian Church in Fayetteville, Onondaga County, N. Y. It was a small but
pretty village, a few miles only from what was then
the larger village and is now the city of Syracuse.
The houses were nearly all detached, with gardens
or grounds of their own, and were scattered along
one main street, with two or three short branches.
There were trees everywhere ; grass and mayweed
and dock and thistles had their own way with the
roadsides and fence corners, and even invaded the
sidewalks ; and it was not at all easy to mark the
line where any wayfarer passed out of the village
into the country. The marvellous prosperity of
Central New York had already made a good beginning, but its full tide had not come. Roads and
bridges were so defective that toll-paying " plank
roads" were constructed along the most frequented
highways, as if in memory of the corduroys which
had answered the purposes of the early settlers, and
had broken their wagons for them. There were almost no able-bodied paupers, but, on the other hand,
there were not many rich men. It was asserted, as

an evidence of the impossible things which might
come true in good times, that there were ten men
in Onondaga County who were each worth a hundred thousand dollars. That was a story over which
sober people shook their heads, but then it was a
remarkable county. At Syracuse, or rather in and
about that part of it which was then the village of
Salina, arose the salt springs which had made the
salt licks of Onondaga Lake a great resort for deer
and for Indian hunters of deer until the Iroquois
were broken and swept away. More salt water was
now obtained by boring wells, and a great industry
was springing up to build a city and to present vexatious questions of protection and free trade to the
politicians of the State and of the nation. East-
ward, not many miles, was the Oneida Reservation
and the "Oneida stone." Southward, a dozen
miles or so, was the Onondaga Reservation, where
a remnant of that once powerful tribe still lingered
around the spot where anciently had burned their
"sacred fire," and where still the pagan half of
their race met yearly to eat the succotash feast and
to burn the white dog to the Manitou of the Onon-
dagas.

Syracuse was the trading centre of the county.
Through it ran the Erie Canal, with several locks at
which boys and girls from the country used to stare
with breathless interest, for each boat that went
through seemed to use up half a pond full of water.
A branch canal ran northward to Oswego, and a
traveller by that could get to the shore of Lake
Ontario.

It was a great country for a boy to grow up in. It was not in any sense new, and some of the houses had moss on their roofs ; but there were plenty of genuine log houses back among the hills whose owners had not yet become sufficiently forehanded to build framed, white-painted dwellings with green blinds, such as might be lived in by men whose farms were nearer to market. It was not a new country, indeed, but it was very young and it was growing tremendously, while in no other part of the United States was there a greater degree of mental activity. It was said that more politics, such as they were, and more religion, such as it was, could be found within twelve miles of Salt Point than in the District of Columbia.

The first four years of any man's life are generally a blank to him, and Grover Cleveland's personal reminiscences may be said to have begun with his journey from Caldwell, N. J., to Newark ; across the ferry to New York City ; on a sailing vessel, a truly wonderful affair, up the Hudson River to Albany ; and thence by a swift packet boat, going often as much as six miles an hour, along the Erie Canal, to Manlius, in Onondaga County. He knew nothing at all of the overland trip to Fayetteville, for it took place during hours of darkness. The family arrived at their new home at about midnight, just in time to escape the peril of travelling on Sunday. Their household goods were not unpacked and put into the parsonage until Monday morning, of course.

Rev. Richard F. Cleveland's Fayetteville pastorate began with the Sunday sunrise. It was to continue during nine years, the very prime of his own life and usefulness, covering also, perhaps, the most important period in the development and formation of the character of his son Grover. The parsonage was a two-story, unpretending structure across the street from the village academy, and was itself the first and most important school. The preparation made in it for subsequent attendance upon the other school over the way began to bear fruit very early. It was natural that a taste for reading should come at once to a boy who learned how to read in such a home. It was also a matter of course that the political and social tendencies and ideas with which its atmosphere was pervaded should take deeper and deeper root year after year.

The common-school system of the State of New York was as yet in a somewhat chaotic condition. There were, indeed, what were called "district schools," but these were of widely varying and fluctuating standards of excellence. Most of them were taught in a straggling and haphazard sort of manner. They were, however, vastly better than no schools at all, and the right kind of boy could get something of value out of them. Their era of reformation and development was sure to come, and a present remedy for their known defects was found in the "academy," with which almost every considerable village was provided.

That of Fayetteville, like the rest, had its primary department, where boys and girls could be received as soon as they had elsewhere acquired the merest

rudiments of education. Grover Cleveland's earliest
recorded ambition was kindled by the idea of some
day becoming a student of the academy, but he had
to endure, first, a preparatory course of two years
in the very red, wooden, unbeautiful district school-
house.   He entered this, for the first time, when he
was eight years old, and the course of study he was
then pursuing included every right good place for
digging bait, or for enticing fish with it afterward,
which a small boy could obtain any knowledge of
and hope to profit by.   Nuts and berries and many
other important elements of natural history were
also receiving thorough and conscientious attention.
Day after day, during those two district school
years, Grover saw the favored students of the academy go and come to and from the dignified belfry
crowned structure so near to his own home, but
seemingly so far from him.   Many of them seemed
to be but a few inches taller than himself.   They
were getting wiser and wiser all the while, he knew,
and they had all sorts of fun, to which he was as yet
an outsider.   He begged his father again and
again for promotion from the district school to the
academy, but those few inches were in the way, and
so were a vague number of months of time, for Mr.
Cleveland had his doubts as to the propriety of such
very early scholarship.   Even in the cradle, however, it is said that Grover exhibited signs of uncommon persistency and strength of will, and his
life-long characteristic now came out buoyantly.
He looked and he longed and he envied day after
day, and he continued his ambitious petition until

his father yielded. The necessary books were procured, and then the academy benches received one more new boy. He was very young—barely eleven ; he was sturdy rather than large for his age, and he was brimming with exultation over the important victory he had won in getting there. He was just the boy to become popular among his mates. None of them were more fond of rough sports and games of physical strength, or more ready for any description of schoolboy adventure, in Summer or Winter. At the same time they discovered something very odd about him, for hardly any of them were in sympathy with his precocious liking for books—for even school books. A great many boys can comprehend another fellow's enthusiasm for " Robinson Crusoe," but it is not so easy for a boy who owns a kite and a ball club and a pair of skates to see much beauty in the books which ought to be the only ones in his desk.

The older children of the Cleveland family were already attending the academy before it was entered by Grover, and the younger followed in regular succession. All were well spoken of by the neighbors, but Cecil was understood to be doing uncommonly well in mathematics, while Grover was really distinguishing himself by his rapid progress in Greek and Latin.

A tendency toward reading implies a disposition to the kind of seclusion which any interesting book calls for, but that was the only uncompanionable trait in Grover's schoolboy character. Once the book was put away, he was as ready for fun as was

any other youngster in Fayetteville, and those of
near his own age were even willing to acknowledge
a kind of leadership that was not at all weakened by
his superiority in the recitation room.

There was one dark night, for instance, when the
good people of the village were startled from their
slumbers by the untimely clangor of the academy
bell. It did not seem to be ringing for fire or tolling
for a funeral, but was going on in an insane, tumultuous rattle of its own invention. Everybody knew
that the academy door was locked, that the win-
dows were closed, and that the bell had been shut
up for the night, with no business before it until nine
o'clock next morning.

It was not altogether the fault of the bell. An
examination detected a rope attached to its hammer, and that rope went out from the belfry window
to the branches of a tree many feet from the building. Grover Cleveland and his brother William
were at the end of the rope, and there is no precise
record of the remarks which were made to them
about it.

The school days passed busily and merrily away,
and came to an end in 1849. Grover had won for
himself an exceedingly good reputation as a bright,
intelligent, and trustworthy boy. The family was
large, however, and the minister's salary was moderate. It was necessary for its younger members to
begin early to think of contributing to the common
fund and to prepare for making their own way in
the world. Grover was only twelve years old, but
he was eager to do his part. Deacon McViccar, of

his father's church, kept a "country store" in the village, and was ready to give the minister's son an opportunity. The establishment contained the customary assortment of commodities—drugs, dry goods, patent medicines, groceries, and whatever else the deacon could foresee a customer for among his neighbors. Grover had been about the youngest boy at the academy, and now he became the youngest merchant's clerk in Fayetteville. He had not by any means abandoned his books, however. The love of them had grown with his growth, and he now gave to them all the hours which were not demanded by Deacon McViccar and his customers. There were not many other boys just entering their 'teens who worked as hard all day and then pored over printed pages to so late an hour in the evening. He won the esteem and good will of his employer, while he persistently continued the educational process which was preparing him to profit by every opportunity which the course of events might afterward offer him.

Only a little more than a year was passed in this first employment, and the unknown future had in store a rapid succession of changes. The Cleveland family had been more than commonly united, husband and wife, brothers and sisters, deserving and receiving sincere and devoted affection ; but it was soon to be scattered. The first premonition came in the failing health of Mr. Cleveland, rendering regular pastoral work severe and burdensome. He was glad to accept an offer of duties under the American Home Missionary Society, with a salary of a thousand dollars a year and a residence at Clinton, N. Y., where his sons could avail themselves of the preparatory school, of Hamilton College, and of Houghton Seminary.

The removal to Clinton was made in 1851. The elder son, William, was already in the college, from which, in due time, he went out to follow his father's profession and keep up the clerical traditions of that branch of the Cleveland family. The rest of the family settled at once in their new home, but Grover took advantage of the kind of vacation given him to make what was for him an exceedingly important journey. He had an uncle named Lewis F. Allen, who owned a great stock farm near Buffalo, N. Y., away off in the dim western regions along the shore of Lake Erie, and a visit was determined upon. It was a romantic pilgrimage for a boy to make, and it was filled with all sorts of adventures going and coming. Five or six weeks were expended among the varied attractions of the Allen farm, the grand fishing to be had near it, and the great sights to be seen along the Niagara River. No wonder was it that Grover's pocket money almost all ran away from him. He did not ask his uncle for any, but managed to work his way home along the canal, making friends as he went. That journey, as a whole, was but one stage in a trip he as yet knew nothing about. On his return he entered the preparatory school, fully expecting to pass from it into college. He had been doing almost too well with his books, and he now studied harder than ever. He was ready to pass the required examination before the right year of his life arrived, and his childhood victory in the matter of the academy could not be repeated at Hamilton. His father suggested to him that he had been giving his mind to his studies after a fashion which rendered a change advisable, and that he might profit by temporary attendance at a school of practical business. The family finances had also something to do with the fact that Grover applied for and obtained employment as a clerk once more in the store of Deacon McViccar, at Fayetteville. The cash part of his remuneration was to be fifty dollars the first year and one hundred dollars the second, and the father's heavily burdened strength was sensibly relieved. He needed relief, for his new duties were by no means light in the hands of a man who could not help attending to them with conscientious fidelity. It was among their unpleasant features that they required much travel, with frequent and protracted absences from home ; and what Mr. Cleveland's health demanded was repose.

Grover finished his two years in the Fayetteville store, giving entire satisfaction to his employer, reading diligently, and making a man of himself, while the other children also grew, walking in right paths, and the older of them were fast becoming men and women. At the end of the time contracted for, the clerk returned to Clinton, hoping to become again a scholar ; but he was disappointed. His father had determined to give up his position under the Home Missionary Society, for which he no longer had physical strength, and to accept a call to

the pastorate of the Presbyterian Church at Holland
Patent, a village on the Black River Railroad, a few
miles north of Utica, N. Y. He had been failing,
failing, but neither he nor his family had any idea
but what a change, less work, less care, would enable him to rebuild and to continue the good work
to which he had given himself. The new home was
reached in September, 1853, but it was not to contain, even at the first, the entire family. William
had obtained a position as instructor in the Institution for the Blind in the city of New York ; Ann,
the elder daughter, was already married, and the
second daughter, Mary, was making preparations
for her wedding. Another change came quickly
and unexpectedly.

The pastor preached in the village church one
Sunday, and the next, and the next. The wedding
was to take place that week, and Grover and his
sister Mary drove over to Utica one day to make
some of her required purchases. They were walking in a street of that town when a sombre message
which had followed caught up with them. Their
father had passed away, and their widowed mother
needed them at home. A shadow and part of the
heavier responsibilities of human life had fallen
very suddenly upon a boy of sixteen.

CHAPTER III.

*A Year in New York City—Ambition Taking Shape
—A Friend in Need—Westward Ho!—An Uncle
Worth Having—Short-Horn Literature—Rod and
Gun.*

LIKE many another faithful pastor, Richard
Falley Cleveland died poor. To the small property
he left behind him, the good people of the churches
in Fayetteville, Clinton, and Holland Patent added
the gift to his widow of the homestead in the latter
place, and here she remained until her appointed
time came.

All the children of the Cleveland family had been
brought up with a clear idea that they were to work
their own way in the world, but some of them were
too young to make a beginning when their father
was taken away. The rest were ready to help their
mother and each other, but they could not accomplish anything worth while by remaining at home.

The Institution for the Blind, in which William
was an instructor, was managed by a board presided
over by Hon. Augustus Schell, long well known and
influential in the political and business circles of
New York. With a little help from him, Grover
also obtained immediate employment as an accountant and assistant instructor in the institution.
It provided him with the means of support for the

time being, but it offered no opening for the future. It was a temporary makeshift, and that seemed to be all ; but it was not so.   A boy so bright, already so uncommonly well prepared to receive impressions and ideas, could not possibly remain, as Grover Cleveland did, during an entire year, in such a place and among such surroundings, without undergoing educational processes as important as they were exceptional.   Apart from the more subtle effects upon mind and character to be produced by daily association with and observation of the people who knew no difference between day and night, it was ' in after time to be of value to the general welfare that the son of Pastor Cleveland was early made, familiar with the methods and management of great public charities.   Moreover, up to this time he had been a country boy, brought up in a little rural world—parsonage, school, congregation, village— which was certainly very good, but which was necessarily narrow.   The great city was now around him, with its palaces and its poverties, with its commerce, and its business, and its politics, and its confusing Babel of all the nations of the earth mingling in one community.   It was an epitome of the great world, and the boyish eyes that studied it were by no means blind.   They saw whatever they could see without any cash outlay, but not any of the amusements or pleasures of the metropolis which involved expense, for every cent which could be saved by close economy went to eke out the slender resources of the widowed mother in her country home.

Too much of life could not be spent in such a manner by a youth into whom the idea and expectation of rising in the world had been instilled from his very cradle. His vague ambition was beginning to take the shape of a determination to become a lawyer, but how that was to be accomplished was apparently an insoluble problem. It was, at all events, one which could not be solved in the New York Institution for the Blind, and the great city itself seemed to offer no opening. All its pathways were thronged, and a crowd of applicants waited before every door of possible opening. There was said to be more room and there might be a better hope for an enterprising boy in the West, if he could find means for getting there. Grover pondered the matter well, and, at the end of the year, he gave up his position in the institution and went home to his mother's house in Holland Patent. She, of course, could give him nothing more than her loving sympathy and her advice, while money was required for a fortune-seeking journey. It was a good thing for a boy in such a strait to have inherited a good man's name and the honor belonging to it, and to have established for himself a high character. Capable men who have made money are apt to know how to keep it, and any liberality they may have does not go out to the vicious, the reckless, and the shiftless. There is a high degree of pleasure to be obtained in helping a young fellow, but it sours into disgust if he does not then go ahead and help himself. When Grover Cleveland applied to Hon. Ingham Townsend for a loan of twenty-five dollars to

carry him westward he was precisely the boy to
obtain it, almost as a matter of course, from a man
who was known to be fond of lending a helping
hand. Mr. Townsend's terms as a money lender
were peculiar. Grover was not really expected to
return the money, but if, in after time, he should
find another young fellow in need of a lift, as he
himself was then, the money, if Grover should be
able to spare it, was to be transferred to him upon
similar conditions. It may be that Mr. Townsend
borrowed the idea from Benjamin Franklin, who
sent a number of small sums upon their benevolent
travels in very much the same manner. Grover
gave his note, as a matter of form, and he kept his
contract in more ways than one. He does not seem
to have made any report of the sums of money,
smaller or larger, which he gave or loaned to the
young or the old during the next dozen of years,
but at last Mr. Townsend received from him the
following letter, dated at Buffalo, N. Y., January
23d, 1867 :

" I am now in condition to pay my note which you hold, given
for money borrowed some years ago. I suppose I might have paid
it long ·before, but I have never thought you were in need of it,
and I had other purposes for my money. I have forgotten the
date of the note. If you will send me it, I will mail you the principal and interest. The loan you made me was my start in life,
and I shall always preserve the note as an interesting reminder of
your ·kindness. Let me hear from you soon. With many kind
wishes to Mrs.·Townsend and your family, I am yours, very re-
spectfully,

" GROVER CLEVELAND."

Ingham Townsend lived to the age of eighty-one

years, dying in 1883, after he had seen the boy to whom he had given a "first start in life" elected governor of the State. The phrase contains a fallacy, after all, since if Grover had not already made a very good start indeed he would not have received that twenty-five dollars.

There was another boy in Holland Patent who had made up his mind to go West, and Grover had company when he set out. He had decided not to waste any of his precious money, and he searched through the young city of Utica for any kind of work that would help him in his plan. He sought there in vain, went on to have a similar experience in Syracuse, and then determined to try Buffalo, although the destination really in his mind was the city of Cleveland, O. Whether or not he was attracted by the name as well as by the well-understood prosperity of the latter place, he had made up his mind that it must contain a law office into which he could manage to work his way. He had no friend there, not even an acquaintance, and his plan of operation was to the last degree cloudy and undefined. The very fact that he had formed it, however, and the courage and force with which he was proceeding to carry it out, won for him at once his next step upon the ladder of success.

Grover Cleveland had already made one memorable visit to Buffalo, and he could not now pass through without going to see his aunt and uncle. Mr. Lewis F. Allen was a lawyer by profession and a farmer and stock breeder by preference. He was a man of high social standing, good financial circumstances, and of uncommon intelligence. He became in after days a radical Republican in politics, and was elected to the Legislature by that party in his district.

The suburb of Black Rock had not yet been absorbed by Buffalo, and Grover left his young companion in the city, while he walked out into the country to see his relations.

The Allen homestead was a handsome, solidly built stone house of two stories, and was every way an inviting place for a boy visitor. Only a part of Mr. Allen's farming and breeding operations were carried on at this place, however, for he had another establishment, with a farm of about one thousand acres, on Grand Island, in the Niagara River, where he kept a herd of about fifty short-horned Durham cattle, which were his especial pride. The house itself, standing at no great distance from the river bank, had been built, in 1817, by General Peter B. Porter, Secretary of War in the Cabinet of John Quincy Adams, and afterward a major-general of New York militia during the War of 1812. Without and within it bore testimony to the character and the tastes of its present owner. The rooms were commodious and well furnished, and it is declared that there were books, books, books, everywhere.

Here the young adventurer, going West to study law, received a warm and appreciative welcome. In a spirit of sturdy self-reliance, if not of boyish pride, he had not come to ask for any help from his uncle. He did not ask for any, and it was offered to him in an exceedingly acceptable shape. Mr. Allen had his own opinion of the fortunes and misfortunes of the Cleveland family, or rather of that branch of it of which Rev. Richard F. Cleveland had been the head. He is reported as saying at a later day :

" Grover's father was a good man. He was highly respected as a minister, and was a preacher of fine abilities. But his modesty killed him—I mean that he didn't have push enough. He was conscientious and devoted to his work, but he could never take advantage of his opportunities for advancement. He never got along in the world as he might have done if he had been a little more worldly. He had a large family. After he left college he went to teach school in Baltimore, and found his wife there. They had nine children. Cecil and Fred, the two who were lost at sea, went into the army when the Civil War broke out. All the daughters are living. Four of them are married. The youngest one has inherited her father's literary abilities."

Unworldliness and diffidence had stinted the prosperity of the father, in his opinion, but here was one of the sons with " push" enough to carry him right out into a strange country, afoot and alone. It was an appeal to precisely the right spot in the heart of a self-helpful man like Mr. Allen.

" Stop here, my boy," he said. "·The law business is of no use in Ohio. If you stop here, I will try and find you a place."

He added that he had work enough for such a boy, in his own house and study, to keep him busy until the following Autumn, at a fair compensation, and that it would be time enough then to hunt up a law office.

So good an offer was closed with at once, and

Grover walked back to the city, found his companion, explained the change in his plans, and said
good-by to him, for he went on westward, according
to his original purpose.

So, in the Spring of the year 1855, the road to a
law office began to open through a noble stock farm
and through a miscellaneous mass of papers from
which Mr. Allen was laboriously compiling the second volume of " The American Short-Horn Herd
Book." Grover was diligent, painstaking, and
every way capable of relieving his uncle of a large
part of the drudgery entailed by such a work. He
did his share so efficiently that his connection with
it was not permitted to cease with that volume.
Six years later, when the fifth of the series was
printed, Mr. Allen said in its preface :

" In the compilation of the second, third, fourth, and fifth volumes of this work, I take pleasure in expressing my acknowledgment to the kindness, industry, and ability of my young friend and
kinsman, Grover Cleveland, Esq., of Buffalo, a gentleman of the
legal profession, who has kindly assisted my labors in correcting
and arranging the pedigrees for publication ; and to him is a portion of the credit due for the very creditable display which our
American short-horns make before the agricultural public."

The herd book may have been somewhat tiresome literary digging, but the stock farm itself fully
justified the enthusiasm of its owner, while the
shooting and fishing to be had were the best that
Grover had yet known, and he was as healthily fond
of both as ever. When he had work to do, he did
it well, as his uncle testified of him, but when he
and his cousins could get over upon Grand Island,

most of their work was done with rod and gun. There was, after all, something like a vacation and a long picnic about that Summer of 1855, passed in so pleasant a home, with such friends, relieved from care as to the present and almost as to the future. No wonder that health and spirits rose to running over and that Grover meddled with strange oxen until he was kicked across the stable, or with a big muscalonge until they had to pry open the creature's mouth with a stick to rescue a badly bitten finger. Short-horns, or strange fish, or the heaps of books in his uncle's library—whatever came in the way was sure to be investigated persistently. The five months required by the volume undergoing compilation slipped away with great profit to mind and body, and left Pastor Cleveland's son in excellent condition for beginning a much longer and more difficult apprenticeship than that which he had in this manner served to agricultural literature. Of the sixty dollars cash earned, the greater part went to the widowed mother at Holland Patent.

CHAPTER IV.

Cleveland a Law Student—All Night among the Books—The Drift of Politics—Admitted to Practice—First Success—The Civil War—Two Brothers in the Army and One to Care for their Mother— Steady Advances.

LONG before Autumn arrived Grover had won a fixed and settled place in the good-will of his uncle. Mr. Allen knew all the lawyers in Buffalo, as he himself asserted, and he pondered well beforehand his nephew's choice among them. He selected a gentleman named Hibbard, who was entirely unaware of the compliment thus paid him, and who received the young applicant for a clerkship in a manner which cut off the application at once. There was probably no intentional rudeness, but Grover, although only eighteen, was a trifle high-strung, and he thought he heard a reason for turning on his heel and instantly leaving Mr. Hibbard's office. The latter did not even guess what sort of clerk he had missed getting ; and Mr. Allen, on hearing Grover's report, expressed a gruff determination to make the next inquiry in person, instead of sending his too sensitive nephew. As he relates the matter :

"Then I went to town and saw Rogers—Rogers, Bowen & Rogers it was then ; they are all dead now but one, who is in

Europe—and asked him if they didn't want a boy in the office. Rogers said they 'didn't want any one, though they liked smart boys. I told him there was a smart boy at my house who wanted to come in and see what he could do. ' Well,' said Rogers, ' there's a table,' pointing to one in a corner. That's the way Grover went into their office. Rogers took him in as a favor to me, without seeing the boy at all. But they soon found out he was smart, and then they wanted to keep him. I told them to pay him what they could afford to pay.''

No pay at all came until after the new clerk had fully proved his value to the office, but his circumstances were by no means unpleasantly straitened. In after years Mr. Allen's indignation was hotly aroused over sensational stories printed concerning the hardships and privations which his young relative had undergone in his desperate struggles to obtain a legal education. He was as well dressed as other young men, for his uncle had a pride about that, and paid for three or four suits of clothes as they were needed. During the first part of his relations with Rogers, Bowen & Rogers he continued to board with his uncle, and the only drawback was the walk of two miles, going and coming, since part of the way was over a badly made and badly kept country road, which might at times be a slough of mud and at other times heavily drifted with snow. The walk was duly taken, however, storm or shine, and it was noted that no other person about the office was more regularly punctual than was the new clerk and student. There was but one other law student and a copyist, and these managed to give Grover a remarkable experience at the very outset of his legal career. The head of the firm, the senior

Mr. Rogers, was a man of few words, except, perhaps, before a jury or in engineering a point of law.
His first indication to the new-comer of a course of
study to be pursued consisted in banging down before him upon the table the first volume of Blackstone's Commentaries, remarking : " That's where
they all begin !"

Whether or not the story belongs to that very
day and night, Grover picked up the book and began. It was not a novel, but it was absorbingly interesting to a youth who regarded it as the gate
through which he must pass to success in life, to
wealth, and to honorable fame. There was no
doubt but what he yet would master a treatise
which for the hour so completely mastered him. It
was for more than one hour, however. He forgot
all about the time of day, and the other people in
the office, lawyers and clerks, forgot all about him.
They completed their own tasks, locked the doors
behind them, and went away to whatever else might
be waiting for them. Young Cleveland knew nothing of their going or of any other mundane matter
but Blackstone's Commentaries, until the fading
light warned him that he must tear himself away
from that book. Then the locked doors informed
him that for one night he was to be imprisoned,
without supper or breakfast, and with no better
company than a large law library and the accumulated papers of the firm's extensive practice. He
knew that the family out at Black Rock would wonder what had become of him, and he was sure of
being made fun of when let out next morning, but

"THERE'S WHERE THEY ALL BEGIN"

he had a remarkably fine opportunity for silent and solitary meditation over what he had been reading and over any and every other subject which might come to him for consideration.

The board and clothing which he received from Mr. Allen did not come in a manner to offend a spirit of independence, for work upon the herd book went on from time to time. There was simply no money in the young man's pocket, and he could well afford to wait a while for that to come. Up in the morning for an early breakfast. Off in all weathers in time to be punctual at the office. Scrupulously diligent there in the discharge of every duty placed upon him and in further delving into Blackstone and his fellows in the law library. All the way back to Black Rock for supper and for an evening over his uncle's papers, or any reading which might take their place. There was no time for mere amusement, but the obstacles to success in life gave way rapidly before such iron industry.

One day, not long after the course of law study began, Mr. Allen asked his nephew how he was getting along.

"Pretty well, sir," said Grover, "only they don't tell me anything."

Mr. Allen was determined that that boy should have everything that belonged to him in any man's law office, and he went at once to his friend Mr. Rogers with what seemed to him so serious a complaint. "If the boy has got any brains," replied the crusty counsellor, "he will find out for himself without any telling."

No better satisfaction could be had, and young Cleveland was compelled to find his own way through the tangled wilderness of legal learning. During two entire years the compensation allowed him did not rise above four dollars per week. Then higher duties came and better pay, and a small attic room was hired in the Southern Hotel, in Buffalo. It was by no means equal to the pleasant quarters out at Black Rock, but there was a saving of time as well as of toil in escaping from so long and rough a walk. It was a hotel much patronized by cattle dealers, among whom the sub-editor of the "Short-Horn Herd Book" already had many acquaintances. He now continued his habit of early rising, and his breakfast was generally eaten with the drovers, by candle light at some seasons. The little attic room was a capital place for study, and its tireless occupant had no fear of any interruption after reaching it. He possessed an uncommonly tough and vigorous constitution, strengthened now by long years of thoroughly good and regular habits, and he found it capable of enduring without harm the merciless drain of the work he put upon it.

Political party excitement ran very high in the first year which Grover Cleveland passed with the Buffalo law firm, but he was not yet a voter, and he could do no more than hear and read and watch the course of events. The National Democratic Convention met in May, at Cincinnati, and nominated James Buchanan for President and John C. Breckinridge for Vice-President. The People's Party, which quickly took the name of Republican, held a

National Convention at Philadelphia on June 18th, and nominated John C. Frémont for President and William L. Dayton for Vice-President. The remnant of the old Whig Party, taking up the candidates previously named by the Convention of the American, or Know-Nothing Party, nominated, in September, at Baltimore, Millard Fillmore and Andrew Jackson Donelson.

The Whig and Democratic press and public speakers were agreed in one vehement declaration that the success of the Republican Party then or at any subsequent Presidential election would bring upon the country civil war and the dissolution of the Union. The Republicans replied that no such consequence ought to come or would come and that a question relating to human rights could not be decided by a threat or even a peril of violence. The political campaign ended in the election of Mr. Buchanan, but the Republicans secured one hundred and fourteen electoral votes out of two hundred and ninety-six, and it was evident that they were rapidly gaining strength. They had exhibited much more than any but their most sanguine leaders had expected.

The first year of Mr. Buchanan's administration went by without any perceptible lull in the general excitement. Events in Kansas and the course of legislation in Congress were strengthening the Republican Party at the North and feverishly stimulating the development of the Secession movement at the South. All over the United States, during that year of hot debate and anxious forecast, thou-

sands of young Americans became of age and prepared to form their first political affiliations.
Among them was Grover Cleveland, and with the
year 1858 began his active membership in the Democratic Party. ·He did more than merely go to the
polls and vote at the November election.   He went
with a pocket full of tickets and remained at the
polls all day, as a volunteer distributor, a service for
which his hearty and genial manners peculiarly
qualified him.   There is a social and political evil
in the fact that too many bright young fellows
feel a sort of unwholesome reluctance in following so excellent an example, or have no political ideas and convictions to sustain them in such
an exhibition of patriotic energy.   Grover Cleveland's work for the party in whose usefulness he
believed did not cease with that first day at the
polls.   He made a continuing practice of faithful
attendance on election day from that time forward
until he was chosen governor of the State.   He
thereby made himself widely acquainted with his
fellow-citizens, and the rigid fairness with which he
served his own party and his repudiation of trades
and tricks with tickets won him an important degree of confidence among his immediate antago-
nists.. He was in full accord with the Democratic
Party as it then existed, and he was vigorously preparing for usefulness in a political future which none ·
could then foresee.

Another year went by, and in May, 1859, four
years after beginning his course of study, Mr. Cleveland was admitted to the bar.   He had won the en-

tire confidence of his employers, and they now placed him in charge of the office, with what was considered the very good salary of six hundred dollars a year, speedily raised to one thousand. A gentleman who was at that time one of his office associates afterward wrote of him :

" Grover won our admiration by his three traits of indomitable industry, unpretentious courage, and unswerving honesty. I never saw a more thorough man at anything he undertook. Whatever the subject was, he was reticent until he had mastered all its bearings and had made up his own mind, and then nothing could swerve him from his conviction. It was this quality of intellectual integrity more than anything else, perhaps, that made him afterward listened to and respected, when more brilliant men who were opposed to him were applauded and forgotten."

To have an established position and a sufficient support immediately upon admission to the bar is a success which does not come to many young lawyers, and Grover Cleveland was but twenty-two years of age when he reached this result of his persistent study and work. It placed him at once in the front rank of the younger members of his profession in the city of Buffalo, and gave his admiring uncle and aunt good reason to be proud of the manner in which they had taken him up. It is said that he had very little of the " personal magnetism" ascribed to many men who achieve eminence and to some whose winnings are not altogether desirable, but he had a noteworthy faculty for attracting to himself the strong good will of the best men with whom he became associated. Year by year the circle of these esteems and friendships widened, and

it was well, with reference to a large part of them,
that he held aloof from extreme partisanship in
politics and gave himself entirely to the business in
his hands.

No man of any force of character, nevertheless,
could fail to take a distinct political position of
some sort in Erie County in the years 1859, 1860.
It had been an ancient stronghold of the Whig
Party, and had sent Millard Fillmore, year after year,
to the State Legislature and then to Congress, and
it now contained thousands of men who fully agreed
with him in his earnest prophecies of trouble to
come.   Not a few who, at least half way, believed
him added sturdily, "Let it come," and passed
over into the swelling ranks of the Republican
Party.   Among these was Mr. Allen himself, but
not his nephew, and when the party lines were
drawn for the campaign of 1860, they found themselves upon opposite sides of the great question of
the day.   One section of the Democratic Party,
standing alone for that campaign only, nominated
Stephen A. Douglas for President and Herschel .
V. Johnson for Vice-President.   The Whigs who
in 1856 had voted for Millard Fillmore now dropped their old party name and reappeared as the
Constitutional Union Party, with John Bell and
Edward Everett as their candidates.   Both of these
political factors, Whig and Democratic, were to
be quickly absorbed by the two great parties, to one
of which every man among them really belonged.
Of these, the Republican Party, already controlling
a large majority of the Northern States, nominated

Abraham Lincoln and Hannibal Hamlin, while the regular "old line" Democracy nominated John C. Breckinridge and Joseph Lane. Every vote cast in a Northern State for either Douglas or Bell might nearly as well have been cast for Lincoln, so far as the electoral college and the Presidency were concerned. That of Grover Cleveland was not among them. He was faithful to the doctrines he had already imbibed, and he acted with the party which, in his opinion, offered the only hope of escape from the evils threatened by a Republican success. Now that all is over, it is easy to discern that any such hope was fallacious, that the moral and social forces in operation in 1860 were too powerful for possible control, and that the time of an inevitable revolution had fully come. The political crisis was not then so easily to be comprehended, and the Republican Party itself contained not many men who would have voted as they did if they had at all believed that the Sumter gun, the campaigns of the Potomac, the Mississippi, the Cumberland, the Tennessee, and the James were to follow. Even the most conservative Democrats had no prophetic anticipation of the vast proportions of the Civil War, but they voted for Breckinridge and Lane and against what they termed a sectional party, and then and afterward they preserved in vigorous activity a political organization whose inestimable value to the country is evident to every student of constitutional government.

Law business went on as usual in the office of Rogers, Bowen & Rogers, in the courts of Erie

County, and in the other courts throughout the United States during the political campaign and through the sombre Winter which followed. Then Spring came, and Lincoln was inaugurated, and the thunder of the coming storm began to mutter among the heavy clouds along the Southern horizon. Day after day and week after week it became more plainly evident that disunion meant forcible secession and that the doubtful slave States were drifting helplessly into the great tide that was sweeping all on toward what seemed to be a national shipwreck. The fall of Fort Sumter came at last, and the first call for troops, and the battle of Bull Run, and then the startled, staggering, wrathful but relentlessly determined nation, through its chosen and lawful President and its Congress, shouted its ringing summons for five hundred thousand volunteers.

There were four brothers in the Cleveland family, sons of Pastor Cleveland, but the elder son, William, was a minister of the Gospel, and only three were liable to military duty.

It was plain that a time had come when every young American owed service to his country, without reference to any party vote he ever had cast or yet might give, and the three brothers considered the matter. Grover was in a position which would enable him, better than the others, to contribute to the support of their widowed mother, and he had also more to lose than they by breaking up his business connections. It was decided, therefore, that Richard Cecil and Lewis Frederick should answer

the call for volunteers and that Grover should remain a civilian. Taking the country through, there
were not many families whose membership did better than this.

The volunteers marched away, the war went on,
with its varying record of disaster and success, and
all the political elements at the North which had
predicted and dreaded its coming drew together in
a strong and solid opposition which criticised, denounced, and at times almost hampered and hindered the party in whose hands was the administration of the Government and the direction of the
armies. Between the two political extremes, mod-
erating each in turn, was a fluctuating mass of conservative men, some of whom were known as War
Democrats and some by other names. Among these
it is safe to class the young Democratic Buffalo lawyer, who had two brothers in the army and who
would have been there himself if not prevented by
a manifest and sacred duty.

From somewhere among these first years after
Grover Cleveland was admitted to practice and before any great prosperity came to him there has
floated down a legend in explanation of the fact
that he afterward so long remained a bachelor. It
is a story of a fair face that frowned and then that
smiled, and of a light that passed away—of a white
stone and a green mound in the cemetery. It is
one of those closed doors along the corridor of life
before which biography will not linger, because of
the withered moss-roses that are scattered on the
threshold.

There are anecdotes, more or less authentic, relating to skilful management of law cases and a singularly methodical and faithful performance of dry details of professional business. There are other floating waifs which tell of social qualities, personal kindliness, and liberality. Putting them all together, they do but indicate in the usual way the well-known processes through which a rising man steadily obtains the hold upon his fellow-citizens which they themselves at last discover and make of public or party use.

CHAPTER V.

Mr. Cleveland Assistant District-Attorney—Drafted as a Soldier—A Defeated Candidate—Rising at the Bar—Elected Sheriff—Two Executions.

MR. CLEVELAND'S duties in connection with the business of Rogers, Bowen & Rogers were of a limited nature, and did not constitute him in any sense a member of the firm.   He was, therefore, free to accept and attend to any private practice which might offer.   Some did offer, from time to time, and was managed in a manner which gave him the confidence of his clients and their friends, while winning the professional approval of older practitioners.   There is rarely any opportunity for brilliant display in the minor cases which drift within the reach of a very young lawyer.

In 1863, the fourth year of this mingling of office work and general business, the information that an assistant district-attorney for Erie County was soon to be selected went the rounds of the Buffalo law circles.   It was an appointment much to be desired by any young lawyer, as opening a pretty sure gate to reputation and practice.   There were, of course, a number of bright young men eager to obtain the prize, and they and their friends for them reached out for it as best they might.   There was, nevertheless, a kind of undertone of common opinion, making itself heard, that Grover Cleveland was the right man for the place. He made no effort, presented no application, keeping aloof from the current discussion of the matter, while the claims and qualities of the several aspirants were almost necessarily compared with his own. The result of such a process of the selection of the fittest brought him an unsought offer of the appointment. He was able to accept it, therefore, without bringing upon himself any of the injurious consequences of a rivalry and a contest.

There were especial reasons why the Buffalo bar desired an assistant district-attorney from whom they might expect diligence and capacity. The law did not require that the district-attorney himself should be a resident of the city of Buffalo, where most of the business of the office was transacted. Mr. Cyrenius C. Torrance, who then held the position, was in delicate health, and his home was at Gowanda, a country village thirty miles from Buffalo. So far, therefore, as the ordinary routine of work might be concerned, Grover Cleveland became district-attorney, and all his ambition was aroused to the thorough performance of every duty which Mr. Torrance was compelled to leave in his hands. He began to make his mark at once. Case after case, as he took it up, in its order, was handled in a manner which testified to the good results of previous fidelity. Nothing was permitted to take him away from the increasing and even oppressive demands of his public duties. While in the office of Rogers, Bowen & Rogers, members of the firm and others had frequently invited him to their houses, and in other ways had tried to draw him out into society. It was not only a testimony of their personal esteem, but a kindly expression of their idea that he was confining himself too closely to the hard-work part of human life. He had almost uniformly refused to be turned aside, even in so pleasant a manner, from the one aim before him, and he now did the same. Cordial and kindly to all who came and ready to respond heartily to every friendly greeting, he had that upon his hands which demanded every hour of time and every ounce of strength, and to all social enticements he gave a courteous but firm denial.

The course of the Civil War and the management of national affairs by the Lincoln administration and by the Republican majority in Congress during the years 1861 and 1862 had been greatly misunderstood by the people of the country. The very magnitude of the terrible struggle for national life and unity confused the minds of men. All disasters to the Union arms were painted darkly, while the most important successes, vitally affecting the final result, were either undervalued or ignored. The burdens of the war, its awful cost in human life and in what seemed fabulous treasure, sickened the very hearts of a multitude. The South was putting forth its utmost strength, heroically, and it was needful that the Union armies in the field should be renewed and heavily re-enforced ; but volunteers did not now come forward as at the first. Even heaped-up bounties did not offer a sufficient stimulus.

The Autumnal elections of 1862 sent out a voice of political warning also. The Democratic Opposition, absorbing now the conservative elements of the old Whig Party, notably the Fillmore Whigs of Erie County, N. Y., gained a strength which gave it the control of several Northern States and of many important municipalities. One of the seemingly minor and almost unimportant fruits of the political change had been the election of Mr. Torrance to be District-Attorney of Erie County, that Grover Cleveland might receive his first public employment in the following year.

President Lincoln and the strong men who stood around him were equal to the emergency. Warned by the soldiers of the South and by the voters of the North that the war must be pushed with even the vigor of desperation, the response of the national Executive and the national Legislature was grandly energetic. Already, September 22d, 1862, just before the adverse elections, the President had issued his first Proclamation of Emancipation, and the second followed at the end of the specified ninety days. Another proclamation declared the suspension of the Writ of Habeas Corpus in specified cases arising in connection with the Civil War. The succeeding session of Congress strengthened the national finances by the National Bank Act and by other measures, and provided unlimited re-enforcements for the army by the Draft Act. A year of unprecedented military activity was planned, and it was well understood that 1863 would witness a trial of strength between the contending forces which

the South, at least, could never hope to repeat, unless her arms should prove phenomenally successful.
The machinery of the Draft Act was prepared with
extraordinary rapidity and efficiency, and in mid-
Summer it began to reach out its iron hands for its
harvest of living men. The successive measures of
the Administration were bitterly, wrathfully criticised by the orators and press of the Opposition.
There were muttered threats of forcible opposition
to the draft in many places. In New York City its
enforcement was made the occasion of a riot, in
which fourteen hundred men were killed, but there
was little real trouble elsewhere. The day for its
pitiless lottery came in Buffalo, and the first name
drawn from the wheel was that of Grover Cleveland.

There could not be one moment of hesitation as
to what was his duty as a patriotic citizen. President Lincoln wanted one more rifleman, tallying
with that slip of paper drawn from the wheel containing the list of serviceable citizens of Erie County.
He did not especially require an assistant district-
attorney who already had two brothers in the
army. Mr. Cleveland quietly provided a substitute,
as permitted by the law, and went on with the increasing mass of important public law cases in his
hands. The fact that he was now the sole support
of his mother received a pointed commentary in the
fact that the money required to procure a substitute
was borrowed of Mr. Torrance.

Mr. Cleveland's duties as assistant district-attorney began with the year 1863, at a salary of
only six hundred dollars, the real advantages ex-

pected being strictly professional and largely in the future. His moderate partisanship, in connection with his efficient services as a " working Democrat," were given yet another recognition in that year. The old Second Ward of Buffalo contained a large German population, and was Republican by a pretty regular majority of about two hundred and fifty. The local Democracy insisted upon nominating Grover Cleveland for supervisor, without much idea of electing him ; but, to the astonishment of all men, he only fell short of success by thirteen votes, while the rest of the party ticket was as badly beaten as ever. Perhaps there were shrewd political managers in Buffalo even then who took notes for future reference concerning a man who could bring out all the strength of his own party and at the same time borrow votes from the other side.

The military events of the year 1863 included the victory at Gettysburg and the complete success of General Grant's campaign in the West, but their effect upon the popular mind was not fully comprehended until the close of the Presidential campaign of 1864. It was a matter of course that Abraham Lincoln should be renominated for President by the Republican Party. Andrew Johnson was named with him for Vice-President. The Democratic Party drew into its ranks every element of Northern opposition to the Lincoln administration, expressed its criticisms and complaints vehemently in its platform, but nominated as its candidate for President General George B. McClellan, with George H. Pendleton, of Ohio, for Vice-President. They were able to win but twenty-one votes in the electoral college against two hundred and twelve given to Lincoln and Johnson, and they failed to elect a sufficient number of members of Congress to answer the purposes of legislative "opposition" required for political health under all known forms of constitutional and representative government by the people.

With the year 1865 the official term of Mr. Torrance, and so of his energetic assistant, was to expire by limitation, and there was no question whatever as to who should then be the Democratic candidate for district-attorney. Mr. Cleveland was nominated, as a matter of course, in the hope that his personal popularity and his known fitness for and familiarity with the duties of the position might carry him through, in spite of the disaster which the party had suffered in Erie County at the election in 1864. He ran very well, although he positively refused to take any personal part in the canvass. He attended court and argued cases while his friends electioneered for him. They did their best, but the odds against them were too great, and his close personal friend, the Republican candidate, Lyman K. Bass, was duly elected.

It was no disaster whatever to Grover Cleveland that he was defeated in the canvass for district-attorney. He had won all that he could win in connection with that office, and it was time for him to strike out into general practice. His course during the years in which he had been in charge of a large and important part of its business had given him a very desirable prominence before the public as well

as a good rank at the bar, and it was certain that
private practice of all sorts would now come to him.
His arrangements for business were speedily made,
and he formed a partnership, in January, 1866, with
Isaac K. Vanderpoel, a lawyer of excellent standing and reputation, formerly Treasurer of the State
of New York. The firm of Vanderpoel & Cleveland
continued until August, 1869, when it was dissolved
by the election of its senior member as Police Justice of Buffalo. A new firm was formed at once,
consisting of A. P. Laning, Grover Cleveland, and
Oscar Folsom. They were warm personal friends
as well as business associates, and this, too, was yet
to be an important factor in the career of Mr. Cleveland. The firm of Laning, Cleveland & Folsom
found its hands at once full of important business.
In that very first year, 1869, they were counsel for
the defence in the most noted libel suit which, until
then, had occurred in that part of the State—that of
Hon. David S. Bennett against the Buffalo *Commercial Advertiser*. The damages claimed were one
hundred thousand dollars, and the various points at
issue—the nature of the case, the standing of the
parties, the business interests involved—all attracted
to it an uncommon intensity of popular interest. Its
management was especially in the hands of Mr.
Cleveland, and to him, in general estimation, was
given the credit of gaining an unexpected triumph
for his clients and, at the same time, for correct
business methods and for the freedom of the press.
There are a number of cases on the docket during
1868, 1869, and 1870 whose importance, character,

and history go far toward explaining what would otherwise be the enigma of the strong position held by Mr. Cleveland in the city and county at this early day. It was a kind of strength deserving a careful study by the managers of political parties, for it is readily and thoroughly understood by the clear-headed common people of America. Once it is gained, to any exceptional degree, by any man in one county—for instance, in Erie County—any other county, to whose voters the fact and its nature are made plain, becomes as the first county with reference to that man. Men feel that they know him, and they speak of him as an acquaintance and a neighbor, and unless they are altogether opposite to him in their political opinions, they are very likely to vote for him as soon as an opportunity offers. Daniel Webster's genius and learning do not present so strong an appeal for the confidence and support of a voter who can form no satisfactory mental picture of them and to whom their possessor looms up as a kind of myth, rather than as a familiar and friendly human being.

In the year 1870 the Democratic Party was aware that the Congressional district constituted by Erie County was Republican by a small and doubtful majority, which might be overcome by judicious nominations and a vigorous canvass. It possessed a strong candidate for Congress in Hon. David Williams, the manager of the Lake Shore Railroad, but any important defect in the list of minor candidates to be voted for at the same election would probably defeat the ticket. This was, therefore, made up with great care. The second office in rank among those to be filled was that of sheriff. The shrievalty nomination was probably to be the turning point between success and failure. The party managers had only one problem before them, and they solved it. They needed a man, well known throughout the county and particularly in Buffalo, against whose personal and business character no just criticism could be made. He must be a Democrat whose party record was without flaw, that he might draw out the full strength of his own somewhat jealous and exacting party. He must at the same time be a man who had not, by extreme partisanship, made it impossible for him to obtain a few hundred votes which might otherwise be cast for a Republican.

It was what is sometimes termed "an off year" in politics, midway between two Presidential campaigns. In the great contest of 1868 General U. S. Grant had been elected President and Schuyler Colfax Vice-President, with two hundred and fourteen votes in the electoral college, but thirty-three of the eighty electoral votes given to Horatio Seymour and Francis P. Blair were those of the State of New York. There were everywhere indications that the old Civil War party lines were breaking, and the Democracy throughout the country determined to send more of its own men to Congress in 1872.

The post of Sheriff of Erie County was known to be very lucrative, and it carried with it an amount and kind of political influence which rendered it sure to be fought for with all the force of the party which already held it. In order to carry the key and central point of the political battlefield, the thoughtful party leaders decided to nominate Grover Cleveland, as being the one man who united in himself all the understood requirements for success. This decision was reached without any consultation with Mr. Cleveland. When the District Convention met and the unsought nomination was made, he strongly protested against the use of his name. Defeat might be in many ways injurious, while success would compel him to give up the growing law practice that was fast fulfilling the boyish dream which had brought him to Buffalo in 1855. His friends, in reply, frankly explained to him the situation, and he was induced to put aside his personal objections. The canvass was made, and a Democratic victory resulted. Mr. Williams went to Congress, and Mr. Cleveland became Sheriff of Erie County on January 1st, 1871, leaving the law business of Laning, Cleveland & Folsom in the hands of his partners. His connection with them could not be instantly and entirely severed, but his new duties prevented his taking, thenceforth, any very active part in the current practice of the firm.

As expected, the sharpest fight of the campaign had been over the sheriff, and not over the Congressman. Mr. Cleveland succeeded by a majority of only about one hundred, but it was distinctly understood that the usual Republican majority had been overcome by a sufficient number of the members of that party, who discerned reasons for preferring the Democratic nominee.

There was a surprise in store for all concerned, for Mr. Cleveland himself expressed surprise at his own election, and then proceeded to remodel the methods of transacting the affairs of the sheriff's office. During a long series of official terms, and in the hands of Whigs, Democrats, or Republicans, there had been an order, or rather a disorder, of things full of loopholes for gross favoritism, extravagance, and corruption. Mr. Cleveland had not come to steal, directly or indirectly, nor was he disposed to permit questionable practices in any part of his official domain. There were men in his own party who imagined that the customary spoils would simply change their destination and be apportioned among good Democrats instead of among equally good Republicans, but they were to be disappointed. The contracts for county supplies, for instance, were no longer awarded by favor, but to the lowest bidders, in fair and public competition, to the great benefit of the county treasury, while every department was subjected to a rigid and business-like censorship, which killed off old-time frauds.

The better elements of both parties looked on approvingly, while certain other elements of each muttered and grumbled. Special care was taken in selections of minor officials connected with the office, and the deputy in immediate charge of it was Mr. W. L. G. Smith, a gentleman of respectable literary attainments, who had been United States Minister to China under President Buchanan.

The term of office for which Mr. Cleveland was elected covered the years 1871, 1872, and 1873, no incumbent being eligible for a consecutive re-election. Although now receiving a considerable income, he made no change in the quiet, bachelor habits to which he had so long been accustomed. He did not even take a more active interest in local politics or exhibit any desire to become better known as a party manager. He had been almost forced into the position which he now held, and he had no ambition which could induce him to act the part only too well known to American electioneering as that of " Boss."

The sheriff of a county has the charge and care of all criminals convicted in the county courts, and in this department also Mr. Cleveland is said to have effected desirable improvements. One duty came to him here, however, which presented a singular test of his steadiness of nerve, or, perhaps, of the entire absence from him of the kind of shuddering sentimentalism which can almost pride itself upon turning over to another hand a disagreeable or painful duty. The laws of the State of New York do not provide for the creation of the social outcast known in other lands and times as the public executioner, the " headsman" or the " hangman." The terrible death penalty is rarely exacted, but in the few extreme cases in which the judge, and the jury, and the State Executive agree that a criminal must no longer live, a mournful effort is made to surround the place of execution with a sombre dignity and solemnity. When the simple but ghastly machinery of a scaffold is all in place for its grim function and the condemned felon stands upon the drop, with the rope at his neck, the end comes with the quick severing of the cord which retains in place the weight or fall. The cutting of that cord is, therefore, the taking of human life. It seems to be done by the hand which holds the axe whose edge comes down upon the hemp, but in that hand are concentrated the moral and legal responsibilities of every official, high or low ; of every detective, or witness, or lawyer ; and of every unknown agency in any manner contributing to the awful result. The jury, and the judge, and the governor, and the sheriff cut the cord as one person, whether or not the latter shrinks from a positive, physical performance of his last duty and commits it to the hand of a temporary deputy, hired at a high price from among the men who are less sensitive in the matter of taking human life. Sheriff Cleveland was unable to discern the imagined sentimental elevation of an officer of the law lifting his hand or dropping his handkerchief, as a signal to another man, above that other man who, at that signal, dropped an edge of steel upon a releasing cord. In the two capital cases which occurred during his term of office he performed the final duty himself, but in each case he accomplished first an important public service. In one, while making no undue effort to secure a pardon, which was plainly not merited, it was at his instance that the governor caused a special inquiry by medical experts as to the sanity of the convict. In both a judicious effort was made on behalf of decent privacy and in resistance of the morbid, pernicious curiosity which is accustomed to haunt the last scenes of a criminal tragedy.

From month to month and from year to year, even the murmurs of the dissatisfied assisted in making the general public uncommonly well acquainted with their sheriff and with the surprising course that he was taking. He went out of the office, at the end of his term, with a very large augmentation of the peculiar reputation and strength which had caused his nomination and secured his election.

There was one interruption to the toilsome routine of Sheriff Cleveland's attention to public duties. His brothers Cecil and Frederick had become lessees of the Victoria Hotel, at Nassau, and had looked forward to an abundant prosperity. One dark day, in the year 1872, however, the news came that the Steamer Missouri, upon which they were passengers, had been burned at sea, and that they had perished with the rest. It was necessary for Mr. Cleveland to leave his office to his deputies during about six weeks, that he might make a mournful voyage to the Bermudas and settle the affairs of his kindred. He went and returned, making his first and only acquaintance with the ocean.

CHAPTER VI.

Defective Financiering—The First Case in a New Law Practice—Capacity for Work—Death of Oscar Folsom—Old Law Cases—Preparing for a National Reputation.

ON leaving the sheriff's office, Mr. Cleveland returned, without any parade whatever, to the law. His old-time practice, with its business connections and channels of increase, had long since passed away from him. He was now in very good circumstances, from former earnings and from the accumulated, unexpended fees of the shrievalty. He would have been a man of considerable property if it had not been for certain noticeable defects of character. One of these, testified to by his partners and associates, was his incapacity for charging and collecting his fees. He simply did not know how to get out of a fat case the professional winnings which might be in it and which it would have yielded to a lawyer of better capacity in that particular field. Another serious flaw in his financial management was a weakness for undertaking the causes of poor men and for paying the current outlays from his own funds. One of his partners, Mr. W. S. Bissell, is reported as saying, years later :

" I am now closing up a case of Cleveland's which has been running on for years, during all which time he has paid all disbursements, such as costs of entry, witness fees, etc., out of his own pocket, because the man was too poor to meet these necessary expenses. And this is only one case out of many that are here on our books. I have often told him that he had no right to accept the praises of the press and the public for his incorruptibility in office, because it was nothing to the credit of a man who cares nothing for money."

Another defect, less serious than these in its injury to his bank account, was a known disposition to keep his old contract with Ingham Townsend and to send out twenty-five dollars, more or less, without any hope or expectation of ever seeing the money again.

In spite of all these drawbacks, which continued to operate in after time, Mr. Cleveland made a new beginning as a lawyer in the month of January, 1874, entirely independent of any immediate profits from his practice. His first case brought him no fee nor any advance of his reputation at the bar. A poor woman, an utter stranger, living out in the country at some distance from Buffalo, came to him with a story of a mortgage upon her home. It was due—overdue, and it was about to be foreclosed by its too grasping owner. The property would be sold under the hammer at a ruinous sacrifice, and she and hers would be left homeless and in poverty. Her husband was sick, unable to attend to work or business, and she had come to Mr. Cleveland for advice in her last extremity. The sum required of her was about fourteen hundred dollars, and she had not even enough to pay a respectable fee to a lawyer for telling her, perhaps, that the law must take its course. Mr. Cleveland gave her very good ad-

vice. He examined the case, and told her to sit
still. Then he went to his bank himself, drew out
the money in greenbacks, hired a horse and buggy,
and sent a messenger to tender payment to the
holder of the mortgage. Her home was rescued
very easily, and there are those whose convictions
would incline them to the idea that such a first case
was an uncommonly hopeful beginning. It is said
by an ancient writer, "The liberal soul deviseth
liberal things, and by liberal things shall he stand."

At about this time an entirely new law firm was
constructed. It consisted of Lyman K. Bass, the
successful Republican candidate for district-attorney
in 1865 ; of Grover Cleveland, the defeated Democratic candidate in that year ; and of a gentleman
named W. S. Bissell. The firm name was Bass,
Cleveland & Bissell, and it was speedily overrun
with business. Two years afterward, in 1876, the
health of Mr. Bass failed, and he went to Colorado
for its restoration, leaving the firm " Cleveland &
Bissell," to be joined, in 1881, by Mr. George J.
Sicard.

During the three years of his term as sheriff of
Erie County Mr. Cleveland had not in any wise
ceased to be a lawyer and a laborious student of
law. He returned to his chosen profession not
rusted by inactivity nor under any necessity of
stumblingly catching up with the times. He was
rather rested and ripened and better than ever prepared to succeed in undertaking business of a high
grade and winning for himself an honorable rank
at the bar. That of Erie County had, from early

days, included some of the most capable lawyers of the State, or of the United States, among whom and in trials of capacity with whom both original and acquired power were requisite to obtain distinction. The position at this time and afterward attained by Mr. Cleveland has been well defined by Hon. George W. Clinton, a son of Governor De Witt Clinton, Vice-Chancellor of the University of New York and Chief Judge of the Superior Court.

" As a lawyer," says Judge Clinton, "he was known both as a counsellor and an advocate, and he often appeared before a jury. In his jury addresses he never fired over the heads of the jury in rhetorical eloquence. He addressed himself to them directly, as an honest, sensible man speaking to his fellows, and he won his verdicts by his close and full arguments and his thorough knowledge of all the evidence in the case. He was strictly honorable, and never endeavored to take petty advantages of the opposing counsellor of the jury. So keen was his sense of honor and justice that it would have been against the grain of his character to have tried to mislead a jury, if justice was opposed to him. I certainly never knew him to make the effort. When he began practice his reputation as a lawyer was respectable. It rose gradually among the profession until, at the time he became mayor, he may truthfully be said to have been eminent at the bar of Erie County."

An all-important element of the swift success which now came to the ex-sheriff was to be found in the unimpaired and exceptional toughness of a constitution which enabled him to endure extraordinary toil without exhibiting outward signs of fatigue. One of the gentlemen at this time associated with him has recorded, concerning his capacity for work :

" He [Mr. Cleveland] was the most industrious man I ever knew in any department of life. I have often said to him that I could not work as he did. Time after time he would remain here all

night in the office working on his cases. . . . He is, moreover, the most self-reliant man I ever saw. When he was here he
never wanted people to assist about him. What he had to do he
would do himself."

So had it been from the beginning, from the time
when a persistent little fellow in a very short jacket
succeeded in becoming a scholar in the Fayetteville
Academy.   Whatever resources of mind, or body, or
of circumstances had been given him, he had made
the most of them, courageously and tirelessly, and
success followed as a necessary result.

In the year 1875 occurred a sad event, which, in
terminating suddenly another life, may have prepared the way for the future entrance of a new element into that of Mr. Cleveland.   The junior partner in the old law firm of Laning, Cleveland & Folsom, Mr. Oscar Folsom, was one of those exceptional men for whom their personal friends feel an
attachment strongly resembling that of kinship.   He
was a graduate of the University of Rochester,
where he had distinguished himself for scholarly
qualities, at the same time that he was about the
most popular man in his class.   After entering the
legal profession he rose rapidly and seemed to have
before him a career of brilliant and solid success.
In the latter part of July, 1875, however, he was
thrown from a carriage, in a runaway, and was almost instantly killed.

A meeting of the bar of Erie County was promptly
called.   It was presided over by Judge Daniels of
the Supreme Court, and was addressed by a number of distinguished gentlemen, eloquently express-

ing deep feeling over so startling a termination of so bright a life. Mr. Cleveland was called upon, and there was something peculiarly touching in the tribute which he paid to the memory of his friend. At the same time, no better example can be given of his oratorical power, apart from his trained capacity for explaining a law point or making a clear argument before a dull or listless jury. It was altogether unpremeditated, but was carefully reported for the press.

" It has been said, ' Light sorrows speak, great grief is dumb,' and the application of this would enforce my silence on this occasion. But I cannot go so far, nor let the hour pass without adding a tribute of respect and love for my departed friend. He was my friend in the most sacred and complete sense of the term. I have walked with him, talked with him, ate with him, and slept with him—was he not my friend?

" I must not, dare not recall the memories of our long and loving friendship. And let not my brethren think it amiss if I force back the thoughts which come crowding to my mind. I shall speak coldly of my friend ; but the most sacred tribute of a sad heart, believe me, is unspoken.

" In the course of a life not entirely devoid of startling incidents, I can truly say I never was so shocked and overwhelmed as when I heard, on Friday night, of the death of Oscar Folsom. I had an engagement with him that evening, and was momentarily expecting him when I received the intelligence of his injury ; and before I reached the scene of the accident I was abruptly told of his death ; I shall not attempt to describe my emotions. Death seemed so foreign to this man, and the exuberance of his life was so marked and prominent, that the idea of his dying or his death seemed to me incongruous and out of place. And before I saw him dead I found myself reflecting, ' How strange he would look, dying or dead.'

" I had seen him in every other part of the drama of life—but this—and for this he seemed unfitted.

" His remarkable social qualities won for him the admiration of all with whom he came in contact, while his great, kind heart caused all to love him who knew him well.   He was remarkably true in his friendships, and having really made a friend he 'grappled him with hooks of steel.'   Open and frank himself, he opposed deceit and indirection.   His remarkable humor never had intentional sting ; and though impulsive and quick, he was always just.   In the practice of his profession and in the solution of legal questions he saw which was right and just, and then expected to find the law leading him directly there.

"It is not strange to find joined to a jovial disposition a kind and generous heart ; but he had, besides these, a broad and correct judgment and a wonderful knowledge of men and affairs ; and the instances are numerous in my experience when his strong common-sense has aided me easily through difficulties.   Such was my friend.

"The sadness of his taking off has no alleviation.   I shall not dwell upon the harrowing circumstances.   On Friday afternoon Oscar Folsom, in the midday of life, was cherishing bright anticipations for the future.   Among them, he had planned a home in an adjoining town, where he calculated upon much retirement and quiet.   He had already partially perfected his arrangements, which were soon to be fully consummated.   Within forty-eight hours he reached the town of his anticipated residence.   But God had intervened.   The hands of loving friends bore him to a home, but not the home he had himself provided.   He found peace in the home that God provides for the sons of men, and quiet—ah ! such quiet—in the grave.   I know how fleeting and how soon forgotten are the lessons taught by such calamities.   'The gay will laugh, the solemn brow of care plod on, and each one as before pursue his favorite phantom.'   But it seems to me long, long years will intervene before pleasant memories of his life will be unmingled with the sad admonitions furnished by the death of Oscar Folsom.

"Let us cherish him in loving remembrance and heed well the lesson of his death ; and let our tenderest sympathy extend to a childless father, a widowed wife, and fatherless child."

His own course with reference to these was yet to prove the utter sincerity of his utterances before the Buffalo bar.

There is nothing generally interesting in old law cases. Their dry mummies, in the form of court records and heaps of old papers, seem as if there could never have been any life in them ; yet they all once belonged to the lives of men and women. They are dramas, many of them tragedies, of hope and disappointment, of strife and sorrow, of passion and of crime. The career of any busy lawyer, notably such a career as had thus far been that of Grover Cleveland, needs but to be put into story by a skilful hand to exceed in interest any possible creation of a novelist. Imagination falls short of the reality, always ; but these true stories will never be told, for who shall read and interpret the hearts on both sides of any case and trace the relation of their stilled or quickened beatings to the dry and formal papers and the action of counsel and of court ?

Year after year, in a long succession of cases, lesser and greater, Mr. Cleveland firmly established his reputation as one of the leading lawyers of Western New York. As one of his professional friends remarked of him, "He was the strongest man I ever knew without a national reputation."

When such a statement can truthfully be made of any man, it is hardly less than a prophecy of national fame to come, for the individual making the assertion cannot have been the only keen-eyed observer who has discovered so important a fact. There were really several thousands of men, in Buffalo alone, who had already formed very much the same opinion and were only waiting a suitable opportunity to give it practical expression, by ballot or otherwise.

CHAPTER VII

Politics after the Civil War—The New Vote—The New Democratic Party—Mr. Cleveland Talked of for Alderman—Elected Mayor of Buffalo.

IT was necessary that a new generation should arise before the United States could come out from under the dark shadow of the Civil War. It was almost necessary that the old generation should entirely pass away. Strangely enough, some of the worst effects of the great struggle were thrown off vastly more readily by men who had borne arms on either side than by other men who had but talked or written about the war. There were sound reasons, beyond any dispute, for the nation's decision, at the polls, that its government should, for a time, at least, be carried on by the men who had conducted the war to a successful conclusion. Equally wise, however, were the local constituencies who were beginning to strengthen the hands of the hitherto almost overwhelmed Opposition in Congress.

This Opposition retained, from political necessity, the name of the Democratic Party, although it now included men who had sat in the Chicago Convention of 1860 ; many who had been prominent supporters of the Lincoln administration ; with a long list of the best soldiers of the Union armies. In most of the Southern States it held an unquestionable preponderance—from its curious inheritance of the entire " secession" vote—which was detrimental to the best interests of those commonwealths and to the position of the party at the North.

In the year 1872, while Mr. Cleveland was sheriff of Erie County and took no unduly active part in politics, although working steadily and efficiently with his own party, the Presidential campaign was less vigorously contested than usual. From its beginning to its end not many men had any serious doubt of a Republican victory, but thoughtful politicians studied the election returns for indications of the drift of public opinion and for omens of the political future.

The Republican Party renominated General Grant for President and named Senator Henry Wilson, of Massachusetts, for Vice-President. The Opposition declared itself a coalition of the regular Democratic Party and the Liberal Republicans, and nominated Horace Greeley for President and B. Gratz Brown for Vice-President. Undoubtedly a large number of dissatisfied Republicans voted for that ticket, but a vastly larger number of Democrats, who took no interest in such an election, quietly remained at home. In 1868 the popular vote had shown an almost parallel rate of increase for both parties, with the advantage in favor of the Democracy.

In 1872 the popular vote seemed to say that while the Republican Party had gained five hundred and eighty-one thousands of voters, the Democratic Party had gained only one hundred and twenty-four thousand. The death of Mr. Greeley before the

meeting of the electoral colleges of the several
States yet farther disturbed the elements for making calculations. The electoral votes gave the
prophesied result even more decisively than had
been expected : two hundred and eighty-six for
Grant and Wilson ; forty-two for Thomas A. Hendricks for President and forty-seven for B. Gratz
Brown for Vice-President, and the remainder scat-
tering confusedly. The coalition had failed to
carry any Northern State. It had not really been
a coalition. It had been rather a marvellously blind
and blundering attempt to discover and to organize
the elements which all competent politicians knew
to be in existence for a strong and efficient Opposition. One of those elements would not support a
memory of the secession movement, in the person
of any leader, Northern or Southern. Another
was as positive in its rooted aversion to any memory of abolitionism, represented, for instance, by
even so moderate and capable a man as Horace
Greeley. Yet another important element saw or
felt that the right time had not come, and if it
voted at all it did not urge anybody else to do so.
The executive and the legislative branches of the
National Government were apparently turned over
by the people, to the compact and powerful party
which had saved the Union and the life of the nation ; but the reaction had but been delayed, and
in the Autumn of 1874 the House of Representatives contained a strong Democratic majority. The
Presidential term wore away, and 1876 came, and once
more the Republican Party and the Opposition held

their national conventions, but in the mean time tremendous changes had taken place. In 1872, out of three hundred and sixty-six electoral votes, seventeen for President and fourteen for Vice-President had been rejected for reasons growing out of the as yet defective reconstruction of the Southern commonwealths. In 1876, Colorado, with three votes, having been added, there were to be three hundred and sixty-nine electoral votes, with no known reason why any should fail of being counted. Minor elections throughout the country showed that the Republican Party had lost nothing in numerical strength, but at the same time proved that the Opposition was making greater relative gains and taking vast strides toward power. It was grasping the lion's share of all naturalized immigrants, and it was sweeping in every form and shade of disaffection with the long and stringent rule of the old Republican Party. Evidently a new political era was dawning, and the most sagacious calculators and prophets confessed that the future was an insoluble problem.

The Republican Party nominated Rutherford B. Hayes for President and William· A. Wheeler for Vice-President.

The Democratic Party nominated Samuel J. Tilden and Thomas A. Hendricks. There was an omen of coming trouble, however, in the almost chaotic condition of the Southern vote and in the fiercely jarring factions of the Republican Party. The Opposition did not as yet feel strong enough to indulge in the luxury of factions. There had been a Democratic Party, just before the Civil War, which had elected Abraham Lincoln by insisting upon running two candidates of its own, and the lesson was not likely to be soon forgotten. The returns of the election of 1876 were startling. The Republican Party had gained four hundred and thirty-six thousand eight hundred and eighty votes over its record for 1872, while the Democratic gain was one million four hundred and fifty thousand eight hundred and six, and it held a majority of more than a quarter of a million above its old antagonist. This majority, however, was not so distributed as to insure a preponderance in the electoral college. There was, at first, an apparent decision in favor of the Democratic candidate, with a remaining doubt out of which was quickly born one of the most bitter and perilous contests in American political history. The settlement of the many points in dispute required the creation, by act of Congress, of what was known as the Electoral Commission, a new court of appeals with specific powers. Its judgment was rendered only just in time to authorize the inauguration of President Hayes on March 4th, 1877, and the States were declared to have given him one hundred and eighty-five electoral votes, against one hundred and' eighty-four for Mr. Tilden. A majority of one was sufficient, and all the nation drew a breath of relief; but the title of President Hayes was not considered without flaw until June 14th following, when it was so declared by an overwhelming vote in Congress.

The difference of a million and a half between its

vote of 1872 and its vote of 1876 was a notification to the old-time Democratic leaders that a new party had arisen, and that it must look around for new men to place before the people, or that it must expect defeat. A sort of enigma was propounded, seeing that as yet it had no apparent means for indicating by name the right individual among its tumultuous four and a quarter millions. Hopeful Democrats assured each other that the coming man would show his marks before long, but not any of them dreamed of looking for him in a busy law office in Western New York, and in the person of a very quiet bachelor, who as yet had held no office higher than that of county sheriff. A year or so later, he was, indeed, talked of for alderman of his own ward in the city of Buffalo. The story of that is told by a leading citizen, one of his strong personal friends, but a stanch Republican. They were at breakfast together at the City Club.

" He [Mr. Cleveland] said that the people of his ward were badgering him to run for alderman ; that the ward was a Republican one, and they thought he might carry it. He thought it was his duty to run ; that he would be able in that way to give control of the council to the Democrats, and ' in that way keep those fellows (the other aldermen) straight.' He seemed to be annoyed that the people should put it on the ground of obligation, as he did not want to give his time to it, nor was it congenial to his tastes to accept such a place. He thought it would interfere with his business.

" I said to him : ' Cleveland, I would not take the place ; you have the right idea of it ; your professional career is of vastly more importance than the wrangling position of alderman ; but I'll tell you what, Cleveland, I am a Republican ; but if you will run for mayor I will vote for you.' I do not think he anticipated the nomination of mayor."

The preponderance of duty was against the aldermanic canvass, but Mr. Welch had given an unpremeditated, conversational expression to an idea that was ready to take form in the minds of many hundreds of other Republicans who knew Mr. Cleveland.

The Presidential campaign of 1880 came, and found a noteworthy condition of affairs. The Republican Party, solid and firm in spite of its factions, had again increased by more than four hundred thousand votes, as if by the regular growth of a healthy body. The Democratic Party, however, had failed to absorb all the elements of the Opposition this time, and was in a minority of nine hundred and fifteen, so nearly were the great powers equalized, while a third ticket, a "Greenback" fantasy, carried away three hundred thousand of the quadrennial increase. The Republican candidates, James A. Garfield and Chester A. Arthur, both of whom were to fill the Executive chair, received two hundred and fourteen electoral votes against one hundred and fifty-five given to General Winfield S. Hancock and William H. English, the Democratic nominees. The Opposition had made two blunders. It had failed to unite the prevalent disaffection against the dominant party, and it had discovered · no new men. Its candidate for President was only a very brilliant military record, singularly devoid of political strength, and its candidate for Vice-President was a resurrected memory of the old party strifes of the days before the Civil War.

The thirty-five electoral votes of the State of New York, which had been given to Tilden in 1876,

were cast for Garfield in 1880. Erie County was
yet Republican, and the city of Buffalo was a veri-
table stronghold of that party.

The course of Mr. Cleveland during all these successive trials of party strength had been such as to
identify him firmly and consistently with the doctrines and fortunes of the growing new party, whose
several branches, North and South, had been so
successfully grafted into the old, deeply-rooted stem
which had borne the same name under altogether
different political conditions. He was a Democrat
of the unquestionably regular denomination from
his boyhood up, but capable of a broad and liberal
treatment of those opposed to him upon any point,
that left them entirely free to agree with him and
to act with him with reference to any other. His
list of personal friends, beginning with his uncle,
contained a large number of well-known Republicans. At the City Club, and other places of public
resort for gentlemen, citizens of character and influence were beginning to discuss with growing earnestness a topic, and a list of topics, which could be
separated, somewhat, from the field of State and
national party issues.

Even the games of whist at the club—and Mr.
Cleveland was said to be an uncommonly good
whist player — were sometimes interfered with,
broken up by gusts of indignant commentary upon
the wretchedly corrupt condition of the municipal
management of the city of Buffalo.   .

Somewhat similar was the state of affairs in many
other cities and large towns throughout the country.

A number of these, and even several of the States of the Union, were rapidly drifting into bankruptcy and repudiation through reckless extravagance and shameless jobbery. It was not a fault of any party, but a disorder of a feverish and over-stimulated time. Its most prominent and disgraceful representative had been the Democratic "Tweed Ring" of New York City, broken up at last by a combination of the honest elements of both political parties. A reformation of abuses existing in the city of Buffalo called for a like combination in the year 1881.

The Republican rule in Buffalo had been sustained by majorities ranging from twenty-five hundred to five thousand, nearly related, from one campaign to another, to the recorded votes given to State and national party tickets. There was no use whatever in any Democrat running for the office of mayor simply as a Democrat. There could be no benefit won by the party, on the other hand, in raising the cry of "reform," unless it should place before the people a candidate sufficiently well known as capable of embodying that idea and fit to be trusted with the fulfilment of its promise. The rank and file of the Republican Party, with all the personal following of its candidates, good or bad, would surely go with and for any straight party ticket nominated. Democratic success called for a name which would attract at least two thousand of the best and most thoughtful Republicans of Buffalo. When the Democratic City Convention met it was a sort of Diogenes, searching with an uncommonly anxious lantern. the streets and lanes of its own organization all over Buffalo.

Mr. Cleveland was not a member of the convention. He was interested in its proceedings and in their result, for he had long been in the habit of strongly expressing his public-spirited indignation over the known waste and misappropriation of the municipal funds, and over grave defects in the administration of the people's business. On that day, however, he was trying a case in court, while the convention made its search and discovered the name it was in need of. He was nominated for mayor as a Democrat, but particularly as the Democratic citizen whose personal character carried in it an assurance of something more than mere partisanship.

As soon as the nomination was made and the applause with which it was received had subsided, a committee was appointed to go to the court room and notify the candidate of what had been done. He heard them when they came, expressed a simple and modest assent, and returned with them to the hall of the convention.

Here he was received with enthusiasm, but he had no speech to make. While heartily and hopefully accepting the nomination, his address was unexpectedly brief, and was devoid of all attempt at any oratorical effect. In fact, it was thoroughly business-like and commonplace, and as soon as he could punctuate it with a bow to the convention he went back to the court room and finished his suspended argument. A more formal acceptance, constituting also the " platform" upon which he proposed to be brought before the people, was quickly afterward transmitted and published. It was as follows : •

"GENTLEMEN OF THE CONVENTION : I am informed that you have bestowed upon me the nomination for the office of mayor. It certainly is a great honor to be thought fit to be the chief officer of a great and prosperous city like ours, having such important and varied interests. I hoped that your choice might fall upon some other and more worthy member of the city Democracy, for personal and private considerations have made the question of acceptance on my part a difficult one. But because I am a Democrat, and because I think no one has a right, at this time of all others, to consult his own inclinations as against the call of his party and fellow citizens, and hoping that I may be of use to you in your efforts to inaugurate a better rule in municipal affairs, I accept the nomination tendered me.

" I believe much can be done to relieve our citizens from their present load of taxation, and that a more rigid scrutiny of all public expenditures will result in a great saving to the community. I also believe that some extravagance in our city government may be corrected without injury to the public service.

" There is or there should be no reason why the affairs of our city should not be managed with the same care and the same economy as private interests. And when we consider that public officials are the trustees of the people, and hold their places and exercise their powers for the benefit of the people, there should be no higher inducement to a faithful and honest discharge of public duty.

" These are very old truths ; but I cannot forbear to speak in this strain to-day, because I believe the time has come when the people loudly demand that these principles shall be, sincerely and without mental reservation, adopted as a rule of conduct. And I am assured that the result of the campaign upon which we enter to-day will demonstrate that the citizens of Buffalo will not tolerate the man or the party who has been unfaithful to public trusts.

" I say these things to a convention of Democrats, because I know that the grand old party is honest and they cannot be unwelcome to you.

" Let us, then, in all sincerity promise the people an improvement in our municipal affairs ; and if the opportunity is offered us, as it surely will be, let us faithfully keep that promise. By this means, and by this means alone, can our success rest upon a firm foundation and our party ascendency be permanently assured. Our opponents will wage a bitter and determined warfare, but with united and hearty effort we shall achieve a victory for our entire ticket.

"And at this day, and with my record before you, I trust it is unnecessary for me to pledge to you my most earnest endeavors to bring about this result ; and if elected to the position for which you have nominated me, I shall do my whole duty to the party, but none the less, I hope, to the citizens of Buffalo."

The canvass was, as he anticipated, "bitter and determined," but it was soon discovered to be something more than a mere party struggle. The Republicans of Buffalo had no thought of changing their relations to their great national organization, but a very large number of them could not be persuaded that the abuses spoken of in Mr. Cleveland's letter of acceptance were a correct expression of Republicanism. They therefore voted for the Democratic nominee, and he was elected by a majority of three thousand five hundred over his competitor. Many of even those who voted against him were well satisfied with the result, while more were disposed to watch him with lynx-eyed jealousy and see if he really meant anything by his promises of reform. On the whole, they did not believe it would all amount to anything more than the ordinary bait in every political platform trap that is set to catch voters. They had been too sharp to be caught, they said to themselves, and so they were prepared to be the more deeply and permanently influenced by the fact that Mayor Cleveland kept his word.

CHAPTER VIII.

*The Mayor's Reform Message—The First Veto—
Skirmishing—The Great Fight Over the Sewer—
The Street-Cleaning Contract—Minor Vetoes—The
Semi-Centennial of Buffalo.*

" A CITY set upon a hill cannot be hid." A human character may possess the qualities for which other men are seeking, and yet its value will fail of general recognition until it shall be placèd upon some elevation where it can be seen by other eyes than those which have been close by it in some hollow. The work done by Grover Cleveland in the law office of Rogers, Bowen & Rogers had been understood by the narrow circle of observers who soon selected him for assistant district-attorney. The field of recognition steadily widened, and he became Sheriff of Erie County. The direct operation of the same law of human society had now carried him into the mayor's chair.

The commerce of the fresh-water inland seas of North America is enormous and is rapidly increasing. Its best connection with the commerce of the great world is through the natural and artificial channels provided by the State of New York, central among which are the Hudson River, the Erie Canal, and their auxiliary railway lines. At the Atlantic terminus of this great avenue of trade and transportation is.the great city known as New York and Brooklyn, arbitrarily but conveniently divided by the East River and by existing charters into two municipalities. Second to this among the cities of the Empire State is the city of Buffalo, at the lake end of the avenue, and the fact that the latter has a population bordering upon a quarter of a million does not adequately express its commercial connections, its manufacturing importance. and its political prominence among the cities of the United States.

The city of New York does not govern itself, but is jealously provided by the State with a system of "boards of commissioners," greatly diminishing the power and responsibility of its mayor and aldermen. It is otherwise in Buffalo, and the provisions of the city charter provide a wide field for the exercise of local executive and legislative ability. It was a field very thickly grown with offensive weeds in the year 1881.

The city is politically divided into thirteen wards, and the majority which elected Mr. Cleveland was not well distributed among them. Each ward was entitled to two aldermen, and in only five was the opposition to the old order of things able to elect its candidates. The Common Council consequently contained only ten "reform" members, against sixteen who were, at least, prepared to resist innovation. The minority of ten was sufficient, however, to protect the veto power of the mayor, and to prevent a two-thirds vote from carrying obnoxious legislation over his head. If, therefore, he was not at once in position to originate and carry into effect reform measures, he could immediately present an impassable barrier to unlawful or otherwise objectionable proceedings on the part of the Common Council.

Mr. Cleveland entered upon the discharge of his new duties on January 2d, 1882, and the public waited eagerly for his first official utterance. It came in the shape of the customary message from the mayor to the council. Its reading before that body by their clerk was listened to with profound but somewhat agitated attention, and the newspapers of Buffalo which published it sold many more copies than usual, for something like a gust of pure air seemed to come with it.

" *To the Honorable the Common Council of the City of Buffalo :*

" In presenting to you my first official communication, I am by no means unmindful of the fact that I address a body, many of the members of which have had large experience in municipal affairs ; and which is directly charged, more than any other instrumentality, with the management of the government of the city and the protection of the interests of all the people within its limits. This condition of things creates grave responsibilities, which I have no doubt you fully appreciate. It may not be amiss, however, to remind you that our fellow citizens, just at this time, are particularly watchful of those in whose hands they have placed the administration of the city government, and demand of them the most watchful care and conscientious economy.

" We hold the money of the people in our hands, to be used for their purposes and to further their interests as members of .the municipality ; and it is quite apparent that, when any part of the funds which the taxpayers have thus intrusted to us are diverted to other purposes, or when, by design or neglect, we allow a greater sum to be applied to any municipal purpose than is necessary, we have, to that extent, violated our duty. There surely is no difference in his duties and obligations, whether a person is in-

trusted with the money of one man or many. And yet it sometimes appears as though the officeholder assumes that a different
rule of fidelity prevails between him and the taxpayers than that
which should regulate his conduct when, as an individual, he holds
the money of his neighbor.

" It seems to me that a successful and faithful administration of
the government of our city may be accomplished, by bearing in
mind that we are the trustees and agents of our fellow citizens,
holding their funds in sacred trust, to be expended for their benefit ; that we should at all times be prepared to render an honest
account to them touching the manner of its expenditure, and that
the affairs of the city should be conducted, as far as possible, upon
the same principles as a good business man manages his private
concerns.

" I am fully persuaded that in the performance of your duties
these rules will be observed. And I, perhaps, should not do less
than to assure your Honorable Body that, so far as it is in my
power, I shall be glad to co-operate with you in securing the faithful
performance of official duty in every department of the city government."

It is a severe and sufficient commentary upon the
previous and current management of Buffalo public
affairs, that such words as these were not only
necessary, but were resentfully regarded by some of
those who heard them as a prophecy of a revolution
at hand. The message went on to criticise in vigorous terms the jobbery, the " shameful. neglect of
duty," " the wasting (to use no stronger term) of
the people's money," and the mismanagement prevailing in several departments of the municipal service. At the end of its caustic arraignment of the
street-cleaning department, one alderman could
endure it no longer and moved that the further
reading of so extraordinary a document be dispensed
with, but a majority of the council decided to let it

go on. The clerk proceeded with the mayor's man-
uscript, and abuse after abuse and evil after evil
was set forth in terse, unsparing directness of speech.
Even the public schools had suffered, and they and
their needful buildings and appliances had been
made the instruments of dishonesty. The neglected
health of the city received sharp commentary, and
a condition of its drainage indicated by the fact
that thirty-six per cent of its annual deaths were
caused by preventable zymotic diseases. The immediate construction was recommended of a sewer
in the lower part of the city, and the abatement of
at least one great source of injury. The public
printing, the duties of the city auditor, the hours of
work of clerks and other officials in the employ of
the city, and matters relating to their pay-rolls,
with other subjects, were dealt with after a manner
which testified to the care and thoroughness with
which Mr. Cleveland had prepared himself for the
important task which he had undertaken. The
closing paragraph of the message was as follows :

"In conclusion, I desire to disclaim any dictation as to the performance of your duties. I recognize fully the fact that with you
rests the responsibility of all legislation which touches the prosperity of the city and the correction of abuses. I do not arrogate
to myself any great familiarity with municipal affairs, nor any
superior knowledge of the city's needs. I speak to you not only
as the chief executive officer of the city, but as a citizen, proud of
its progress and commanding position. In this spirit the suggestions herein contained are made. If you deem them not worthy
of your consideration, I shall still be anxious to aid the adoption
and enforcement of any measures which you may inaugurate, looking to the advancement of the interests of the city and the welfare
of its inhabitants."

Perhaps he was right in disclaiming any spirit of dictation, but his suggestions were terrifically pungent. They contained something plainly resembling a declaration of war, and they aroused the good people of Buffalo to a continued interest in their own affairs equal to that which had been stirred up at the election. The customary reaction and subsidence into a limp and plundered state did not take place. No after opportunity was given for stagnation, as the mayor's voice was quickly heard again.

The Common Council adjourned, and went home to digest the message. When they came together again they tried their legislative skill upon a scheme which had been long in preparation for the establishment of a city "morgue." According to the received ideas of the public service, the science and art of it called for the creation of offices with pay and perquisites as a kind of municipal skeleton to the several bones of which official duties might be attached at leisure. The aldermen, therefore, voted that there should be a keeper of the morgue, fixed his salary, named the man who was to draw the pay, and felt that they had made a good beginning. The city of Buffalo was on its way to the possession of a place of keeping for anybody who might thereafter be found dead. The morgue was founded, and the first piece of new legislation went to the mayor. At the next session of the council, however, there it was before them again vetoed, with remarks which were sadly like an appendix to the message. What they had done was briefly rehearsed, including "a resolution of the council di-

recting the Superintendent of Public Buildings to
provide accommodations for such morgue in the
building occupied as police headquarters ;'' but the
point of the veto was aimed rather at what they had
failed to do.

" The above, so far as I can find," said the mayor, " is all that
has been done toward establishing the proposed house of the dead.
The precise objects of its establishment ; the conditions under which
subjects shall be received into it ; how they shall be cared for while
there, and under what regulations they may be taken away ; what
disposition, under various circumstances, shall be made of them ;
the care and disposition of property which may be found upon the
persons of the dead, and many other things necessarily incident to
the conducting of such an institution, are left entirely unprovided
for."

They had intended to do all of that some day,
and more, too, and the man that kept the morgue
would have found out what to do with anything
that might be brought to him, and there was no
call for a veto to stop the pay and leave any poor
dead body without a home to go to.   It was very
polite of the mayor to add, however :

" Might it not be well for your Honorable Body to review the
proceedings already had, with a view to such future action as shall
be necessary to accomplish the objects which I have indicated ?

" I commend the whole subject to your careful consideration,
with the assurance of my cordial co-operation in perfecting an
establishment which, if not an absolute necessity, may prove to be
a great public convenience."

With the assistance of their committee on ordinances and of the city attorney, the morgue legislation was in due time put into good shape, but no
official's pay began until his work also began.

The Buffalo people enjoyed a quiet laugh over that first veto, but the next bit of municipal news made them open their eyes. The public printing, up to date performed under quiet arrangements made with favored parties, was now given out to the lowest bidder in public competition, and it was discovered that its former cost had been from fifty to eighty-five per cent more than the new contract price.

The next veto came soon and dealt with a resolution of the council providing for the publication in certain German newspapers of a synopsis of their proceedings. The mayor had been expected to sign this, since no enlightened demagogue, with an eye open to his own political future, would be rash enough to offend the large and influential German vote. It may be that there was forgetfulness of the fact that our thrifty German Americans have even less willingness than others to pay money in useless taxes, and are the last men to take offence at being relieved from fraudulent exactions. The mayor's remarks were moderately bitter, for he said :

" The effect of the resolution under consideration is to give these newspapers eight hundred dollars each for doing no more than they will in a sense be obliged to do without it. This comes very near being a most objectionable subsidy, which, I think, a little reflection will satisfy us all we ought not to encourage, and which, I am sure, the people are not prepared to tolerate."

Before the first month of Mr. Cleveland's term ended, proper attention had been paid to several of his recommendations, including that with reference to pay rolls and methods of payments. It was all good and important work, but it was like skirmishing in comparison with some things which were to follow.

One important subject shortly overshadowed all others. The mayor's message had not given the people of Buffalo their first information that there was a needless aggregate of sickness among them, and that their death-rate was murderously high. There were many who were unwilling to believe the worst, and who almost resented such an aspersion upon the fair fame of the city. Even its business and its growth might suffer if the outside world should obtain an impression that it was a place for well men to get sick in. When, therefore, the professional medical adviser of the Board of Health made to that commission a report which told the truth, they ordered him to present, in writing, his authority for his unpleasant assertions, "and to point out, if possible, the causes which have produced the unusual mortality reported, . . . in order that proper measures may be adopted to diminish our unnecessarily large death-rate."

He was entirely prepared to reply. His authority, he stated, was the National Board of Health at Washington, and his presentation of facts did not admit of any dispute. He added to it :

" The explanation, I think, is not difficult, and happily it can be remedied. Buffalo should be what we once supposed it was, one of the healthiest cities in our land. Our climate is delightful and healthful excepting during two or three spring months. The land upon which it is built is sufficiently high to give good drainage.

Our water is not excelled in quality, and in quantity it is absolutely inexhaustible. What, then, are the causes that run up our mortality rate as compared to other and less favorably situated cities ? As chief causes I would mention insufficient sewerage, and as a natural consequence poisoned well water ; uncleanliness of houses and surroundings, the keeping of large numbers of cattle, crowded together in poorly ventilated buildings ; overcrowded schoolrooms, and, lastly, the Hamburg Canal.

" Perhaps many citizens would have placed my last-mentioned cause first as a destroyer of life. I have placed it last advisedly, believing, as I do, that it produces less sickness and death than the others named. It is, however, a great nuisance, and undoubtedly causes a large amount of sickness.

" The remedies are self-evident, and only require money intelligently expended. I would provide a way to thoroughly sewer every part of the city, then close up every well, and prohibit the digging of any new ones. This would necessitate the introduction of Niagara water into every house ; oblige citizens to keep their houses and surroundings clean ; prohibit the keeping of large numbers of cattle or other animals in the populated portions of the city ; build more school houses, and push forward to early completion the intercepting sewer.

" Nothing that I have suggested is impracticable, and unless these suggestions are carried out in whole or in part, Buffalo may some day rival in the death-rate Salt Lake City with its polygamous institutions."

With reference to drainage, something had already been projected. The previous Common Council had voted that an intercepting sewer should be constructed, and had even advertised for proposals. Somehow or other, the lowest bid obtained was one of one million five hundred and sixty-eight thousand dollars, and nothing more had been accomplished. The actual sewer was as far away as ever, though daily becoming more needful, and so the mayor told the council in a message. He told

them, also, that the people of Buffalo could not intrust them and the various officers working under
them with the performance of so important a work
and the expenditure of so much money. He advised
that the entire matter should be turned over to a
special commission, to be selected with care from
among the best citizens of Buffalo.

"I am satisfied," he said, "that a commission, properly selected, to prosecute this work, would be the means of saving much
time and money, and that the sewer would be better and more
thoroughly built than in any other way.

"I therefore recommend that measures be taken to secure the
passage of a law organizing such a commission, with full control
of the construction of this sewer ; and that in the same bill such
provisions may be incorporated as are necessary to provide for the
payment of the expenses of the work."

Here was an innovation, indeed, and a direct proposition to curtail the power of the legislative branch
of the city government. A million and a half of
dollars was to be spent, perhaps more, and not an
alderman was to have any power over its expenditure. The most active and influential party workers
would have no control over the employment of
men, the letting of sub-contracts, the purchases of
materials, or any other part of the great job. What
was the use and where the profit of politics, as a
trade, if the best thing under the city government
for a long time was to be stolen from the aldermen in such an outrageous manner as this ?

The public press had spoken approvingly of the
mayor's advice, and it was well for the aldermen to
act, at first, with moderation. A report—a sort of

protest—made to the council by the city engineer, even went so far as to say that there would be no objection to an advisory Board of Commissioners, provided these should be without power of practical interference. He also declared that the plans and construction of the proposed work involved no problems which could not be readily and successfully solved in his own office, and the council at once passed a vote in his favor, of which the mayor said, in a message dealing vigorously with the entire subject :

" This action of your Honorable Body I cannot approve, as I do not see why it does not allow the engineer to increase his force of assistants in his discretion. This is, of course, a power that ought not to be conferred on any city officer.

" It seems to me that the good taste of the engineer is not conspicuous in thus putting forward his official pride as a reason why any particular plan, looking to the accomplishment of this very important work, should not be adopted. At a time like this, when everybody is or should be anxious to be speedily rid of our city's disgrace, no such consideration ought to intervene.

" But I am utterly amazed to learn at this late day, from the engineer's communication, that the job we have on hand is such an easy one."

All the points at issue were sharply touched, but a much more important step had already been taken by the mayor. Through State Senator Titus, of the Erie district, a bill had been introduced in the State Legislature, providing for the establishment of the Sewer Commission, with ample power of every kind. The council came together in wrath, and adopted a preamble and resolutions protesting against the passage of the bill, and asking Senator

Titus to withdraw it. They were building better than they knew. They were not building a sewer, indeed, but a State reputation for Grover Cleveland, for their action began to advertise liberally his single-handed fight for the reform of the city of Buffalo. There were constituencies in other parts of New York, and beyond its boundaries, whose local circumstances prepared them to be well pleased in hearing that such a man had been discovered in Erie County.

The mayor's reply to the action of the Common Council contained his own criticisms upon the bill prepared by Senator .Titus, and suggested improvements in its provisions, but firmly and politely dissented from their own course.

" I have no doubt," he said, " the rights and interests of the people in this matter, so far as State legislation is concerned, can be safely left in the keeping of those who represent our citizens in the two branches of the State Legislature."

The press and the people were so strongly with the mayor that the council pretended to yield. They were willing to have a Sewer Commission under a State law, and they at once had a new bill drafted and sent to Albany, as a substitute for the pernicious legislation presented by Senator Titus. It was a carefully-worded bill, designed to protect the vested rights of every Buffalo alderman, and the Sewer Commission it provided would have been merely supervisory if not supervisionary. The mayor sent to the council a message of denunciation of their action and their bill, remarking : " I cannot see that the commissioners contemplated by the act would be more than dignified inspectors of the work therein mentioned. . . . Rather than this, I think it would be better to abandon the idea of a commission entirely."

It was again made evident, through the press and otherwise, that the people were with the mayor. The council once more yielded, and a commission with actual power was obtained. While in the very processes of their slow and grumbling assent, however, the council opened another part of the great drainage which that sewer had been expected to perform. It was to have been the means of obtaining from the State Legislature authority for the issue of city bonds to pay for the construction of the work. Other fortunate cities had obtained such powers, from time to time, and had been able to issue no end of bonds after the stream began to run. The council adopted a resolution asking for the required legislation, and sent it to the mayor for his signature, but it came back with a veto. He said that ten years were to be required for the construction of the sewer, and the city was rich enough to pay as it went without adding to the city debt. It began to dawn upon the minds of some men who read that message, that this Buffalo lawyer, who had turned out so remarkable a mayor, was beginning to show symptoms of statesmanship.

By the act of the Legislature, the Sewer Commissioners were to be five in number, nominated by the mayor and confirmed by the Common Council. All power over the sewer would not be lost by the latter body, if it could compel the mayor to name commissioners acceptable to the aldermen. He had determined, rather, to appoint competent men acceptable to the taxpayers. When he did so, his nominations to the council were laid upon the table, remained there a week, and were then taken up and rejected. During the week which followed, the aldermen had the privilege of hearing and reading the opinions of their fellow citizens concerning the mayor's nominations and their own action, and what they heard and read was full of wholesome instruction. When they came together again they received another of the mayor's politely-worded messages. It renominated the same five gentlemen as before, giving cogent reasons for their selection, and they were at once confirmed by a vote of seventeen to eight. The fight for good drainage and economy was fairly won. The new board employed well-known experts to assist in maturing the required plans, and then let the contract at seven hundred and sixty-four thousand three hundred and seventy dollars—that is, the city was saved over eight hundred thousand dollars upon that job.

There had been an especial cause for the prompt manner in which the Common Council confirmed the Sewer Commissioners upon that day, June 26th, 1882. They were in what is commonly called a peck of trouble over another of their independent dealings with the public funds, and they were expecting yet another message from the mayor. They had voted to give the contract for cleaning the streets of the city, during five years following, to

one George Talbot, for the sum of four hundred and
twenty-two thousand five hundred dollars per
annum, although it was publicly well known that
responsible men were offering to do precisely the
same work at a much lower price.

There had been much bargaining and dickering
over that job, and several aldermen had actually
become ashamed of themselves. Hardly had they
organized for business, upon June 26th, before
the penitents were on their feet, hastening to explain, to retract, to express their disapproval of
their previous action, and to say how sincerely they
wished that they had never done anything of the
kind. The regular order of business, however, required that any message from the mayor should
take precedence, and there was no opportunity
given then to wash their political hands and faces
before it became the duty of their clerk to read to
them the following uncommonly interesting letter
from Grover Cleveland :

"I return without my approval the resolution of your Honorable Body, passed at its last meeting, awarding the contracts for
c'eaning the paved streets and alleys of the city for the ensuing
five years to George Talbot, at his bid of four hundred and twenty-
two thousand five hundred dollars.

"The bid thus accepted by your Honorable Body is more than
one hundred thousand dollars higher than that of another perfectly
responsible party for the same work ; and a worse or more sus-
picious feature in this transaction is that the bid now accepted is
fifty thousand dollars more than that made by Mr. Talbot himself
within a very few weeks, openly and publicly to your Honorable
Body, for performing precisely the same services. This latter cir-
cumstance is, to my mind, the manifestation on the part of the
contractor of a reliance upon the forbearance and generosity of

your Honorable Body, which would be more creditable if it were less expensive to the taxpayers.

" I am not aware that any excuse is offered for the acceptance of this proposal, thus increased, except the very flimsy one that the lower bidders cannot afford to do the work for the sums they name.

" This extreme tenderness and consideration for those who desire to contract with the city, and this touching and paternal solicitude lest they should be improvidently led into a bad bargain, is, I am sure, an exception to general business rules, and seems to have no place in this selfish, sordid world, except as found in the administration of municipal affairs.

" The charter of your city requires that the mayor, when he dis-approves any resolution of your Honorable Body, shall return the same with his objections.

" This is a time for plain speech, and my objection to the action of your Honorable Body, now under consideration, shall be plainly stated. I withhold my assent from the same, because I regard it as the culmination of a most bare-faced, impudent, and shameless scheme to betray the interests of the people, and to worse than squander the public money.

" I will not be misunderstood in this matter. There are those whose votes were given for this resolution whom I cannot and will not suspect of a wilful neglect of the interests they are sworn to protect ; but it has been fully demonstrated that there are influences, both in and about your Honorable Body, which it behooves every honest man to watch and avoid with the greatest care.

" When cool judgment rules the hour, the people will, I hope and believe, have no reason to complain of the action of your Honorable Body. But clumsy appeals to prejudice or passion, insinuations, with a kind of low, cheap cunning, as to the motives and purposes of others, and the mock heroism of brazen effrontery which openly declares that a wholesome public sentiment is to be set at naught, sometimes deceives and leads honest men to aid in the consummation of schemes which, if exposed, they would look upon with abborrence.

" If the scandal in connection with this street-cleaning contract, which has so roused our citizens, shall cause them to select and watch with more care those to whom they intrust their interests, and if it serves to make all of us who are charged with official

duties more careful in their performance, it will not be an unmiti-
gated evil.

" We are fast gaining positions in the grades of public stewardship. There is no middle ground. Those who are not for the
people, either in or out of your Honorable Body, are against
them, and should be treated accordingly."

The vetoed contract had no friends remaining.
The street-cleaning was subsequently let out, for
the same term of years, at three hundred and thirteen thousand five hundred dollars per annum—that
is, at a net yearly saving of one hundred and nine
thousand dollars.

Some weeks before the culmination of the long
struggle over the sewer and street-cleaning contracts, one veto message sent in by the mayor had
seemed, to the eyes of ordinary politicians, as if he
were determined upon committing political suicide.
The Common Council had voted a gift of five hundred dollars to the Fireman's Benevolent Association, and the only fault to be found was that they
had plainly violated a clause in the State Constitution.   They had at the same session voted to take
five hundred dollars from the Fourth of July fund
and apply it to the expenses of celebrating Decoration Day, and in this had been merely guilty of a
misdemeanor expressly provided against in the city
charter.   In disapproving of this part of the council's liberality, the mayor wrote to them :

" I deem the object of this appropriation a most worthy one.
The efforts of our veteran soldiers to keep alive the memory of
their fallen comrades certainly deserves the aid and encouragement of their fellow citizens.   We should all, I think, feel-it a duty
and a privilege to contribute to the funds necessary to carry out

such a purpose. And I should be much disappointed if an appeal to our citizens for voluntary subscriptions for this patriotic object should be in vain.

" But the money contributed should be a free gift of the citizens and taxpayers, and should not be extorted from them by taxation. This is so, because the purpose for which this money is asked does not involve their protection or interest as members of the community, and it may or may not be approved by them."

More was said, very well and very plainly, and the leading Republican journal of Buffalo, the *Express*, uttered an important prophecy of changes which were shortly to come when it made the following commentary :

" A whole volume of sound sense and just principles of municipal government will be found condensed in a brief veto sent to the council yesterday by Mayor Cleveland. It is refreshing to read the message. Appropriations of the public funds must not be made except in accordance with law. Safeguards provided by the constitution and the charter must be respected. The money raised by taxation must not be diverted from its legitimate objects. However worthy the sentiment recognized in any misappropriation, justice, not generosity, must prevail. When the council wrongfully votes away the people's money, there is no credit in the act, because the money, having been extorted from the people, is not a free gift from that body. The city government is a business establishment, and must be conducted on business principles. All these golden rules are laid down in disapproving a vote of five hundred dollars for Decoration Day—a small sum for a worthy object ; but, as the mayor shows, it is not the amount of the appropriation, nor the merit of it, but the principle involved, which must be considered. Private bounty ought to be equal to such a call, and then, to prove that he thinks so, Mr. Cleveland privately contributes one tenth of the whole sum needed, thus supplementing excellent principle by liberal example."

The work went bravely on, and there were minor vetoes, called for by widely-varying specimens of lcose and wasteful legislation. As one citizen pointedly remarked, Mr. Cleveland seemed to regard the city as his client, for whose every interest, large or small, he was bound to make a fight. Among those interests, not the least in social importance, was that of the street children, to the evils of whose sad condition his attention was especially directed by the Society for the Prevention of Cruelty to Children.

During month after month, the citizens of Buffalo became more and more proud of their reform mayor. They talked about him to strangers, somewhat as if he had been a local rarity which distinguished Buffalo above all the less fortunate municipalities of the State and of the Union. They wrote letters about him to the journals of New York, Chicago, and other great cities, which were to be pitied because of their supposable poverty at that time in their mayor department.

It was in the year 1882 that Buffalo completed its first half century of existence, for it was only a young lady of a city after all. It was determined to have a grand celebration of the occasion, and to combine the anniversary of the locality with that of the nation. Since the Fourth of July was that year to come upon a Sunday, its parade was necessarily transferred to the 3d of the month. Every effort was made to express the pride felt by the citizens of Buffalo in the character and prosperity of their community. There was a grand procession of the military, the firemen, the police, the many societies, and the citizens. The portrait of the first mayor

was borne through the streets side by side with that
of the mayor for 1882, and the latter made an address, during the festivities of the evening, which
cannot well be omitted from the record of these
phenomenally important months of his career.

" LADIES AND GENTLEMEN : I ought, perhaps, to be quite content on this occasion to assume the part of quiet gratification. But
I cannot forbear expressing my satisfaction at being allowed to
participate in the exercises of the evening, and I feel that I must
give token of the pleasure I experience in gazing with you upon
the fair face of our queen city at the age of fifty. I am proud with
you in contrasting what seems to us the small things of fifty years
ago, with the beauty, and the greatness, and the importance of to-
day. The achievements of the past are gained ; the prosperity of
the present we hold with a firm hand ; and the promise of the
future comes to us with no uncertain sound. It seems to me to-
day that of all men the resident of Buffalo should be the proudest
to name his home.

" In the history of a city, fifty years but marks the period of
youth, when all is fresh and joyous. The face is fair, the step is
light, and the burden of life is carried with a song ; the future,
stretching far ahead, is full of bright anticipations, and the past,
with whatever of struggle and disappointment there may have
been, seems short, and is half forgotten. In this heyday of our
city's life, we do well to exchange our congratulations, and to revel
together in the assurances of the happy and prosperous future
that awaits us.　　　　　　　　　　　.

" And yet I do not deem it wrong to remind myself and you,
that our city, great in its youth, did not suddenly spring into existence clad in beauty and in strength. There were men fifty
years ago who laid its foundations broad and deep ; and who,
with the care of jealous parents, tended it and watched its growth.
Those early times were not without their trials and discouragements ; and we reap to-day the fruit of the labors and the perse-
verance of those pioneers. Those were the fathers of the city.
Where are they ? Fifty years added to manhood fills the cup of
human life. Most have gone to swell the census of God's city,
which lies beyond the stream of faith. A few there are who list-

lessly linger upon the bank, and wait to cross, in the shade of trees they have planted with their own hands. Let us tenderly remember the dead to-night, and let us renew our love and veneration for those who are spared to speak to us of the scenes attending our city's birth and infancy.

"And in this, our day of pride and self-gratification, there is, I think, one lesson at least which we may learn from the men who have come down to us from a former generation.

"In the day of the infancy of the city which they founded, and for many years afterward, the people loved their city so well that they would only trust the management of its affairs in the strongest and best of hands ; and no man in those days was so engrossed in his own business but he could find some time to devote to public concerns. Read the names of the men who held places in this municipality fifty years ago, and food for reflection will be found. Is it true that the city of to-day, with its large population and with its vast and varied interests, needs less and different care than it did fifty years ago ?

"We boast· of our citizenship to-night. But this citizenship brings with it duties not unlike those we owe our neighbor and our God. There is no better time than this for self-examination. He who deems himself too pure and holy to take part in the affairs of his city, will meet the fact that better men than he have thought it their duty to do so. He who cannot spare a moment in his greed and selfishness to devote to public concerns, will, perhaps, find a well-grounded fear that he may become the prey of public plunderers ; and he who indolently cares not who administers the government of his city, will find that he is living falsely, and in the neglect of his highest duty.

"When our centennial shall be celebrated, what will be said of us ? I hope it may be said that we built and wrought well, and added much to the substantial prosperity of the city we had in charge. Brick and mortar may make a large city, but the encouragement of those things which elevate and purify, the exaction of the highest standard of integrity in official place, and a constant, active interest on the part of the good people in municipal government, are needed to make a great city.

"Let it be said of us when only our names and memory are left in the centennial time, that we faithfully administered the trust which we received from our fathers, and religiously performed

our parts in our day and generation, toward making our city not
only prosperous, but truly great."

Less importance attaches, apparently, to his remarks upon the occasion of the laying of the corner-
stone of the building erected for the uses of the
Young Men's Christian Association, but an extract
from them will bear a close examination, although
entirely devoid of any attempt at oratorical effect :

" We this day bring into a prominent place an institution which,
it seems to me, cannot fail to impress itself upon our future with
the best results.   Perhaps a majority of the citizens have heard of
the Young Men's Christian Association, and perchance the name
has suggested, in an indefinite way, certain efforts to do good and
to aid generally in the spread of religious teaching.   I venture to
say, however, that a comparatively small part of our community
have really known the full extent of the work of this association,
and may have thought of it as an institution well enough in its way
—a proper enough outlet for a superabundance of religious enthusiasm—doing, of course, no harm, and perhaps very little good.
Some have aided it by their contributions from a sense of Christian duty, but more have passed by on the other side.   We have
been too much in the habit of regarding institutions of this kind as
entirely disconnected from any consideration of municipal growth
of prosperity, and have too often considered splendid structures,
active trade, increasing commerce, and growing manufactures as
the only things worthy of our care as public-spirited citizens.   A
moment's reflection reminds us that this is wrong.   The citizen
is a better business man if he is a Christian gentleman, and surely
business is not the less prosperous and successful if conducted on
Christian principles.

" This is an extremely practical, and perhaps not a very elevated view to take of the purposes and benefits of the Young Men's
Christian Association, but I assert that if it did no more than to
impress some religious principles upon the business of our city, it
would be worthy of generous support.   And when we consider the
difference, as a member of the community, between the young
man who, under the influence of such an association, has learned

his duty to his fellows and to the State, and that one who, subject to no moral restraint, yields to temptation, and thus becomes vicious and criminal, the importance of an institution in our midst which leads our youth and young men in the way of morality and good citizenship must be freely admitted.

" I have thus only referred to this association as in some manner connected with our substantial prosperity. There is a higher theme connected with this subject which touches the welfare, temporal and spiritual, of the objects of its care. Upon this I will not dwell. I cannot, however, pass on without invoking the fullest measure of honor and consideration due to the self-sacrificing and disinterested efforts of the men, and women, too, who have labored amid trials and discouragements to firmly plant this association in our midst upon a sure foundation. We all hope and expect that our city has entered upon a course of unprecedented prosperity and growth. But to my mind not all the signs about us point more surely to real greatness than the event which we here celebrate. Good and pure government lies at the foundation of the wealth and progress of every community. As the chief executive of this proud city, I congratulate all my fellow citizens that to-day we lay the foundation stone of an edifice which shall be a beautiful ornament, and, what is more important, shall enclose within its walls such earnest Christian endeavors as must make easier all our efforts to administer safely and honestly a good municipal government.''

CHAPTER IX.

*Widening Fame—The Buffalo Pattern Bolt—The
Cleveland Boom—Nominated for Governor of New
York—The Scratchers—A State Canvass Watched
by the Nation—A Great Majority and a New Star
in American Politics.*

IN his message to the Common Council denounc-
ing the street-cleaning contract, Mayor Cleveland
told them : '' We are fast gaining positions in the
grades of public stewardship.''

He could plainly see the grade and position won
for themselves by men who were manifestly betraying their trusts, but as yet he had no perception of
the prominence which his fight for honest stewardship was acquiring for himself. His course had been
approved by the citizens and by the public press of
Buffalo, with small reference to mere party lines.
The Republicans who had repudiated their own
party nominations to vote for him and make him
mayor were especially grateful to him for the manner in which he had justified their independent action. While all Democrats were claiming him and
advertising him as a representative Democrat, a fine
specimen of what their party really consisted of, his
Republican supporters were even more eagerly pro-
claiming, throughout the State, that the reform of
Buffalo had been accomplished by their own public

spirit and by the acumen which had enabled them
to find and help so great a rarity as an honest Democrat. He was a man, they said, who could be
trusted by any body of Republicans who might wish
to administer at any time another rebuke to their
own party management. There was a tremendous
array of facts in support of this defence of themselves by the Buffalo Independents, and it was read
or listened to with deep interest by the sagacious
chiefs of the Democratic Party.

The latter were becoming better and better aware,
from month to month, in the year 1882, that the
Republican Party was preparing a grand opportunity for a well-led Opposition movement, patterned,
for instance, very much like that which had succeeded so well in the city of Buffalo.

In 1879 the Democratic candidate for governor
of the State had fallen forty-two thousand votes behind his Republican competitor, Governor Cornell,
but in 1880 General Hancock had received only
three thousand less votes than were given to General Garfield. Nevertheless, the entire official
patronage and influence of the national and State
governments being now in the hands of the Republican Party, with what seemed a reasonably safe
majority for any respectable ticket it might choose
to nominate, there appeared to be no hope whatever for the election of a Democratic governor in
1882. The appearance was not deceitful, and there
was no such hope or prospect whatever. A regular
Democratic nomination, pitted against a regular
Republican nomination, would have been swept

away by a much larger majority than that which
had given the electoral vote of New York to Garfield and Arthur. No such contest was to occur,
however, in 1882, and the Republican Party was
not to have the privilege of voting for a candidate
of its own selection. A large majority of its membership wished the re-election of Governor Cornell,
but their will was overruled by a knot of powerful
party chiefs, and their State Convention was so
manipulated, not to employ any stronger term, that
a member of President Arthur's Cabinet, Judge
Folger, a very capable and excellent gentleman,
was placed at the head of the State ticket.

There was a loud and angry murmur of rebellion
from one end of the State to the other. Men who
had voted for Frémont, and for Lincoln, and for
every regular Republican nomination set before them
since 1856, rushed into print with unstinted denunciations of the unpardonable dictation attempted
and the outrageous processes through which it had,
apparently, succeeded. By so doing, they placed
before the Democratic leaders the exciting question, " Have we among us any man.for whom these
insulted and enraged Republicans can be induced
to vote ?"

There was a long list of distinguished gentlemen
to be pondered over, but the best known among
them were men too intensely Democratic, and of
the others it was almost evident that as yet they
had made no record which would answer the requirements of the hour. Immediately a number of
prominent citizens of Erie County responded en-

thusiastically that Buffalo could solve the problem. They had the very man, and there were in their city hundreds of Republicans, as angry as any of their brethren elsewhere, who would be ready to tell the anti-Folger bolters that it was entirely safe to vote for Grover Cleveland. They asserted that in case of his nomination, a fourth part of the assumed Republican majority of twenty thousand would disappear along the shore of Lake Erie.

Editorial articles, correspondence, anecdotes of the Buffalo municipal reform, began to appear in the columns of leading Republican newspapers, and even portraits of Mr. Cleveland, not all works of art, were pretty generally distributed, that other constituencies than his own might make a kind of personal acquaintance with him.

Much of this work had actually preceded the meeting of the Republican Convention and the nomination of Judge Folger, but it burst into sudden and swift energy as the consequences of that political error became apparent. There had been " Cleveland Clubs" in a number of places, but more now sprang into existence, like mushrooms. The Democratic State Convention had been called to meet at Syracuse on September 22d, 1882, and as the day drew near, the press teemed with more numerous eulogies of the reform Mayor of Buffalo. What the party slang of the day describes as a " boom" was taking place, and the prospects of other candidates were fast ebbing away.

When the convention assembled, its first duty was the adoption of a platform of resolutions, and

these did not fail to severely criticise the nomination
of Judge Folger, and to open a gate for any Republican voters whose views of it were thus set forth.
Specified reforms in State and national administration were demanded, and the dominant party
was vigorously arraigned for alleged defects in its
methods of dealing with important interests. Previous Democratic platforms had done the same, with
at least equal vehemence of expression, and yet
sweeping Republican victories had expressed the
popular doubt concerning the sincerity of the party
bringing the indictments. Something more than
ringing phrases and bitter denunciations would have
to be offered if a different result were now to be
hoped for. It would be entirely easy to nominate
a good and distinguished Democrat, for whom even
angrily dissatisfied Republicans would refuse to
vote, and few of the latter had any personal objection to Judge Folger.

. When the resolutions had been read and adopted,
the really most important work of the convention
began. Half a dozen or so of names were offered
as candidates for nomination for governor of the
State, and in behalf of each a eulogistic speech was
made. The name of Grover Cleveland was presented by Hon. Daniel N. Lockwood, of Buffalo,
the same gentleman who, in 1881, had moved his
nomination for mayor. He had prepared a speech
which answered the purpose in hand admirably, for it
was made to appear that the platform already adopted,
no less than the error of the Republican Party, had
been made to fit the nomination of Mr. Cleveland.

The first ballot taken in any such nominating convention, not overshadowed in advance by one great name, is apt to have two predominant characteristics. Part of its votes are often purely complimentary, expressing local good-will for a favorite citizen. More distinctly, however, is the first ballot a vote of inquiry into the relative strength of the candidates before the convention. The result was eminently satisfactory to the eager gentlemen from Erie County. Only one more ballot of investigation was required in order to satisfy everybody else that the right man had been discovered, and then, on the third ballot, Grover Cleveland was nominated. His party had decided that his was the one name around which its own most orthodox element and all the other elements required for success could be drawn together.

The real platform of the Democratic Party, in the animated canvass which followed, was Mr. Cleveland's record as reform Mayor of Buffalo and his letter accepting the nomination. The latter was as follows :

" BUFFALO, October 7, 1882.

" *Hon. Thomas C. Ecclesine, Chairman, etc.*

" DEAR SIR : I beg to acknowledge the receipt of your letter, informing me of my nomination for Governor by the Democratic State Convention, lately held at the city of Syracuse.

" I accept the nomination thus tendered to me, and trust that, while I am gratefully sensible of the honor conferred, I am also properly impressed with the responsibilities which it invites.

" The platform of principles adopted by the convention meets with my hearty approval. The doctrines therein enunciated are so distinctly and explicitly stated that their amplification seems scarcely necessary. If elected to the office for which I have been nominated, I shall endeavor to impress them upon my administration and make them the policy of the State.

" Our citizens for the most part attach themselves to one or the other of the great political parties ; and, under ordinary circumstances, they support the nominees of the party to which they profess fealty. It is quite apparent that under such circumstances the primary election or caucus should be surrounded by such safeguards as will secure absolutely free and uncontrolled action. Here the people themselves are supposed to speak ; here they put their own hands to the machinery of government ; and in this place should be found the manifestations of the popular will. When by fraud, intimidation, or any other questionable practice, the voice of the people is here smothered, a direct blow is aimed at a most precious right, and one which the law should be swift to protect. If the primary election is uncontaminated and fairly conducted those there chosen to represent the people will go forth with the impress of the people's will upon them, and the benefits and purposes of a truly representative government will be attained.

" Public officers are the servants and agents of the people, to execute laws which the people have made and within the limits of a constitution which they have established. Hence the interference of officials of any degree, and whether State or Federal, for the purpose of thwarting or controlling the popular wish, should not be tolerated.

" Subordinates in public places should be selected and retained for their efficiency, and not because they may be used to accomplish partisan ends. The people have a right to demand, here as in cases of private employment, that their money be paid to those who will render the best service in return, and that the appointment to and tenure of such places should depend upon ability and merit. If the clerks and assistants in public departments were paid the same compensation, and required to do the same amount of work, as those employed in prudently-conducted private establishments, the anxiety to hold those public places would be much diminished, and, it seem to me, the cause of Civil Service Reform materially aided.

" The system of levying assessments for partisan purposes on those holding office or place cannot be too strongly condemned. Through the thin disguise of voluntary contributions, this is seen to be naked extortion, reducing the compensation which should be honestly earned, and swelling a fund used to debauch the people and defeat the popular will.

" I am unalterably opposed to the interference by the Legislature with the government of municipalities. I believe in the intelligence of the people when left to an honest freedom in their choice, and that when the citizens of any section of the State have determined upon the details of a local government, they should be left in the undisturbed enjoyment of the same. The doctrine of home rule, as I understand it, lies at the foundation of Republican institutions, and cannot be too strongly insisted upon.

" Corporations are created by the law for certain defined purposes, and are restricted in their operations by specific limitations. Acting within their legitimate sphere, they should be protected ; but when by combination or by the exercise of unwarranted power they oppress the people, the same authority which created should restrain them and protect the rights of the citizens. The law lately passed for the purpose of adjusting the relations between the people and corporations should be executed in good faith, with an honest design to effectuate its objects and with a due regard for the interests involved.

" The laboring classes constitute the main part of our population. They should be protected in their efforts peaceably to assert their rights when endangered by aggregated capital, and all statutes on this subject should recognize the care of the State for honest toil and be framed with a view of improving the condition of the workingman.

" We have so lately had a demonstration of the value of our citizen soldiery in time of peril, that it seems to me no argument is necessary to prove that it should be maintained in a state of efficiency, so that its usefulness shall not be impaired.

" Certain amendments to the constitution of our State, involving the management of our canals, are to be passed upon at the coming election. This subject affects diverse interests and, of course, gives rise to opposite opinions. It is in the hands of the sovereign people for final settlement ; and as the question is thus removed from State legislation, any statement of my opinion in regard to it, at this time, would, I think, be out of place. I am confident that the people will intelligently examine the merits of the subject and determine where the preponderance of interest lies.

" The expenditure of money to influence the action of the people at the polls, or to secure legislation, is calculated to excite the gravest concern. When this pernicious agency is successfully employed a representative form of government becomes a sham ; and laws passed under its baleful influence cease to protect, but are made the means by which the rights of the people are sacrificed, and the public treasury despoiled. It is useless and foolish to shut our eyes to the fact that this evil exists among us ; and the party which leads in an honest effort to return to better and purer methods will receive the confidence of our citizens and secure their support. It is wilful blindness not to see that the people care but little for party obligations, when they are invoked to countenance and sustain fraudulent and corrupt practices. And it is well for our country and for the purification of politics that the people, at times fully roused to danger, remind their leaders that party methods should be something more than a means used to answer the purposes of those who profit by political occupation.

" The importance of wise statesmanship in the management of public affairs cannot, I think, be overestimated. I am convinced, however, that the perplexities and the mystery often surrounding the administration of State concerns grow, in a great measure, out of an attempt to serve partisan ends rather than the welfare of the citizen.

" We may, I think, reduce to quite simple elements the duty which public servants owe, by constantly bearing in mind that they are put in place to protect the rights of the people, to answer their needs as they arise, and to expend for their benefit the money drawn from them by taxation.

" I am profoundly conscious that the management of the diverse interests of a great State is not an easy matter, but I believe, if undertaken in the proper spirit, all its real difficulties will yield to watchfulness and care.

                    " Yours respectfully,

                              " GROVER CLEVELAND."

The varying figures of the election returns of previous years had been of such a nature that almost any sort of prognostication could be drawn from them. There had been Democratic factions as in-

subordinate as any now supposed to exist in the
Republican camp and elections had been disas-
trously influenced thereby. In several successive
Presidential campaigns, New York had been the
most uncertain factor in any forecast of the probable
result. There were forces now at work, however,
which were undoubtedly underestimated by the
most capable politicians of both parties. Everybody desired an improvement in the administration
of the affairs of the State, but not many men were
prepared to forget all their experiences and expect
perfect sincerity in that direction from any party
organization with which they were acquainted.
Precisely the same desire for improvement, for reform, had existed before, but it had exercised only a
moderate influence over election returns. The
voters who had wished, but had not hoped, now became widely awakened to read with surprised interest the messages of Grover Cleveland to the Common Council of Buffalo, and even indifferent stay-
at-homes were stirred up to the experiment of cast-
ing a ballot for him. As to the disaffection in the
Republican Party, the leaders whose arrogance had
aroused it scoffed at it, at first, as a chronic discontent, which was not likely to do any more mischief
in this case than in others. At a comparatively recent election, the name of " Scratchers" had been
applied to several thousands of Republicans who
dropped one name or more from their regular ticket
without inserting any substitute. To these came
the entirely pertinent example and assurances of
the "reform" Republicans of Buffalo. What had

been done for a town might as well be done for a
State, and the Scratchers became energetic workers
for Grover Cleveland.

The Republican leaders who had scoffed at the
murmurs against the nomination of Judge Folger
were presently dismayed by the storm they had created. They had been accustomed to manage and
to command and to find their well-disciplined party
following them in compact column. They were dismayed, but they were also bitterly angry. The men
who now turned away from them and from their
brilliant records, legislative, administrative, or military, to find something better in the name and fame
of a mere country lawyer, a county sheriff, a city
mayor for, as yet, only half a year—those men were
declared to be either lunatics or deserters, hardly a
shade better than traitors. The canvass grew hot-
ter, from day to day, and it rapidly assumed an aspect of national importance. New York is the
most wealthy and populous of the States of the
Union. It contains the largest city ; its journals
are the most widely read of any, while its closely
balanced politics and its large· factorship in the
electoral college concentrate upon it the most anxious scrutiny of the thoughtful citizens of every
other American commonwealth and community.
All the nation, therefore, read with deep interest
the story of the manner in which Mayor Cleveland
had beaten the aldermen, and it was felt pretty generally that what the whole country needed was some
sort of intercepting sewer, rightly planned and constructed. An additional importance was given to

one phase of the situation by a peculiarly unwise movement on the part of the more extreme Republicans. In the Democratic State Convention, the Chairman of the Committee on Resolutions, preparing and reporting the party platform, was a gentleman, Roger A. Pryor, who had been a general in the Confederate Army during the Civil War. An effort was made, with this as one of its texts, to connect the existing Democratic Party with the Rebellion of 1861, as if it were or had been in sympathy with secession and disunion. The recoil was destructive, for many of the supporters of Mr. Cleveland were able to show uncommonly good war records, while adding that the return of Confederate soldiers to active and distinguished citizenship was of itself the greatest triumph won for the Union armies.

The few short weeks of the canvass went swiftly by and the November polls were opened. When they closed, at sunset, Grover Cleveland had been elected Governor of New York, by the largest majority known to its history—one hundred and ninety-two thousand. More than a hundred thousand Republicans had evidently decided that their private convictions and their public duty required them to vote for him. A new name, a star of the first magnitude, had swiftly arisen in the political sky. There was something so startling about it as to entirely justify the remark made by one cynical observer, who sneered : " Well, yes ; he's gone up like a rocket, but he'll come down like the stick."

There were, indeed, many who spoke of the ex-

ceeding suddenness with which Grover Cleveland
had obtained a national reputation, but in so doing
they were forgetful of both the earlier and later history of their own country.

The United States is only an aggregate of many
small election districts, and a man who is well known
in one of these can seem as an old acquaintance to
the voters of the district next adjoining within one
week's time, if his friends and the local newspapers
work efficiently.   Moreover, at every election, quite
a respectable number of freemen cast their intelligent ballots for men of whom they really know
nothing whatever,

CHAPTER X

The Fruits of the Victory—Extraordinary Expenses
of the Mayor's Office—The Dinner at the Manhat-
tan Club—Speech of the Governor-Elect—Going to
Work at Albany—The First Message to the Legis-
lature.

THE combined Opposition gained an amazing victory at the polls in November, 1882. The precise
nature of their triumph, however, was by no means
hidden from acute politicians of either party, and it
was yet to be seen whether or not the Republican
ascendancy in New York had received a permanently
shattering blow. Of course, the Democratic strength
had been augmented and consolidated, and was
likely to be kept well in hand for some time to
come, but the future action of its auxiliary force of
temporarily disaffected Republicans was by no
means certain, while that party was known to be
gaining and not weakening in other parts of the
country. It was almost a tradition of American
politics that a reaction against the party in power
should take place half way between two Presidential
elections, and that then the pendulum of the doubtful vote should swing back again. How far it was
now about to swing was likely to depend largely
upon the use which might be made by Grover Cleveland of his opportunities as Governor of the State

of New York. Keen-eyed calculators saw that there
were dangers ahead. If he should undertake in
stupid earnest to fulfil his promises of reform, he
would surely array against himself, one after another, as many powerful interests as the course of
defective legislation should throw in his way. It
was to be hoped, rather, that he would inaugurate
an "era of good feeling," and rally around him all
the clans of all the available political tribes, including especially any refugees in any typical Republican or Democratic cave of Adullam.

The Democratic Party leaders made an exceedingly judicious use of the immediate occasion.
During the brief but exciting canvass, Mr. Cleveland had remained in Buffalo in the daily performance of his duties as mayor. He had seemed to be
about the most cool and undisturbed Democrat in
Erie County, not to mention any of his Independent
Republican friends. He received the news of his
election with steady equanimity, one of its most
pleasing features to him being the fact that his own
county gave him six thousand six hundred and fifty-
three more votes than it had given for the Democratic candidate for governor in 1879. His exact
majority there was seven thousand three hundred
and forty. As soon as the results were declared,
he began to make all necessary preparations for the
extraordinary change which was before him. If
among the members of the Board of Aldermen of
Buffalo there were any who felt a degree of personal
relief and pleasure upon receiving what they were
assured was the last message ever to be sent to

them by Grover Cleveland, there was not one who did not instantly vote for the cash appropriation it requested of them. He asked that a warrant should be authorized for the payment of the incidental and extraordinary expenses of the mayor's office during the year 1882. The sum total of his outlay, advanced from his own pocket, had been twenty-five dollars and twenty-four cents, and the warrant on the Treasury was drawn ; but one alderman wondered why Cleveland did not make the odd cents up to a round quarter, somehow. His public and private business affairs were quickly in good shape to be left behind him, and he accepted an invitation which he had received to visit the city of New York, as the guest of the Manhattan Club.

The social standing and personal character of this organization, thoroughly and representatively Democratic, rendered it the most fitting instrumentality for putting a species of seal upon the record which had been made by and for the governor-elect. A grand banquet was given by the club, on December 6th, 1882, and of the two hundred and fifty gentlemen whose presence was invited, an ample proportion had not been previously associated with Democratic victories.

Perhaps the banquet was intended, without the governor-elect's knowledge, as a species of brilliant interrogation. It may have served to ask the momentous question : "Is not this the right man for New York to uphold as its selection for the next Democratic Presidential nomination ?"

Whatever may have been its purposes, other than

social and complimentary, it offered Mr. Cleveland an excellent opportunity, of which he took an all but unsparing advantage. It enabled him to publish his clear perception of the true nature of the popular movement which had given him his phenomenal majority. There were afterward features of his official and political course and conduct which required for their perfect interpretation a reference to his reply to his enthusiastic welcome by the Manhattan Club. To the distinguished assembly gathered in his honor, he said :

"We stand to-night in the full glare of a grand and brilliant manifestation of the popular will, and in the light of it how vain and small appear the tricks of politicians and the movements of partisan machinery. He must be blind who cannot see that the people well understand their power, and are determined to use it when their rights and interests are threatened. There should be no scepticism to-night as to the strength and perpetuity of our Government. Partisan leaders have learned, too, that the people will not unwittingly and blindly follow, and that something more than wavering devotion to party is necessary to secure their allegiance. I am quite certain that the late demonstration did not spring from any pre-existing love for the party which was called to power, nor did the people put the affairs of the State in our hands to be by them forgotten. They voted for themselves, and in their own interest. If we retain their confidence, we must deserve it, and we may be sure they will call on us to give an account of our stewardship. We shall utterly fail to read aright the signs of the times if we are not fully convinced that parties are but instruments through which the people work out their will, and that when they become less or more, the people desert or destroy them. The vanquished have lately learned these things, and the victors will act wisely if they profit by the lesson. I have read and heard much of late touching the great responsibilities cast upon me, and it is certainly predicated upon the fact that my majority was so large as to indicate that many not members of the party to which

I am proud to belong, supported me. God knows how fully I appreciate the responsibilities of the high office to which I have been called, and how much I sometimes fear that I shall not bear the burden well. It has seemed to me that a citizen who has been chosen by his fellows to discharge public duties owes no less nor more to them whether he is selected by a small or a large majority. In either event he owes to the people who honored him his best endeavors to carefully protect their rights and further their interests. An administration is only successful in a partisan sense when it appears to be an outgrowth and result of party principles and methods. These honored doctrines of the Democratic Party are dear to me. If honestly applied in their purity I know that the affairs of the Government will be fittingly and honestly administered, and I believe that all the wants and needs of the people would be met. They have survived all changes, and good, patriotic men have clung to them through all disasters as the hope of political salvation. Let us hold them as a sacred' trust, and not forget that the intelligent, thinking, reading people will look to a party which they put in power to supply all their various needs and wants, and that the party which keeps pace with the developments and progress of the times, which keeps in sight its landmarks, and yet observes the things which are in advance, and which will continue true to the people as well as to its traditions, will be the dominant party of the future. My only aspiration is to faithfully perform the duties of the office to which the people of my State have called me, and I hope and trust a proud endeavor will light the way to a successful administration."

At every point the great banquet was a complete success, and the response of Governor Cleveland was read by a wider and more deeply interested public than has often studied an after-dinner speech in this country.

Three weeks later the Executive Mansion at Albany was ready for its new occupant, and, on January 1st, 1883, in company with his law partner, Mr. Bissell, the governor-elect came from Buffalo to take possession. A greater than ordinary public

curiosity had been aroused with reference to the
inauguration ceremonial, and there were crowds of
people around the State Capitol the next morning.
They were awaiting the arrival of the new governor,
and the retiring governor, Mr. Cornell, was in the
Executive Chamber of the Capitol, also waiting to
receive him.   Unannounced, and all but unnoticed,
a pair of quiet gentlemen on foot pushed their way
among the throng until they disappeared through
the costly, very costly portal of the Capitol.   One
of them was Grover Cleveland, and the other was
his private secretary, Daniel S. Lamont.   There
had been no parade whatever ; nothing but a quiet
and business-like coming to the performance of an
appointed task.

   Success in that performance, or failure, and the
degree of either, would surely have a direct and important effect upon the future of the Democratic
Party and of Mr. Cleveland's own career, while the
situation had its peculiar difficulties.   Immediately
behind him lay the record of Governor Cornell, and
the people of the State had found very little fault
with the conduct of that public servant.   The great
mass of his own party had been so well satisfied with
his administration, that his putting aside, unjustly,
for personal and not for public reasons, had prepared the way for Mr. Cleveland's election.   It appeared fairly evident that Mr. Cornell's successor
was not likely to shine by any express comparison
with him.   Hundreds of citizens who had loudly
extolled, for campaign purposes, the reforms accomplished by the Mayor of Buffalo, openly expressed

their doubt if he had in him enough of natural-born statesmanship to spread equally well over the affairs of a great State. Perhaps the first noticeable feature of the new administration was the fact—to be discovered in his message to the Legislature—that he had not taken the trouble to entertain and consider that doubt. Whatever were the other features of the message, it was ringing with self-reliance, without containing one sentence which consciously asserted it.

There were a few words in the opening clause of the message which reminded other men that he might require a little time for the study of this case, in which the State had retained him, for he said :

"I transmit this, my first annual message, with the intimation that a newly-elected executive can hardly be prepared to present a complete exhibit of State affairs, or to submit in detail a great variety of recommendations for the action of the Legislature."

The exhibit, and the recommendations which he was called upon for and was prepared to make at once, included all which might belong to the chief executive of a nation, with the exception of anything relating to foreign affairs and matters of war and peace.

The finances of the State, as evidenced by reports from the comptroller's office, were in good condition, but the system of taxation by means of which they were rendered so left it "notoriously true that personal property not less remunerative than land and real estate escapes to a very great extent the payment of its fair proportion of the expense incident to its protection and preservation under the law." So said the governor in the next section of his message, and there were gentlemen familiar with the subject who shook their heads a little, even while they assented to his declaration of "the imperfection of our laws touching the matter of taxation and the faulty execution of existing statutes."

The manner in which the State canals were dealt with showed that careful study had been given to that subject, while in connection with it the governor advised the creation of some tribunal answering the general purposes of a court of claims. By this, it was made to appear, several existing offices could be dispensed with or condensed and a saving of thirty thousand dollars yearly could be accomplished.

The public schools were mentioned with an expression of approval of their condition and management. Better methods and more thoroughness in the supervision of savings banks and of insurance companies was recommended. Attention was asked to needed improvements in the drill and instruction of the uniformed militia.

Attentive readers of the message reached this part of it without discovering anything unusually interesting. There were those, however, who had voted for "reform" with an idea that it was to have especial reference to the State prisons and the uses made of convict labor. These now discovered that their grievance was one of the matters with which the governor was as yet unprepared to deal. He said :

" If these penal institutions are self-sustaining, without injury or embarrassment to honest labor, it is a matter for congratulation ; but it is, at least, very questionable whether the State should go further and seek to realize a profit from its convict labor.   In my judgment it should not, especially if the danger of competition between convicts and those who honestly toil is thereby increased, and the overcrowding of any of the prisons, with its attendant evils, is the result."

Attention was asked to insane asylums and other charitable institutions.

The fees and charges imposed upon commerce at the port of New York by existing laws were sharply remarked upon, and reform here was plainly asked for.   Other matters were touched, including the State Capitol building, the State judiciary, and the reapportionment of the State into convenient Congressional districts.

With reference to the subject of Civil Service Reform, so widely discussed during the political canvass, the message said :

" It is submitted that the appointment of subordinates in the several State departments, and their tenure of office or employment, should be based upon fitness and efficiency, and that this principle should be embodied in legislative enactment, to the end that the policy of the State may conform to the reasonable public demand on that subject."

The ex-Mayor of Buffalo knew something about municipal affairs, and he was ready to give an opinion concerning the best remedy for known evils. He said :

" The formation and administration of the government of cities are subjects of much public interest, and of great importance to many of the inhabitants of the State.   The formation of such governments is properly matter for most careful legislation. They should be so organized as to be simple in their details and to cast upon the people affected thereby the full responsibility of their administration. The different departments should be in such accord as in their operation to lead toward the same results. Divided counsels and divided responsibility to the people, on the part of municipal officers, it is believed, give rise to much that is objectionable in the government of cities. If, to remedy this evil, the chief executive should be made answerable to the people for the proper conduct of the city's affairs, it is quite clear that his power in the selection of those who manage its different departments should be greatly enlarged.''

Large parts of the membership of both of the great political parties had loudly complained of their inability to make themselves heard at all in party management, and a note of reform was sounded in the message :

'' The protection of the people in their primaries will, it is hoped, be secured by the early passage of a law for that purpose, which will rid the present system of the evils which surround it, tending to defraud the people of rights closely connected with their privileges as citizens.''

A general exhortation to watchfulness and fidelity closed the first communication of Governor Cleveland to the Legislature. Some men said that he had laid out too much, or more than was at all likely to be accomplished during his term of office, and they were right enough, since he was not the legislative, but the executive, servant of the people. Other men, eagerly expecting something sensational and exciting, declared that his message was a very tame affair. Any kind of governor might have said all that was in it and not set up for a reformer at all.

Perhaps there were others who discerned an un-looked-for maturity and an acquaintance with public affairs beyond what might have been expected from a mere "ward politician," as Mr. Cleveland's opponents had contemptuously termed him.

The great mass of the citizens of the Empire State, if they read the message at all, did so and then went about their business with that curious willingness to let things take care of themselves until next election which is so marked a feature of American politics. They had provided themselves with a Legislature, a governor, and with nobody knew just how many other officials, and so long as the great social machine jolted along without hurting any man, his place was to let it jolt. Perhaps this new man from Erie County might run against something, if he should try to keep his promises, and if he did the newspapers would have something to say about it. There had been a real busy campaign, to be sure, but it was all over now.

CHAPTER XI.

Bachelor's Hall in the Executive Mansion—The Executive Chamber—Open Doors—Retained for the State—Habits of Business—A Legislative Critic and Editor—Veto Messages—The Five-Cent Fare Bill—The Mayor's Bill.

FOR the first time in his life Grover Cleveland found himself keeping house. He had decidedly too much house to keep, considering the facts that he was a bachelor and that his dwelling was the commodious residence provided by the State of New York for its governors. There was something peculiarly lonesome about it, for although the mansion has no claim to magnificence, it is amply large enough for a numerous family as well as for private and public hospitalities. During all his years of professional and official life in Buffalo, since leaving his uncle's house at Black Rock, he had lived very unostentatiously, beginning with his attic room at the Southern Hotel. After that he had had some experience of boarding-houses, but had been best satisfied with his later apartments, well furnished and comfortable, in the same building with his law office and exceedingly convenient to all his work and business.

In those days any person seeking him was most likely to find him, at almost any hour, toiling away among the books and papers in his office. The endless procession of his fellow citizens now pouring toward him discovered that he was forming a strictly similar habit of life in Albany. The Executive Chamber at the Capitol was his work room, and there was his time to be spent, as the work upon his hands called for all the trained, methodical, tireless industry which had been the one secret of his success in life. All the circumstances of his education and career had inclined him to a dislike of ceremonial formality and of the guarded etiquette which is often so useful, so necessary a protection to men in positions of authority. He now somewhat hastily swept away any barriers which might surround the Executive Chamber, for he gave the attendants a sweeping direction to "admit any one who asks to see the governor."

The requirements of public business and of a conscientious economy of time, with the help of a few dozens daily of useless intruders, would surely obtain the reform of so unwise a law as that ; but the order indicated character, and the fact of its utterance gave sincere pleasure to a multitude of simple people who had no idea of ever going to Albany.

Grover Cleveland was governor as completely as he had been sheriff or mayor, but it was speedily evident that he had taken up his duties with an idea of their nature and of his relations to them which corresponded with rare accuracy to his own individuality. He was really the attorney and counsellor retained in the great case of the State and People of New York *v.* Whomsoever-it-may-concern.

That direct and comprehensive view of the matter simplified everything for him, and it also throws a helping light upon his course of action as governor. It would be a needlessly stupid misconception to suppose that the uses of the State executive were in this manner narrowed or that they lost anything of their dignity.

The multiform ramifications of the "great case" in hand were found to require a transfer of the work-a-day routine of the Buffalo apartments and law office to the Executive Mansion and Chamber. These latter were less than a mile apart, just a good, bracing walk after a seven-o'clock-in-the-morning breakfast. On reaching the Chamber business began, with heaps of documents and correspondence already prepared by a hard-worked private secretary. Sooner or later, as the work in hand might indicate, visitors were admitted, but at one o'clock the governor walked out and went home for luncheon. Punctually at two o'clock he was again in the Chamber to toil until six, and that hour was apt to terminate any reception of callers. Dinner had to be walked home after and eaten, that Governor Cleveland might be back at his work by eight o'clock in the evening. Precisely how late in the night it might be before another walk home could be taken was not always easy to guess beforehand, but word went out through the city of Albany that "This here new governor's a right down hard-working sort of man. Doesn't make any fuss, neither. He walks, too ; doesn't seem to have any use for a carriage."

The Legislature of 1882 had provided for a "Civil Service Reform" Commission, and Governor Cleveland's appointments in compliance with the law gave very general satisfaction. Only moderate and almost inevitable criticisms were made upon his other appointments. With reference to such fault as was found, he was doubtless entitled to the defence made for President Lincoln in the matter of military commanders : "Well, but you know he had a good deal on his hands, and he hadn't time to make a lot of new men. He had to pick and choose among such an assortment as there was on hand, and some of 'em were odd patterns."

Any sketch of a public man still before the people, if it happen to be prepared for party purposes, may properly contain a minute record of his public acts, but biography, designing to present a just view of character and career, does not require such minuteness.

Merely-local success attained by Grover Cleveland, within what was deemed a narrow area, had only prepared the minds of men to watch with more than ordinary curiosity for any further indications of the broader grasp of mind and will, the dignified requirements of executive statesmanship, which are not often discovered, but which, when found, are of such vast value.

Mr. Cleveland had absolutely no parliamentary experience. He had not sought legislative duties or honors. It may be that his distaste for them grew out of an instinctive perception in his own mind that he lacked the peculiar qualifications of a parliamentary leader.

In any legislative assembly there were weaker and more flexible men who could out-manœuvre him. It now remained to be seen whether or not his capacity and training fitted him for the important and responsible post of State critic and revising editor of the huge volume of current legislation at Albany, for that is precisely what the law demands that the governor shall be.

Upon questions affecting the entire nation, the new governor's record was as yet simply that of his party. His speech before the Manhattan Club, however, with his first message as its commentary, testified that he was prepared to take an independent position. He was a man who was in the habit of thinking for himself and having the courage of his convictions. Beyond that, his earlier utterances did not go, and each executive act, positive or negative, followed its immediate predecessor without anything resembling a prophetic warning. It was not long before a number of disturbed and anxious lobbyists were heard to remark, in one form or another, "There is no telling what Grover Cleveland will do next. Any kind of bill must take its own chances with him."

The intense toil performed in the Executive Chamber was measured precisely by what the friends of each particular bill, large or small, described as its "chances," omitting from these all considerations outside of the public uses, the legal structure, and the constitutionality of the measure itself. Almost, if not quite, for the first time in the history of the Legislature, it found the governor acting as its law counsel, as well as critic and editor, for really well-meaning bills, with defects only of construction, came quietly slipping back unvetoed, to be tinkered up for signature. There was rarely any extended discussion or delay in such cases, and nobody was disposed to say that the governor was "exercising an undue influence over legislation."

Owing to the rapid growth of the State in wealth and population, the rise of hamlets into villages and towns, and the swift expansion of new settlements into prosperous cities, the work of successive Legislatures has largely consisted of experimental "charter" manufacturing and mending. The city of New York alone has furnished an all but ceaseless run of business of this sort—largely job work. Governor Cleveland's declarations concerning municipal reforms pointed directly at local self-government and local responsibility. In this he was pretty well sustained by public opinion, except with reference to the great seaport, where no local majorities could be intrusted with focalized interests which are worldwide rather than municipal.

Only a month or so after the inauguration, "An act to amend and consolidate the several acts relating to the city of Elmira," was returned with a veto message which denounced it as "special legislation of the most objectionable character," and designed to "establish a different rule to govern the liability of the city of Elmira in cases of injury caused by negligence, than that which prevails in other parts of the State."

A bill relating to the city of Lyons was returned with specific reasons for its disapproval, and with general remarks relating to the class of measures to which it evidently belonged.

"There are other sections of this charter," said the governor, "which might be criticised, to which I will not refer. It is quite apparent that something should be done to prevent the introduction, or, at any rate, the passage of such bills as this. They seem often to be prepared without any care, or without any appreciation of the evils to be remedied, or the manner of accomplishing improvements. Once here, they attract but little attention, because they are supposed to be of no importance to the Legislature, being local in their nature. And then they are good-naturedly allowed to pass and to reach the executive, a mass of impracticable inconsistencies and incongruous and useless crudities, which, if allowed to go upon our statute books, would be a disgrace to the State and the law-making power."

There were other vetoes which exhibited the same readiness to protect any public purse throughout the State, from such overflowing patriotism as had induced the aldermen of Buffalo to give away other men's money for the celebration of Decoration Day. For example, the Legislature was carefully given the constitutional reasons why it had no power to authorize the county of Chautauqua to appropriate for the construction of a soldiers' monument, money raised for general purposes by taxation.

An unnecessary act to enable the Fayetteville supervisors to borrow money to buy a fire engine was sent back with as scrupulous care as was any more important measure.

The character and minuteness of Governor Cleveland's examination of legislation brought before him, as well as his very thorough study of the general subject of local self-government by the people, do not appear so manifestly in any of his earlier or later veto-messages as in the reasons given by him for approving and signing what was known as the Mayor's Bill, enacting a notable change in the conduct of New York City affairs. There was a very powerful opposition to this measure, and its most active opponents were prominent members of the Democratic Party. To them and to the general public, the governor argued the entire case, in a message dated March 17th, 1884, but which had evidently been long in course of preparation. He had knowledge of the kind of work which might sometimes be expected from a board of aldermen, whether Buffalo Republicans or New York Democrats, and he knew that the people of the latter city had generally shown good sense in the selection of their mayors. The message may be dull reading to many, but the man who prepared and sent it can be better understood by its perusal. Any practised student of human character will hardly fail to note a high degree of philosophical sincerity in Governor Cleveland's analysis of the bill. He wrote :

" The interest which has been aroused regarding the merits of this bill, and quite a determined hostility which has been developed on the part of those entitled to respectful consideration, appear to justify a brief reference to the principles and purposes which seem to me to be involved in the measure, and an incidental statement of the process of thought by which I have been led to approve the same.

" The opponents of the bill have invoked the inviolability of the rights of the people to rule themselves, and have insisted upon the preservation of a wise distribution of power among the different branches of government ; and I have listened to solemn warnings against the subversive tendency of the concentration of power in municipal rule, and the destructive consequences of any encroachment upon the people's rights and prerogatives.

" I hope I have not entirely misconceived the scope and reach of this bill ; but it seems to me that my determination as to whether or not it should become a law does not depend upon the reverence I entertain for such fundamental principles.

" The question is not whether certain officers heretofore elected by the people of the city of New York shall, under the provisions of a new law, be appointed. The transfer of power from an election by the people to an appointment by other authority, has _already been made.

" The present charter of the city provides that the mayor ' shall nominate, and by and with the consent of the Board of Aldermen appoint the heads of departments.'

" The bill under consideration provides that after the 1st day of January, 1885, ' all appointments to office in the city of New York now made by the mayor and confirmed by the Board of Aldermen shall be made by the mayor without such confirmation.'

" The change proposed is clearly apparent.

" By the present charter the mayor, elected by all the people of the city, if a majority of twenty-four aldermen elected by the voters of twenty-four separate districts concur with him, may appoint the administrative officers who shall have charge and management of the city departments.

" The bill presented for my action allows the mayor alone to appoint these officers. This authority is not conferred upon the mayor now in office, who was chosen without anticipation on the part of the people who elected him, that he should exercise this power, but upon the incoming mayor who, after the passage of the act, shall be elected, with the full knowledge on the part of the people, at the time they cast their votes, that they are constituting an agent to act for them in the selection of certain other city officers.

" This selection under either statute is delegated by the people. In the one case it is exercised by the chief executive acting with twenty-four officers representing as many different sections of the municipality ; in the other by the chief executive alone.

" I cannot see that any principle of Democratic rule is more violated in the one case than in the other. It appears to be a mere change of instrumentalities.

" It will hardly do to say that because the aldermen are elected annually, and the mayor every two years, that the former are nearer the people and more especially their representatives. The difference in their terms is not sufficient to make a distinction in their direct relations to the citizen.

" Nor are the rights of the people to self-government in theory and principle better protected when the power of appointment is vested in twenty-five men, twenty-four of whom are responsible only to their constituents in their respective districts, than when this power is put in the hands of one man elected by all the people of the municipality with particular reference to the exercise of such power. Indeed, in the present condition of affairs, if disagreement arises between the mayor and the aldermen, the selection of officers by the representative of all the people might be defeated by the adverse action of thirteen representatives of thirteen aldermanic districts. And it is perfectly apparent that these thirteen might, and often would, represent a decided minority of the people of the municipality.

" It cannot be claimed that an arrangement which permits such a result is pre-eminently democratic.

" It has been urged that the proposed change is opposed to the principle of home rule. If it is intended to claim that the officers, the creation of which is provided for, should be elected, it has no relevancy, for that question is not in any manner presented for my determination. And it surely cannot be said that the doctrine of home rule prevents any change by the Legislature of the organic law of municipalities. The people of the city cannot themselves make such change ; and if legislative aid cannot be invoked to that end, it follows that abuses, flagrant and increasing, must be continued, and existing charter provisions, the inadequacy of which for the protection and prosperity of the people is freely admitted, must be perpetuated. It is the interference of the Legislature with the administration of municipal government, by agencies arbitrarily created by legislative enactment, and the assumption by the law-making power of the State of the rights to regulate such details of city government as are or should be under the supervision of local authorities, that should be condemned as a violation of the doctrine of home rule.

" In any event I am convinced that I should not disapprove the bill before me on the ground that it violates any principle which is now recognized and exemplified in the government of the city of New York.

" I am also satisfied that as between the system now prevailing and that proposed, expediency and a close regard to improved municipal administration lead to my approval of the measure.

" If the chief executive of the city is to be held responsible for its order and good government, he should not be hampered by any interference with his selection of subordinate administrative offi- cers ; nor should he be permitted to find in a divided responsibility an excuse for any neglect of the best interests of the people.

"The plea should never be heard that a bad nomination had been made because it was the only one that could secure con- firmation.

" No instance has been cited in which a bad appointment has been prevented by the refusal of the Board of Aldermen of the city of New York to confirm a nomination.

" An absolute and undivided responsibility on the part of the appointing power accords with correct business principles, the appli- cation of which to public affairs will always, I believe, direct the way to good administration and the protection of the people's interests.

" The intelligence and watchfulness of the citizens of New York should certainly furnish a safe guarantee that the duties and powers devolved by this legislation upon their chosen representative, will be well and wisely bestowed ; and if they err or are betrayed, their remedy is close at hand.

" I can hardly realize the unprincipled boldness of the man who would accept at the hands of his neighbors this sacred trust, and standing alone in the full light of public observation, should wil- fully prostitute his powers and defy the will of the people.

" To say that such a man could by such means perpetuate his wicked rule, concedes either that the people are vile or that self- government is a deplorable failure.

" It is claimed that because some of these appointees become members of the Board of Estimate and Apportionment, which determines very largely the amount of taxation, therefore the power to select them should not be given to the mayor. If the question presented was whether officials having such important duties and functions should be elected by the people or appointed, such a consideration might well be urged in favor of their election. But they are now appointed, and they will remain appointive, whether the proposed bill should be rejected or approved. This being the situation, the importance of the duties to be performed by these officials has to do with the care to be exercised in their selection, rather than the choice between the two modes of appointment which are under consideration.

" For some time prior to the year 1872, these appointments were made by the mayor without confirmation, as is contemplated by the bill now before me. In that year a measure passed the Legislature giving the power of appointment to the Common Council. The chief executive of the State at that time was a careful and thorough student of municipal affairs, having large and varied experience in public life. He refused to approve the bill, on the ground that it was a departure from the principle which should be applied to the administration of the affairs of the city, and for the reason that the mayor should be permitted to appoint the subordinate administrative officers without the interference of any other authority.

" This reference to the treatment of the subject by one of my distinguished predecessors in office, affords me the opportunity to quote from his able and vigorous veto message which he sent to the Legislature on that occasion. He said :

" ' Nowhere on this continent is it so essentially a condition of good government as in the city of New York, that the chief executive officer should be clothed with ample powers, have full control over subordinate administrative departments, and so be subject to an undivided responsibility to the people and to public opinion for all errors, shortcomings, and wrong-doings by subordinate officers.'

" He also said :

" ' Give to the city a chief executive, with full power to appoint all heads of administrative departments. Let him have power to remove his subordinates, being required to publicly assign his reason.'

" He further declared :

" ' The members of the Common Council, in New York, will

exert all the influence over appointments which is consistent with
the public good, without having the legal power of appointment,
or any part of it, vested in their hands.'

" In 1876, after four added years of reflection and observation,
he said, in a public address, when suggesting a scheme of municipal government :

" ' Have, therefore, no provision in your charter requiring the
consent of the Common Council to the mayor's appointment of
heads of departments ; *that only opens the way for dictation by the
council or for bargains.* This is not the way to get good men nor
to fix the full responsibility for maladministration upon the people's chosen prime minister.'

" These are the utterances of one who, during two terms, had
been Mayor of the city of New York, and for two terms Recorder
of that city ; and who for four years had been Governor of the
State.

" No testimony, it seems to me, could be more satisfactory and
convincing.

" It is objected that this bill does not go far enough, and that
there should be a rearrangement of the terms of these officers ; also
that some of them should be made elective.   This is undoubtedly
true ; and I shall be glad to approve further judicious legislation
supplementary to this, which shall make the change more valuable
and surround it with safeguards in the interests of the citizens.
But such further legislation should be well digested and conservative, and, above all, not proposed for the purpose of gaining a
mere partisan advantage.

" I have not referred to the pernicious practices which the present
mode of making appointments in the city of New York engenders,
nor to the constantly-recurring bad results for which it is responsible.   They are in the plain sight of every citizen of the State.

" I believe the change made by the provisions of this bill gives
opportunity for an improvement in the administration of municipal
affairs ; and I am satisfied that the measure violates no right of
the people of the locality affected, which they now enjoy.   But the
best opportunities will be lost and the most perfect plan of city
government will fail, unless the people recognize their responsibilities and appreciate and realize the privileges and duties of citizenship.   With the most carefully-devised charter, and with all the
protection which legislative enactments can afford them, the people

of the city of New York will not secure a wise and economical rule until those having the most at stake determine to actively interest themselves in the conduct of municipal affairs."

It was eminently necessary that Mr. Cleveland, as a politician whose name and standing were of value to his party, should present good reasons for approving the Mayor's Bill. It was even more so that he should be able to show ample cause for vetoing the Five-Cent Fare Bill about two weeks earlier in the season. If the former was said to favor concentration of power in a single official hand, the latter appealed to a very active and sensitive popular sentiment.

Jealousy of great corporations and of their increasing wealth and power is by no means confined to the poorer people so often spoken of as "the laboring classes"—in a land where labor is honorable and nearly all men are toilers. Great riches invite envy and anything human reacts with a feeling of resentment from a corporate body with the strength of a machine and the apparent heartlessness of a goblin. Subsequent events have demonstrated the correctness of the popular decision that five cents was enough for a fare upon the elevated railways of New York City. A restriction to that rate, however, would in their beginning have prevented capital from taking the risks incurred in their construction, and they had been given a more liberal source of income by legislative enactments which were as contracts between elevated railway corporations and the State. When, therefore, public sentiment expressed itself loudly through the press and in a bill passed through the Assembly by a vote of one hundred and nine to six, and the Senate by a vote of twenty-four to five, an uncommonly interesting study was thereby laid upon the crowded table in the Executive Chamber. Hardly any better test could have been offered of either capacity as a critic, sincerity as a guardian of law and of rights under the law, or of that unconscious sincerity which is really farsighted, and which delivers its possessor from the ditches blundered into by mere demagogues.

Governor Cleveland returned the bill, March 2d, 1884, with an accompanying message which found more readers and aroused a deeper interest than almost any other public document of the day. He presented a full but condensed history of the legislation under which the elevated railways had been constructed, with references to action taken thereon by the courts ; rehearsed the progressive construction of the novel and important viaducts so provided for, and added :

" I am of the opinion that in the legislation and proceedings which I have detailed, and in the fact that pursuant thereto the road of the company was constructed and finished, there exists a contract in favor of this company, which is protected by that clause of the Constitution of the United States which prohibits the passage of a law by any State impairing the obligation of contracts."

Other legal points were set forth, and the message concluded with :

" If I am mistaken in supposing that there are legal objections to this bill, there is another consideration which furnishes to my mind a sufficient reason why I should not give it my approval.

"It seems to me that to arbitrarily reduce these fares, at this time, and under existing· circumstances, involves a breach of faith on the part of the State, and a betrayal of confidence which the State has invited.

"The fact is notorious that for many years rapid transit was the great need of the inhabitants of the city of New York, and was of direct importance to the citizens of the State. Projects which promised to answer the people's wants in this direction failed and were abandoned. The Legislature, appreciating the situation, willingly passed statute after statute, calculated to aid and encourage a solution of the problem. Capital was timid, and hesitated to enter a new field full of risks and dangers. By the promise of liberal fares, as will be seen in all the acts passed on the subject, and through other concessions gladly made, capitalists were induced to invest their money in the enterprise, and rapid transit but lately became an accomplished fact. But much of the risk, expense, and burden attending the maintenance of these roads are yet unknown and threatening. In the mean time, the people of the city of New York are receiving the full benefit of their construction, a great enhancement of the value of the taxable property of the city has resulted, and in addition to taxes, more than one hundred and twenty thousand dollars, being five per cent in increase, pursuant to the law of 1868, has been paid by the companies into the city treasury, on the faith that the rate of fare agreed upon was secured to them. I am not aware that the corporations have, by any default, forfeited any of their rights ; and if they have, the remedy is at hand under existing laws. Their stock and their bonds are held by a large number of citizens, and the income of these roads depends entirely upon fares received from passengers. The reduction proposed is a large one, and it is claimed will permit no dividends to investors. This may not be true, but we should be satisfied it is not, before the proposed law takes effect.

"It is manifestly important that invested capital should be protected, and that its necessity and usefulness in the development of enterprises valuable to the people should be recognized by conservative conduct on the part of the State government.

"But we have especially in our keeping the honor and good faith of a great State, and we should see to it that no suspicion attaches, through any act of ours, to the fair fame of the commonwealth. The State should not only be strictly just, but scrupulously fair, and in its relation to the citizen every legal and moral obligation should be recognized.   This can only be done by legislating without vindictiveness or prejudice, and with a firm determination to deal justly and fairly with those from whom we exact obedience.

"I am not unmindful of the fact that this bill originated in the response to the demand of a large portion of the people of New York for cheaper rates of fare between their places of employment and their homes, and I realize fully the desirability of securing to them all the privileges possible, but the experience of other States teaches that we must keep within the limits of law and good faith, lest in the end we bring upon the very people whom we seek to benefit and protect a hardship, which must surely follow when these limits are ignored."

CHAPTER XII

The Approval of Good Men—Minor Vetoes—Prisons and Criminals—The Pardoning Power—Rising to a Higher Level of Fame—The Purity of Elections.

WHATEVER amount and degree of hollow popularity an aspiring politician might hope to gain by assuming to be a champion of the people against the greed and power of corporations had been put away from himself by Governor Cleveland in his veto of the Five-Cent Fare Bill. The vote of a man whose mental darkness prevents him from discerning a point of constitutional law, counts as much in any ballot-box as does that of President Andrew D. White, of Cornell University, or of the venerable President Martin B. Anderson, of the University of Rochester, who at once wrote to the governor vigorous letters of approval. Nevertheless, the public support of such men, not at all connected with partisan politics, went far toward neutralizing the effect of an unthinking uproar which found its bitterest expression in journals tainted with anarchism.

If it was worth something to an entirely new fame to find its statesmanship sustained by the ablest scholars and teachers in the State, perhaps it was worth as much to be assailed by the avowed enemies of law and order, of all property, and of all vested interests.

Men who might, indeed, read a veto message, if its matter displeased them, but who could not in any event appreciate its reasoning, were not likely to be won back again by other vetoes more in accord with their narrow prejudices.

On April 2d, 1883, a veto of an act extending the already great privileges of gas-light companies in the use they are permitted to make of the public streets, contained the following :

"Another fatal objection to this bill is found in the provision allowing the corporations therein named to enter upon private property, and erect and maintain their structures thereon, without the consent of the owner. It seems to me that this is taking private property, or an easement therein, with very little pretext that it is for a public use.

"If a private corporation can, under authority of law, construct its appliances and structures upon the lands of the citizen without his consent, not only for the purpose of furnishing light, but in an experimental attempt to transmit heat and power, the rights of the people may well be regarded as in danger from an undue license to corporate aggrandizement."

In returning another bill, framed and passed for the benefit of the Utica Ice Company, he wrote :

"Our laws in relation to the formation of corporations are extremely liberal, and those who avail themselves of their provisions should be held to a strict compliance with their requirements. There is manifestly no propriety in the passage of a special act to relieve a private corporation and its stockholders, as proposed in this bill."

There was something peculiarly discouraging to a large class of political party workers in the reasons given, on April 9th, 1883, for a very prompt return of a bill proposing important changes in the organization and management of the Fire Department of the city of Buffalo. The assembled legislators of the State were almost rudely informed that :

" The purpose of the bill is too apparent to be mistaken. A tried, economical, and efficient administration of an important department in a large city is to be destroyed, upon partisan grounds or to satisfy personal animosities, in order that the places and patronage attached thereto may be used for party advancement.

" I believe in an open and sturdy partisanship, which secures the legitimate advantages of party supremacy ; but parties were made for the people, and I am unwilling, knowingly, to give my assent to measures purely partisan, which will sacrifice or endanger their interests."

The best and purest corner-grocery statesmen listened to such heretical doctrines with an inward dread that the good old times were on the eve of passing away. With it, however, came the comforting assurance that this sort of thing, if lived up to, would be the end of Grover Cleveland. He was making enemies all over the State, and among them were numbers of able-bodied citizens who knew a great deal about the political anatomy of primaries and the natural selection of delegates to party conventions.

Another broad subject which consumed many of the toilsome hours spent in the Executive Chamber was that of crime, and of criminals, and of the treatment of these after the hands of the law had been laid upon them. It was a study more or less familiar to every practising lawyer and peculiarly so to a man who had been a county sheriff. To any ripeness of preparation or of conviction previously attained by Governor Cleveland, there were now added whatever authority the State executive possesses over the management of prisons and of their inmates, and also the solemn responsibility of the pardoning power.

One of the first acts of the governor, after entering upon the discharge of his duties, was an effort in the direction of a more humane and intelligent treatment of convicts. On February 2d, 1883, he wrote to the Superintendent of State Prisons :

"I deem it proper to call your attention to the provisions of Section 108 of chapter 460 of the laws of 1847, which prohibits the infliction of blows upon any convict in the State prisons, by the keepers thereof, except in self-defence or to suppress a revolt or insurrection ; and also to chapter 869 of the laws of 1869, abolishing the punishment commonly known as the shower-bath, crucifix or yoke, and buck. I suppose these latter forms of punishment were devised to take the place of the blows prohibited by the law of 1847.

" Both of the statutes above referred to seem to be still in force, and, in my opinion, they are in no manner affected by the constitutional amendment giving the superintendent ' the superintendence, management, and control of the prisons,' nor by Sections 1 and 5 of chapter 107 of the laws of 1877, providing that the superintendent shall have the management and control of the prisons and of the convicts therein, and of all matters relating to the government, discipline, police, contracts, and fiscal concerns thereof, and that he shall make such rules and regulations for the government and punishment of the convicts as he may deem proper.

" I especially desire to avoid any injurious interference with the maintenance by the prison authorities of efficient discipline ; but I insist that, in the treatment of prisoners convicted of crime, the existing statutes of the State on that subject should be observed."

He afterward made persistent efforts to accomplish whatever good results were possible under the laws providing for remission of penalties and shortening of terms of imprisonment on account of good behavior and indications of reform. At the same time it became evident that mere petitions, their number or their signatures or their urgency, had but a moderate share in determining the effect of any application for the pardon of a convicted criminal. A large number of pardons were granted, but the percentage was less than in the records of previous governors. No hasty letting loose of a doubtful or dangerous character was likely to occur, when each act of pardon carried with it a written statement of the governor's reasons, in evidence that he had fully satisfied his own mind and had done his duty to the general public as well as to mercy.

There were veto messages of several classes, not indicative of anything especial, excepting, perhaps, the general idea that the Legislature had too many irons in the fire, and that some of these were nearly ruined before being taken out and sent to the governor. One of these, and a fairly representative specimen, was known as the Tenure of Office Bill, particularly affecting certain officials of the city of New York. To the Senate and Assembly providing it with the requisite majority vote, the governor remarked, in his message returning the bill :

" Of all the defective and shabby legislation which has been presented to me, this is the worst and most inexcusable, unless it be its companion, which is entitled ' An act to provide for a more efficient government of the department of parks in the city of New York.' "

The honorable body to which that assurance was given, loudly, in the reading of the message by its clerk, would have been entirely justified in asking itself, " Does this man imagine that he is addressing the Buffalo Board of Aldermen ?"

The worst of it was that the leading journals of both parties appeared to agree with the governor, while all the judges of all the courts said, " Amen."

The first year of Governor Cleveland's term of office drew toward its close in the same untiring routine of daily and hourly toil. He had done absolutely nothing which could be described as " brilliant," in the sense in which that term may be applied to fireworks or to a grand cavalry charge. It seemed as if he must have made more enemies than friends, and, so far as might be, he had been the destruction of any " era of good feeling" among the working politicians even of his own party. There were strong indications that he had been too busy to so much as think of them or of their important relations to his future advancement.

Politicians of a higher grade, men of experience and acumen, deeply interested in great problems of party management and success, looked on with better understanding of an important process which was evidently going forward. They perceived that Grover Cleveland was cutting loose from his former position, and was becoming established upon the level of rank and fame which belongs of right to a successful governor of the greatest State of the Union. He was no longer a new man ; no longer an experiment ; all the voters in the land were now able to answer promptly, if unexpectedly asked the question : " What's the name of the Governor of New York ?" There is no more severe and perfect test of the standing and availability of any public man, if a favorable response can also be obtained to the next question : "Well, glad you know ; what do you think of him ?"

The last public paper sent out in that year from the Executive Chamber at Albany, was dated November 2d, 1883. It was a proclamation by the governor, and contained its own warranty.

" The constitution of the State directs that the governor ' shall take care that the laws are faithfully executed.'

" An appeal has been made to the executive, asking that the laws relating to bribery and corruption at elections be enforced. All must acknowledge that there is nothing more important in our form of government than that the will of the people, which is absolutely the foundation upon which our institutions rest, should be fairly expressed and honestly regarded. Without this our system is a sham and a contrivance, which it is brazen effrontery to call a Republican form of government.

" All this is recognized, in theory, by provisions in the constitution of our State, and by stringent penal enactments aimed at the use of money and other corrupt means to unlawfully influence the suffrages of the people and to thwart their will. And yet I am convinced that a disregard of those enactments is frequent, and in many cases shamelessly open and impudent.

" I, therefore, call upon all district-attorneys within this State, and all sheriffs and peace officers, and others having in charge the execution of the laws, to exercise the utmost diligence in the discovery and punishment of violations of the statutes referred to, and they are admonished that neglect of duty in this regard will be promptly dealt with.

" And I request that all good citizens, in the performance of a plain duty, for the protection of free institutions and in their own interests, report to the proper authorities the commission of any offence against the statutes passed to preserve the purity of the ballot."

CHAPTER XIII.

Hospitalities of the Executive Mansion—Neglect of Political Machinery—Balanced Parties—The Presidency—Protection and Free Trade—Second Annual Message of Governor Cleveland—Occasional Public Speeches.

THERE have been governors of the State of New York during whose terms of official residence in Albany the Executive Mansion became a social centre, à house of more or less brilliant hospitalities. It was not so during the time when it was occupied as a " bachelor's hall " by Grover Cleveland. Even as a small boy in Fayetteville Academy he had been sociable and popular without deserting his books for the company of other boys. The earlier years of his manhood had been given to study and toil in a manner which had impelled him to reject every effort made by his friends to draw him out into society. His public duties and his law practice had afterward confirmed the strong habits already formed, and he carried them with him to Albany. Had there been a Mrs. Cleveland in the governor's house, all would have been different of necessity, but, as it was, the ready welcome was circumscribed by natural limitations, and Albany society was more than a little disposed to resent the temporary loss of one of its most important features and resources.

Another and widely different characteristic of the executive workshop was discernible with peculiar distinctness, for Grover Cleveland was governor, and he was very little more. There had been governors who undertook, at the same time, to act as the chiefs and heads of the parties to which they owed their election. Under their administrations the executive office became the inner den of a vast and busy political spider-web. They caught, or failed to catch, all manner of partisan advantages, not to speak of instances wherein the very net had a ruined look at the sunset of some uncomfortable November day. Governor Cleveland did not apparently avail himself of the official opportunity given him to become the leader and manager of his nominal party in the State. Other eminent Democrats were almost disposed to be pleased with the fact that they could discover no purpose of dictation or even of undue urgency in any of his conferences with them. Now and then, however, he said and did things which might well have reminded them of the opening sentences of his address to the Manhattan Club and its guests. He himself apparently remembered, at least, the substance of several pertinent phrases. " We stand to-night," he then remarked, " in the full glare of a grand and brilliant manifestation of the popular will, and in the light of it, how vain and small appear the tricks of politicians and the movements of partisan machinery ! He must be blind who cannot see that the people well understand their power, and are determined to use it when their rights and interests are threatened. There should be no scepticism to-night as to the strength and perpetuity of our Government. Partisan leaders have learned, too, that the people will not unwittingly, blindly, follow, and that something more than wavering devotion to party is necessary in order to secure their allegiance. I am quite certain that the late demonstration did not spring from any pre-existing love for the party which has been called to power, nor did the people put the affairs of the State in our hands to be by them forgotten."

The Democratic Party acting by itself and for itself could not have elected its candidate for governor. Its leaders had not selected Grover Cleveland as their candidate because of "any pre-existing love" for him, and he knew it. He and they were still standing "in the full glare of a grand and brilliant manifestation," of the real nature of the strength and of the triumph which had been added to the Democratic Party when it acquired the sudden sagacity to become the servant of the people and to nominate a man whom the people would trust to serve them, rather than his party or his ambition. If they should find their trust betrayed, no amount of partisan manipulation of political machinery would prevent the effects of their inevitable resentment. So the party, or rather a selfish and stupid mess of factions in the party, grumbled and growled that it could not manage and direct its own governor, manufactured by it out of a Buffalo mayor, while at the same time its better and more genuinely patriotic elements congratulated themselves over the steady growth of a new political force from which great things might be expected. If the general public should go on in the process of absorbing and digesting the idea that Grover Cleveland was not only capable but honest, and likely to continue so in office, there might be a future before the Democratic Party. Otherwise, the political situation had a gloomy look, for the Republican Party was manifesting a tremendous vitality, and had not the least intention of surrendering its long control of the national authority. The best conditions for wise and healthful administration of public affairs were attained by the nation when its two great parties were so nearly balanced, but several unpleasant illustrations of the same political truth were to be obtained by contrasts in States and municipalities wherein the voice of but one party could be distinctly heard.

The Presidential canvass for a successor to Garfield and Arthur began in 1882, and whatever prospect there might otherwise have been for a re-election of Mr. Arthur died away when the stunning defeat of his candidate, Judge Folger, announced that the electoral votes of the State of New York could not be obtained for him. The Republican list from which the party could select its standard bearers was hardly narrowed by that conclusion, since its long predominance in national affairs had made it only too rich in names well known to all men. An especial disadvantage was quickly apparent in the fact that, with reference to any eminent

Republican spoken of as a probable candidate, the Opposition outside of the party and the very free-spoken contestants within it were able to announce at once the weak points of that supposed nomination. It was possible to say of man after man that, in the presentation of his claims to the Presidency, the unwieldy strength of the organization proposing him must submit to be shorn of the active aid at least of this or that important faction and factor.

The beginning of the year 1884 found the great canvass fairly under way. As it progressed, evidence appeared continually that the issue was likely to be of a personal nature first ; secondarily, one of party name, and altogether lastly, of any direct and immediate bearing upon great questions of public policy, financial or otherwise.

The first issue could not be put into definite shape before hearing from the respective party national conventions. The second came to the minds of a vast multitude very much in the form of the question : " Has the Republican Party ruled long enough ?" And there would have been a decidedly sufficient negative response if the inquiry had been permitted to go forth uncomplicated. There were enough of voters whose dread of change, for its own sake, would have turned the scale against the Democracy if the latter had not assumed an attitude of the most cautious conservatism.

As to other matters, the issue of " protection" and " free trade" offers the best example. It was already before the people, under full and continu-

ous discussion, from year to year, with reference to
Congressional elections. It had its place in the
Presidential canvass and in the party platforms.
Many men had ideas and convictions relating to it,
and a great many failed altogether to care much
about a matter which they did not at all understand. Moreover, there were many Protectionist
Democrats, as there had always been, and there were
many Free-Trade Republicans in like manner. The
result of the election might change the course of
legislation upon the tariff, whether a Democrat or
a Republican should be chosen President of the
United States, but no hope or expectation of such
a change in legislation actually turned votes enough
either way to have determined the result. So far
as the tariff was concerned, the November votes of
1884 were counted before any nominations were
made.

Very nearly all, if not all, of the governors of the
States of the Union prepared and sent in to the
several Legislatures their accustomed annual messages in the Winter of 1884. In each commonwealth the message of its chief executive officer was
more or less a matter of general interest, and was
read and commented upon by all the public-spirited
citizens within the State boundary lines laid down
on the map. Just beyond those lines, the interest
and the reading ceased, with one notable exception.
All over the land there were men, of both political
parties, who took means to obtain an early copy of
the message of the Governor of the State of New
York. It was to be his second annual message,

and, perhaps, it would contain something of which use might be made in more ways than one.

Governor Cleveland was ready on January 1st, 1884, and it was almost painfully plain that the document which he sent to the Legislature had been patiently prepared for perusal by the members of that body rather than for general readers in search of sensational literature. With dry and business-like minuteness, its condensed paragraphs toiled from field to field of the several interests of the Empire State. He had evidently mastered all the details of the great case in which the people had retained him, but there was no eloquence whatever in the manner or matter of his summing up. The legislators said that it was a good message. People generally declared that the governor must have spent a deal of hard work in putting all those things together in that shape—that is, unless he got somebody to help him, and most likely he did. Those whose keener vision read between the lines recognized the important truth that this message was written by a man who had expanded, perceptibly, since November, 1882. Responsibility had worked well with him, and he had manifestly risen to a higher plane of thought and of character. That he possessed the born strength to do so was one of the marks which a party or a people might be glad to find upon a public servant. Of only too many very capable men it had been possible to discover almost the date and day when they reached the limit of their growth. Of some it was even possible to say, "Just along here it seems as if they began to shrivel."

Whether or not Grover Cleveland was ever to exhibit signs of the uncertain quality gasped at as
"greatness," he was manifestly as yet advancing,
and the popular instinct acknowledged the personal
fact which it did not attempt to formulate.

The annual message concluded with a summary
of the past year's legislative and executive performance, and with an earnest demand for attention to
one national subject nearly concerning the first commercial State of the Union.

" The people of the State are to be congratulated upon the progress made during the last year in the direction of wholesome legislation.

" The most practical and thorough civil service reform has gained
a place in the policy of the State.

" Political assessments upon employés in the public departments
have been prohibited.

" The rights of all citizens at primary elections have been protected by law.

" A bureau has been established to collect information and sta-
tistics touching the relations between labor and capital.

" The sale of forest land at the source of our important streams
has been prohibited, thereby checking threatened disaster to the
commerce on our water-ways.

" Debts and obligations for the payment of money, owned
though not actually held within the State, have been made subject
to taxation, thus preventing an unfair evasion of liability for the
support of the Government.

" Business principles have been introduced in the construction
and care of the new Capitol and other public buildings, and waste
and extravagance thereby prevented.

" A law has been passed for the better administration of the
emigration bureau and the prevention of its abuses.

" The people have been protected by placing co-operative insurance companies under the control and supervision of the insurance department.

" The fees of receivers have been reduced and regulated in the interests of the creditors of insolvent companies.

" A Court of Claims has been established where the demands of citizens against the State may be properly determined.

" These legislative accomplishments, and others of less importance and prominence, may well be cited in proof of the fact that the substantial interests of the people of the State have not been neglected.

" The State of New York largely represents within her borders the development of every interest which makes a nation great. Proud of her place as leader in the community of States, she fully appreciates her intimate relations to the prosperity of the country ; and justly realizing the responsibility of her position, she recognizes, in her policy and her laws, as of first importance, the freedom of commerce from all unnecessary restrictions. Her citizens have assumed the burden of maintaining, at their own cost and free to commerce, the water-way which they have built and through which the products of the great West are transported to the seaboard. At the suggestion of danger she hastens to save her Northern forests, and thus preserve to commerce her canals and vessel-laden rivers. The State has become responsible for a bureau of emigration, which cares for those who seek our shores from other lands, adding to the nation's population and hastening to the development of its vast domain ; while at the country's gateway a quarantine, established by the State, protects the nation's health.

" Surely this great commonwealth, committed fully to the interests of commerce and all that adds to the country's prosperity, may well inquire how her efforts and sacrifices have been answered ; and she, of all the States, may urge that the interests thus by her protected should by the greater government administered for all be fostered for the benefit of the American people.

" Fifty years ago a most distinguished foreigner, who visited this country and studied its condition and prospects, wrote : ' When I contemplate the ardor with which the Americans prosecute commerce, the advantages which aid them, and the success of their undertakings, I cannot help believing that they will one day become the first maritime power of the globe. They are bound to rule the seas as the Romans were to conquer the world . . . The Americans themselves now transport to their own shores nine tenths of the European produce which they consume, and they also bring three fourths of the exports of the New World to the European consumers. The ships of the United States fill the docks of Havre and of Liverpool ; while the number of English and French vessels which are to be seen at New York is comparatively small.'

" We turn to the actual results reached since these words were written with disappointment. In 1840, American vessels carried 82 9-10 per cent of all our exports and imports ; in 1850, 72 5-10 ; in 1860, 66 5-10 ; in 1870, 35 6-10 ; in 1880, 17 4-10 ; in 1882, 15 5-10.

" The citizen of New York, looking beyond his State and all her efforts in the interest of commerce and national growth, will naturally inquire concerning the causes of this decadence of American shipping.

" While he sternly demands of his home government the exact limitation of taxation by the needs of the State, he will challenge the policy that accumulates millions of useless and unnecessary surplus in the national Treasury, which has been not less a tax because it was indirectly but surely added to the cost of the people's life.

" Let us anticipate a time when care for the people's needs as they actually arise, and the application of remedies, as wrongs appear, shall lead in the conduct of national affairs ; and let us undertake the business of legislation with the full determination that these principles shall guide us in the performance of our duties as guardians of the interests of the people.''

The governor's message contained nothing which could be made use of against either himself or his party. It did not even claim the good legislation accomplished as exclusively Democratic work, nor did it assume credit for the crushing of evil and defective measures. The party press, indeed, asserted all that was needful and opened the way for some pretty keen rejoinders which the governor himself had not invited. Republican journals commented upon his appeal on behalf of American commerce that the disappearance of American shipping from the ocean carrying-trade was an evil for which no party was responsible, and for which no party was prepared to provide a remedy. The operation of causes set on foot by reason of the Civil War had co-operated with the general change from ships of wood to ships of iron, and from the use of side-wheel steamers to the employment of propellers, during a period when American shipyards were idle by compulsion. Nevertheless, did the governor's facts and figures bear an appearance of accusing the dominant party of having done nothing and of being responsible for the existing state of affairs.

When all criticisms had been made and when even party editors had ceased to discuss the message, it dawned upon a great many minds that Governor Cleveland had somehow managed to place himself before the people upon his record, without having made any promises whatever concerning his future course or conduct. It would, therefore, be necessary to go along with him, from day to day, without anything resembling what the railway managers call a " time table."

The Senate and the Assembly settled down to their business, and the Executive Chamber became as much a mere workshop as ever. In both parts of the Capitol a large amount of interesting and important public service was performed during the months immediately succeeding, but not any of it was of a nature to throw new light upon the character or tendencies of the governor. With reference to each and every bill presented to him for signature, his action was thoroughly consistent with his declared principles and previous action. Even partisan watchfulness failed to discern any new features. The large Roman Catholic element was waked up once to listen to his reasons for vetoing an appropriation for the New York Catholic Protectory, but his position was too strong to be disputed, even if ultra-sectarianism winced over the following passage :

"The name of this institution implies that only Roman Catholic children are there provided for. If this be so, that fact furnishes a good reason why public funds should not be contributed to its support. A violation of this principle in this case would tend to subject the State Treasury to demands on behalf of all classes of sectarian institutions, which a due care for the money of the State and a just economy could not concede, and which would yet have a justification in precedent."

More than once was executive courage called for in dealing with bills especially affecting the interests of laboring men, but criticism was disarmed when it was announced that the governor's action was taken after prudent consultation with the recognized representatives of organized labor. In fact, both the friends and enemies of Mr. Cleveland had already learned to expect from him the constant exercise of a very high degree of prudence, and this expectation became a principal ingredient in the partisan and popular confidence which he was more and more acquiring.

It was a matter of course that the presence of the governor of the State should be in demand upon various occasions of public interest, but only a few

of the many invitations received could be accepted
without irksomely diminishing the hours available
for the executive workshop. It was already well
understood that nothing like oratorical display was
to be expected of him, but he never failed to present in good shape for remembrance the one idea by
which he seemed to be possessed.

To the thousands assembled at the Oswegatchie
Fair, at Ogdensburg, for instance, he said :

" While I, in this manner, urge you to claim from the soil all it
has to yield, by the aid of intelligent efforts in its cultivation, I
cannot refrain from reminding you that, as citizens, you have
something else to do. You have the responsibility of citizenship
upon you, and you should see to it that you do your duty to the
State, not only by increasing its wealth by the cultivation and improvement of the soil, but by an intelligent selection of those who
shall act for you in the enactment and execution of your laws.
Weeds and thistles, if allowed in your fields, defeat your toil and
efforts. So abuses in the administration of your government lead
to the dishonor of your State, choke and thwart the wishes of the
people, and waste their substance."

The Principal of the Albany High School one day
invited the governor to come in and take a look at
the boys and girls. When there, it was almost of
course that he should be expected to say something. The brief remarks which he made may seem
almost commonplace, but they were reported and
printed and were widely read, as offering one more
indication of the habitual thought of the man whose
qualifications for high position were fast becoming
so important a matter of national inquiry. Among
other things, he said :

" I never visit a school in these days without contrasting the advantages of the scholar of to-day with those of a time not many years in the past. Within my remembrance even, the education which is freely offered you was only secured by those whose parents were able to send them to academies and colleges. And thus, when you entered this school very many of you began where your parents left off.

" The theory of the State, in furnishing more and better schools for the children, is that it tends to fit them to better perform their duties as citizens, and that an educated man or woman is apt to be more useful as a member of the community.

" This leads to the thought that those who avail themselves of the means thus tendered them are in duty bound to make such use of their advantages as that the State shall receive in return the educated and intelligent citizens and members of the community which it has the right to expect from its schools. You, who will soon be the men of the day, should consider that you have assumed an obligation to fit yourselves, by the education which you may, if you will, receive in this school, for the proper performance of any duty of citizenship and to fill any public station to which you may be called. And it seems to me to be none the less important that those who are to be the wives and mothers should be educated, refined, and intelligent. To tell the truth, I should be afraid to trust the men, educated though they should be, if they were not surrounded by pure and true womanhood. Thus it is that you all, now and here, from the oldest to the youngest, owe a duty to the State which can only be answered by diligent study and the greatest possible improvement. It is too often the case that in all walks and places the disposition is to render the least possible return to the State for the favors which she bestows."

There was an almost stern earnestness in the governor's response to his welcome before the Bar Association, but no honest lawyer could have been unwilling to hear him say :

" I reflected that there would be here an assemblage of my professional brethren, and the impulse was irresistible to be among them for a time, though necessarily brief, and to feel about me the atmosphere from which, for a twelvemonth, I have been excluded. I beg to assure you, gentlemen, that in the crowd of official duties which for the past year have surrounded me, I have never lost sight of the guild to which I am proud to belong, nor have I lost any of my love and care for the noble profession I have chosen. On the contrary, as I have seen the controlling part which the law-yers of the State assumed in the enacting of her laws, and in all other works that pertain to her progress and her welfare, I have appreciated more than ever the value and the usefulness of the legal profession. And when I have seen how generally my pro-fessional brethren have been faithful to their public trusts, my pride has constantly increased.

" And yet, from the outside world I come within the grateful circle of professional life to say to you that much is to be done before the bar of this State will, in all its parts, be what we all could wish. We hold honorable places, but we hold places of power—if well used, to protect and save our fellows ; if prostituted and badly used, to betray and destroy. It seems to me that a pro-fession so high and noble in all the purposes of its. existence should be only high and noble in all its results. But we know it is not so. There is not a member of the bar in this assemblage who has not shuddered when he thought of the wicked things he had the power to safely do ; and he has shuddered again when he recalled those, whom he was obliged to call professional brothers, who needed but the motive to do these very things.

" An association like this to be really useful must be something more than a society devoted to laudation of the profession. It should have duties to perform earnest in their nature, and not the less boldly met because they are disagreeable. Those who steal our livery to aid them in the commission of crime should be de-tected and exposed ; and this association or branches of it should have watchmen on the walls to protect the honor and fair fame of the bar of the State."

There were other addresses, here and there, all brief, none eloquent, yet each in succession adding an unseen strength by reason of the evidence it con-tained that Mr. Cleveland was not in this way shal-lowly fishing for partisan prominence or for electoral votes. One solitary piece of manifest demagogism would have shattered his prospects ; but his watchful critics vainly searched for that one greedy blunder, and so the unsought-for effect was solidly attained.

CHAPTER XIV.

The Presidential Outlook in 1884—Looking for an Available Candidate—The New York Battleground —The Rival Chicago Conventions—The Nominations of Grover Cleveland and James G. Blaine.

THERE were exceedingly peculiar features in the Presidential canvass of 1884. In that of 1880 the Democratic and Republican parties proper had been so nearly balanced that the popular national majority obtained by the latter was but three thousand and thirty-three—a margin to have been washed away by a heavy rain. Outside of the two main bodies, each a little under four and a half millions of voters, there had been cast what some men called a " crank ballot " of about three hundred and nineteen thousand for impossible candidates. The result, in 1884, might depend upon the drift and division of that outside vote, or it might not, and already there had been signs that its tendencies were quite as much Republican as they were Democratic. The puzzle grew deeper and yet more readable upon an examination of the returns of the electoral colleges of the several States. Of these, Garfield and Arthur had received two hundred and fourteen, and Hancock and English had received one hundred and fifty-five. The former aggregate had contained the thirty-five votes of the State of

New York, now entitled to thirty-six votes, under the new apportionment. It was manifest that the Republican Party had held its own fairly well in all the States which it had carried in 1880. There were several in which it had gained ground, and its continued control of the National Government seemed to be assured but for one arithmetical fact. If the votes of New York were now to be transferred from one column of electoral figures to the other, with them would go the Presidency. New York was, therefore, to be the battleground of the canvass. Short-sighted men, knowing really little of the character of Republican strength in the State, pointed at the returns for 1882, and declared that Grover Cleveland could win by a hundred thousand, after losing half of his then majority. No Democratic leader of any prominence and no Republican of any kind gave an assent to that wild calculation.

There were able men in other States who seriously questioned if the "tidal wave" of reform energy which had lifted Mr. Cleveland into the governor's chair had not spent its force, and if it were not perceptibly receding.

To these his friends responded, somewhat curtly : "Not so ; but, at all events, you cannot name another Democrat who can rally votes enough to sweep the State. You can take your choice between Grover Cleveland and any first-rate man whom the Republicans may name."

There were old and new ambitions in other parts of the Union to whose ears this announcement had a harsh and jarring sound, but before them were the facts concerning Hancock and English and some other very interesting campaign information from many recent local elections in the State of New York.

The Democratic National Convention had been summoned to meet at Chicago on July 8th, 1884.

The Republican National Convention had been invited to assemble in the same city on June 3d, and both bodies were to make use of the vast structure erected, near the shore of Lake Michigan, for the great "world's fair," and known as the "Exposition Building." It was as if the striking similarities in the political situations of the opposed organizations were in this manner represented. For each was the great West required to sit in judgment upon the same vital point of party policy. In each, prior to the sitting of the conventions, the voice of great masses of voters made itself heard in favor of one name in preference to all others. Not in either did the name mentioned receive beforehand the entire approval of all factions. There was one marked difference, however. The discords in the Republican Party were open, bitter, and personal in their nature, while the Democratic discontents were of a minor and local character. As to the latter, however, it was hardly surprising that men were found who declared that Mr. Cleveland's course as governor had made enemies for him of important interests in the State of New York. It was roundly asserted that under no circumstances could he obtain the same vote from his own party which had been given to him in 1882, and the declaration was rigidly correct. There were badly vetoed men who were eager to take revenge, and there were considerable squads of voters who were ready to express their condemnation of a party ruler from whose hands they had received no loaves and fishes whatever.

The Republican leaders watched the drift of these disorderly forces with unconcealed satisfaction, overestimating some of them and acquiring a somewhat exaggerated idea of the reaction which was going on in favor of their own party. They believed, correctly, that they had recovered the greater part of the vote which had "bolted" from them in 1882, and they also believed themselves about to recover the remainder of. it, with the addition of several small but important factions of anti-Cleveland Democrats. It was under such impressions, in the minds of many of its ablest men, that the Republican Convention assembled at Chicago. At least a quorum of its membership were on the ground two or three days before the appointed time, feverishly discussing the important business to be transacted, and each new arrival was promptly captured and drawn into the discussion. Whatever decision was to be reached would surely be, therefore, the verdict of a grand jury which had heard the case fully argued. They were an exceedingly able body of men, and their Democratic opponents read the reports of their proceedings with keen and even anxious interest, hoping that they would make a blunder. Some said that they made one, but it was not so. They were forced to determine a knotty point of policy, and they were forced to run a known risk. Sober and careful review compels the admission that the popular voice of the Republican Party and the recorded action of its convention of delegates was both instinctively and deliberately wise. One result of its debates and votes was felt with tremendous force in the Democratic National Convention held soon after, compelling the latter, as a player upon a political chess-board, to make the precise counter-move called for to avoid inevitable checkmate and loss of the game.

Days were consumed in the preliminary and completed organization processes and in the preparation and adoption of a party platform. The name which seemed to elicit most enthusiasm, whenever mentioned, was that of Mr. James G. Blaine, of Maine. Next to him in apparent strength was President Arthur himself, who was personally popular and had during many years held a strong hand upon the very effective machinery of the party organism. There were other Republican leaders with strong personal followings, but none with any prospect of success except in case of something like a tie between Blaine and Arthur. There were delegates from New York who asserted Mr. Arthur's ability to carry that State, in spite of the disastrous defeat of his friend Folger, but to these it was significantly responded : " Not if the Democrats nominate Grover Cleveland and if the men who voted for him then do it once more."

On the other hand, it was discovered that many of the anti-Folger and anti-Arthur delegates from

New York, with their sympathizers elsewhere, were also opposed to Mr. Blaine. It might be that the party would have to go on without them, and a not very prudent attempt was made to ascertain the strength of their independent tendencies. On the 5th, for this purpose, the following resolution was offered :

" *Resolved*, As the sense of this convention, that every member of it is bound in honor to support its nominee, whoever that nominee may be, and that no man should hold a seat here who is not ready so to agree."

A fiercely vehement opposition, largely from New York, at once revealed the state of feeling in the convention, and the resolution was withdrawn.

The platform of resolutions at last reported and adopted rehearsed the record of the party which, during twenty-four years of war and peace, had controlled the executive department of the National Government, and confidently asserted its claim to the continued confidence of the people. Clear and distinct was its utterance upon the issue of protection and free trade, for its fourth " plank" was as follows :

" It is the first duty of a good government to protect the rights and promote the interests of its own people. The largest diversity of industry is the most productive of general prosperity and of the comfort and independence of the people. We, therefore, demand that the imposition of duties on foreign imports shall be made not for revenue only, but that in raising the requisite revenues for the Government, such duty shall be so levied as to afford security to our diversified interests and protection to the rights and wages of the laborer, to the end that active and intelligent labor, as well as capital, may have its just reward and the laboring man his full share in the national prosperity."

It was not until June 7th that the convention was prepared for a first ballot of inquiry into the relative strength of the candidates, whose names were under discussion through all the larger and smaller gatherings in the crowded city, as well as in the journals of all parties and places in all parts of the Union.

Mr. Blaine's first vote gave him nearly a majority, and upon the second and third ballots more and more strength came to him from the rival candidates, while the direct opposition to his nomination became more and more vehement as it narrowed. On the fourth ballot he obtained five hundred and forty-one out of eight hundred and thirteen ballots cast, and his nomination was declared in a storm of tumultuous applause. When this had subsided, however, it was evident that a unanimous vote could not even then be secured for him. The convention adjourned, and the party press generally expressed a hope that the discontented faction would soon cool down into a silent acquiescence in the will of the majority.

So far as the great mass of the party was concerned, this hope was likely to be verified. In New York especially, however, the very element which had resented the nomination of Judge Folger declared a rebellion against that of Mr. Blaine. What ever might now be its numerical strength, there was but one Democrat known for whom its active support could be reasonably anticipated, and the friends of Grover Cleveland asserted that the "Scratchers" and the Mugwumps of his own State were as his personal following.

The representatives of the Democratic Party met, at Chicago, on July 8th, in the vast auditorium afforded by the Exposition Building. There were present eight hundred and twenty delegates, from forty-seven States and Territories and from the District of Columbia. Under the established rule governing the party, a two-thirds vote would be required for a nomination, and preliminary inquiries revealed the fact that this could not be accomplished upon the first ballot.

A large number of the delegates, especially from the West and South, arrived in Chicago under the impression, variously derived, that the nomination of Mr. Blaine had been a fatal blunder on the part of their opponents, leaving a clearer field before the Democracy. They were very firmly informed by their New York brethren that such was not the case and that Republican gains and losses in the Empire State would be so nearly balanced that a full vote might be counted upon by that party for Blaine and Logan. If the Democratic Convention should present any other name than that of Grover Cleveland, they would, it was positively asserted, at the same time present thirty-six New York electoral votes to the Republican nominees.

It was an imposing assemblage of the representatives of the people, for men to whom a great party had intrusted its affairs were fully entitled to be so designated.

The preliminary organization was not attained

until after noon of the first day, and the temporary chairman selected was Governor Hubbard, of Texas, in a distinct acknowledgment of the relations between the reconstructed South and the Democratic Party. Almost the first perceptible variation from the routine processes of preparing for the work of the convention came from the New York malcontents. Previous conventions had established what was known as the "unit rule," compelling State delegations to cast their votes as one body when so instructed. That of New York had been instructed by its State convention to cast its seventy-two votes solidly, and now one of its members moved to suspend the "unit rule." There was something almost ominous in the fact that his motion, though lost, was sustained by three hundred and twenty-two votes. None of the New York men, therefore, could give full effect to their insubordination, but Mr. Cleveland's friends took warning and became more vehement than ever in asserting that their candidate was the only hope of the party. All the arithmetic of the situation argued with them, and they made rapid advances during the remainder of that day. Their labors continued almost through the night, and when the convention reassembled, on the morning of July 9th, the Cleveland fever was spreading rapidly.

The completion of a permanent organization was followed by an eloquent address from its chairman, Colonel W. F. Vilas, of Wisconsin, and it was then agreed that no nomination ballot should be taken until after the adoption of a platform of resolutions.

While, however, the committee to whom that important task had been assigned should be in consultation, with a heap of offered resolutions before them, opportunity was given for the presentation of candidates by State delegations. State after State responded, as the call of the roll of commonwealths proceeded, and each well-known and honored name was greeted with a generous tribute of applause.

New York was called last, and the name of Grover Cleveland was presented, eloquently, by Hon. Daniel N. Lockwood, of Buffalo, who had in like manner nominated him for mayor and for governor. There was nothing of enthusiasm lacking in the rounds of applause called forth by the speech of Mr. Lockwood, and the nomination was heartily seconded by eminent gentlemen from other States ; but after that the convention was forced to listen to the men of New York who had formed opinions adverse to Governor Cleveland. What they said was not altogether pleasant to his friends, but it had a very peculiar effect, for it somehow strengthened him before the convention. If this were, indeed, all that could be said against him by his enemies, argued delegates from a distance, he must be one of the very safest men in the whole country. Just such a candidate was needed, and that fact was presented by Mr. Edgar K. Apgar, of New York, in a speech which gave a somewhat rose-colored view of the strength of the party in that State, but held before the convention, nevertheless, a possible adverse majority of eighty thousand, in case of a blundering nomination. After presenting forcibly

some facts and figures from the history of previous
Democratic National Conventions and New York
State election returns, Mr. Apgar gave a startling
analysis, sufficiently near to arithmetical truth, of
the reasons why the nomination of Governor Cleveland was demanded.   He concluded as follows :

" We have in the State, probably, about six hundred thousand
voters who will vote for the Democratic Party nominee whom you
may nominate.   We have about five hundred and eighty thousand
voters who will vote the Republican ticket under any and all circumstances.   Now, outside of both these organizations there are a
hundred thousand men in the State of New York who do not care
a snap of their finger whether the Republican Party or the Democratic Party, as such, shall carry the election.   They vote in every
election according to the issues and the candidates presented.
These men absolutely hold the control of the politics of New York
in their hands.   They are the balance of power.   You must have
their vote, or you cannot win.   Every time for ten years past when
we have appealed to this element victory has perched upon our
banners.   When we have failed to do so defeat has come.   These
men unitedly, to a man, implore you to nominate to the office of
President Governor Tilden's successor, elected governor for the
same causes.   They ask you to place him in nomination in order
that all the elements opposed to the longer continuance of the Republican Party in power may be united and make its defeat entirely
certain."

He did not put into words the assertion plainly
implied : " If you decide otherwise, you destroy
the hope of the Democratic Party, and make its defeat entirely certain."   The convention heard that
warning plainly, however, and at once adjourned to
take so great a fact into careful and general consideration.

Rarely has any such deliberative body been enabled to discuss and decide such a point so entirely

unembarrassed by any influence other than its convictions of sound policy and prudence. Even Governor Cleveland's warmest advocates were not confused by any false sentiment, the glamour of a popular name, such as has on several occasions determined the selection of Presidential candidates. No military fame, no brilliant oratory, no towering eminence as a jurist, no personal magnetism, no position as the index finger of a great policy, was claimed for Grover Cleveland. He was neither Andrew Jackson, nor Henry Clay, nor Daniel Webster, nor Stephen A. Douglas, nor James K. Polk. They, nevertheless, asserted for him that he represented public confidence and Democratic success, without any useless analysis of the personal character which attracted to him all but one jarring faction of so tumultuous a political constituency.

The convention came together on the morning of July 10th, with a long and hard and hot day's work before it. There were other names to be presented, as the call of the roll was resumed, other eulogistic speeches were to be made, and at their close there was an adjournment until eight o'clock in the evening, to hear the report of the platform committee.

The resolutions composing the platform were many in number and covered the entire field of controversy between the two great parties. It was said, indeed, by critical journalists, that more space was given to the sins and shortcomings of the party in power than to any prospective blessing offered to

the country by the party proposing to take the
power into its own hands.   At all events, the platform was thoroughly Democratic, and after its
adoption the convention almost nervously approached what was well understood to be a ballot of
inquiry.   It was midnight when it was taken, and
when its perplexing figures were announced, the
delegates were instantly ready to adjourn.   Each
carried away with him for studious examination the
following unexpected tabulation :

```
Whole number of votes.........  .............820
Necessary for a choice......................547
Grover Cleveland............................392
Thomas F. Bayard ..........................170
Allen G. Thurman .......................... 88
Samuel J. Randall........................... 78
Joseph E. McDonald ........................ 56
John G. Carlisle............................ 27
R. P. Flower...............................  4
George Hoadly .............................  3
Thomas A. Hendricks .......................  1
Samuel J. Tilden...........................  1
```

It was true that Mr. Cleveland had failed of receiving even a majority of the ballots and that he
seemed far away from obtaining the required two
thirds ; but the one phenomenal feature was that in
thirty-nine out of the forty-seven States and Territories he had a following.   No other name had attracted support from so many widely separated and
various constituencies.   The old, familiar fames of
statesmen to whose life-long labors the party owed
its very existence seemed everywhere to be almost
slighted in favor of this new man, who had never

made stump speeches, never had held a legislative office, and who never had been elected to any position except by the aid of Republican bolters. The latter fact was referred to with wry faces by old-time Democrats of the strictest sect, only to be answered by some eager New Yorker: "Why, bless your soul, my dear fellow, that's what we've got to have now, or we might as well turn around and nominate Jim Blaine."

The convention gathered on the 11th, with its mind very nearly made up. Perhaps the only remaining question with a number of State delegations was as to the precise time and manner of their making known the determination at which they had arrived. Not many waited long after the process of changing votes from other names to that of Grover Cleveland began. At the end of one balloting he was found to have received six hundred and eighty-three votes, against one hundred and thirty-seven for all others. His nomination was declared, as had been that of his competitor, Mr. Blaine, amid storms of enthusiastic and hopeful applause; and the Democratic National Convention adjourned, the discontented delegates from New York carrying home with them rebellious hearts in a remarkably close resemblance to a number of angry Republicans who had visited Chicago in June.

The utterances of the Democratic platform with reference to the tariff did not meet the views of the extreme school of free-trade advocates. These gentlemen criticised sharply the uncertain tone of the following paragraphs, and declared a determination to obtain greater precision of doctrine at the next opportunity :

" But in making reduction in taxes, it is not proposed to injure any domestic industries, but rather to promote their healthy growth. From the foundation of this Government, taxes collected at the custom-house have been the chief source of Federal revenue. Such they must continue to be. Moreover, many industries have come to rely upon legislation for successful continuance, so that any change of law must be at every.step regardful of the labor and capital thus involved. The process of reform must be subject in the execution to this plain dictate of justice.

" All taxation should be limited to the requirements of economical government. The necessary reduction in taxation can and must be effected without depriving American labor of the ability to compete successfully with foreign labor, and without imposing lower rates of duty than will be ample to cover any increased cost of productions which may exist in consequence of the higher rate of wages prevailing in this country. Sufficient revenue to pay all the expenses of the Federal Government, economically administered, including pensions, interest, and principal of the public debt, can be got under our present system of taxation from custom-house taxes on fewer imported articles, bearing heaviest on articles of luxury, and bearing lightest on articles of necessity.

" We, therefore, denounce the abuses of the existing tariff, and, subject to the preceding limitations, we demand that Federal taxation shall be exclusively for public purposes, and shall not exceed the needs of the Government, economically administered."

Whatever might be the precise views held by Mr. Cleveland, he had not as yet formulated and published them.

CHAPTER XV.

The Great Fight for the New York Vote—Governor Cleveland's Acceptance—Partisan Virulence—The Rip Van Winkle Vote—An Astonishing Result— Triumph of the Democratic Party—After the Election.

THE result obtained at Chicago had been generally expected, and the press and the public were prepared to express their opinion of it. As to its political wisdom, there was hardly a dissenting voice in either party outside of the discontented faction in New York. As to that State, there were very erroneous impressions prevailing, and many men regarded it as altogether sure to give Mr. Cleveland its electors. It was anything but sure, and the Republican leaders at once entered upon a canvass unsurpassed for its ability and thoroughness. They were confronted, at the outset, by the avowed defection of prominent men and of influential journals, but the main body of the party seemed disposed to rally with all the greater devotion around the very able chief it had selected.

During the days of the sitting of the Democratic National Convention Governor Cleveland remained at Albany, in the steady performance of the routine duties of his office, and nobody succeeded in eliciting from him any important remark with reference to the prospects at Chicago. Shortly after the arrival of the telegraphic despatch announcing his nomination, the Executive Chamber was thronged with men of all ranks eager to offer congratulations, but not one of them seemed to be so little excited as was the governor himself. The stream of visitors swelled and poured on during nearly three hours, and so did a torrent of friendly telegrams from all parts of the country. There could be no question but what the convention had succeeded in meeting the wishes of the people to whom its work must look for support and success.

In the evening of that day a throng gathered in front of the Executive Mansion, and the governor was peremptorily called upon for a speech. He had not as yet received official notice of his nomination, and his habitual prudence was testified to by the guarded phrases of his brief response. Among them were these :

"The American people are about to exercise, in its highest sense, their power of right and sovereignty. They are to call in review before them their public servants and the representatives of political parties, and demand of them an account of their stewardship.

"Parties may be so long in power, and may become so arrogant and careless of the interests of the people, as to grow heedless of their responsibility to their masters. But the time comes, as certainly as death, when the people weigh them in the balance.

"The issues to be adjudicated by the nation's great assize are made up and are about to be submitted.

"We believe that the people are not receiving at the hands of the party which for nearly twenty-four years has directed the affairs of the nation the full benefits to which they are entitled, of a pure, just, and economical rule ; and we believe that the ascen-

dancy of genuine Democratic principles will insure a better government and greater happiness and prosperity to all the people.

" To reach the sober thought of the nation and to dislodge an
enemy intrenched behind spoils and patronage involve a struggle,
which if we underestimate, we invite defeat. I am profoundly
impressed with the responsibility of the part assigned to me in this
contest. My heart, I know, is in the cause, and I pledge you that
no effort of mine shall be wanting to secure the victory which I
believe to be within the achievement of the Democratic hosts.

" Let us, then, enter upon the campaign now fairly opened, each
one appreciating well the part he has to perform, ready, with solid
front, to do battle for better government, confidently, courageously, always honorably, and with a firm reliance upon the intelligence and patriotism of the American people."

The committee appointed by the convention to
convey to Governor Cleveland the formal announcement of his nomination did not arrive in Albany
until July 28th. Quite a large number of well-
known Democratic politicians got there several days
in advance of them. The committee was headed
by Colonel W. F. Vilas, Chairman of the Convention. It was · received, accompanied by a distinguished escort, in the drawing-room of the Executive Mansion.

The governor was surrounded by personal and
political friends and by members of his family and
guests. His sisters, Mrs. W. E. Hoyt and Miss
Rose E. Cleveland ; his nieces, the Misses Mary
and Carrie Hastings, were with him. Mrs. Folsom,
widow of his old friend, Oscar Folsom, and her
daughter Frances, guests of his sister at the time,
and Mrs. Lamont, wife of his private secretary,
assisted them in adding to the occasion the one
element of refinement and dignity which is too

often absent upon occasions of a similarly important character.

The speech of Colonel Vilas was eminently appropriate. Uttered as the voice of such a body as the Democratic National Convention at Chicago had been, it formulated the highest commendation which can be given to an American by his fellow citizens. It concluded as follows :

" The National Democracy seek a President, not in compliment for what the man is or reward for what he has done, but in a just expectation of what he will accomplish as the true servant of a free people, fit for their lofty trust. Always of momentous consequence, they conceive the public exigency to be now of transcendent importance, that a laborious reform in administration, as well as legislation, is imperatively necessary to the prosperity and honor of the Republic, and a competent chief magistrate must be of unusual temper and power. They have observed with attention your execution of the public trusts you have held, especially of that with which you are now so honorably invested. They place their reliance for the usefulness of the services they expect to exact for the benefit of the nation upon the evidence derived from the services you have performed for the State of New York. They invite the electors to such proof of character and competence to justify their confidence that in the nation, as heretofore in the State, the public business will be administered with commensurate intelligence and ability, with single-hearted honesty and fidelity, and with a resolute and daring fearlessness which no faction, no combination, no power of wealth, no mistaken clamor can dismay or qualify. In the spirit of the wisdom, and invoking the benediction of the Divine Creator of men, we challenge from the sovereignty of the nation his words in commendation and ratification of our choice—' Well done, thou good and faithful servant ; thou hast been faithful over a few things, I will make thee ruler over many things.' In further fulfilment of our duty, the secretary will now present the written communication signed by the committee."

When this duty had in like manner been performed, Mr. Cleveland responded :

" MR. CHAIRMAN AND GENTLEMEN OF THE COMMITTEE : Your formal announcement does not, of course, convey to me the first information of the result of the convention lately held by the Democracy of the nation ; and yet when, as I listen to your message, I see about me representatives from all parts of the land of that great party which, claiming to be the party of the people, asks them to intrust to it the administration of their Government, and when I consider, under the influence of the stern reality which the present surroundings create, that I have been chosen to represent the plans, purposes, and the policy of the Democratic Party, I am profoundly impressed by the solemnity of the occasion and by the responsibility of my position. Though I gratefully appreciate it, I do not at this moment congratulate myself upon the distinguished honor which has been conferred upon me, because my mind is full of anxious desire to perform well the part which has been assigned to me. Nor do I at this moment forget that the rights and interests of more than fifty millions of my fellow citizens are involved in our efforts to gain Democratic supremacy.

" This reflection presents to my mind the consideration which, more than all others, gives to the action of any party in convention assembled its most sober and serious aspect. The party and its representatives which ask to be intrusted at the hands of the people with the keeping of all that concerns their welfare and their safety should only ask it with the full appreciation of the sacredness of the trust and with a firm resolve to administer it faithfully and well. I am a Democrat because I believe that this truth lies at the foundation of true Democracy. I have kept the faith because I believe, if rightly and fairly administered and applied, Democratic doctrines and measures will insure the happiness, contentment, and prosperity of the people. If in this contest upon which we now enter we steadfastly hold to the underlying principles of our party creed, and at all times keep in view the people's good, we shall be strong because we are true to ourselves and because the plain and independent voters of the land will seek by their suffrages to compass their release from party tyranny, where there should be submission to the popular will, and their protection from party corruption, where there should be devotion to the people's interests. These thoughts lend a consecration to our cause, and we go forth not merely to gain a partisan advantage, but pledged to give to those who trust us the utmost benefits of a pure and

honest administration of national affairs. No higher purpose or
motive can stimulate us to supreme effort or urge us to continuous and earnest labor and effective party organization. Let us not
fail in this, and we may confidently hope to reap the full reward of
patriotic services well performed. I have thus called to mind
some simple truths. Trite though they are, it seems to me well
to dwell upon them at this time. I shall soon, I hope, signify in
the usual formal manner my acceptance of the nomination you
have tendered me. In the mean time I gladly greet you all as co-
workers in a noble cause."

It was a public acceptance of the nomination, but
it did not contain anything which diminished a very
general and increasing curiosity as to what would
be the tenor and effect of the formal response promised to the voice of the convention. The platform
of resolutions adopted at Chicago was felt to be
altogether incomplete until it could be printed with
an appendix from the cautious pen of the Governor
of New York. Meantime the great campaign went
busily forward. When the formal letter of acceptance reached the committee, and was by them placed
before the Democratic Party and the people, it was
found to contain a great deal of matter for reflection and for future reference. It received the
prompt and hearty approval of all the men of all
varying political complexions who had been expected to vote for Mr. Cleveland. They were held
together admirably, and the letter itself at once assumed permanent rank as an important State paper.
It was as follows :

" ALBANY, August 18, 1884.
" GENTLEMEN : I have received your communication, dated July
28th, 1884, informing me of my nomination to the office of Presi-

dent of the United States by the National Democratic Convention lately assembled at Chicago.

" I accept the nomination with a grateful appreciation of the supreme honor conferred and a solemn sense of the responsibility which, in the acceptance, I assume.

" I have carefully considered the platform adopted by the convention, and cordially approve the same. So plain a statement of Democratic faith and the principles upon which that party appeals to the suffrages of the people needs no supplement of explanation.

" It should be remembered that the office of President is essentially executive in its nature. The laws enacted by the legislative branch of the Government the Chief Executive is bound faithfully to enforce. And when the wisdom of the political party which selects one of its members as a nominee for that office has outlined its policy and declared its principles, it seems to me that nothing in the character of the office or the necessities of the case requires more from the candidate accepting the nomination than the suggestion of well-known truths, so absolutely vital to the safety and welfare of the nation that they cannot be too often recalled or too seriously enforced.

" We proudly call ours a government by the people. It is not such when a class is tolerated which arrogates to itself the management of public affairs, seeking to control the people instead of representing them.

" Parties are the necessary outgrowth of our institutions ; but a government is not by the people when one party fastens its control upon the country, and perpetuates its power, by cajoling and betraying the people instead of serving them.

" A government is not by the people when a result which should represent the intelligent will of free and thinking men is, or can be, determined by the shameless corruption of their suffrages.

" When an election to office shall be the selection by the voters of one of their number, to assume for a time a public trust instead of his dedication to the profession of politics ; when the holders of the ballot, quickened by a sense of duty, shall avenge trusts betrayed and pledges broken, and when the suffrage shall be altogether free and uncorrupted, the full realization of a government by the people will be at hand. And of the means to this end, not one would, in my judgment, be more effective than an amendment to the Constitution disqualifying the President from re-election.

When we consider the patronage of this great office, the allurements of power, the temptation to retain public place once gained, and, more than all, the availability a party finds in an incumbent whom a horde of office-holders, with a zeal born of benefits received and fostered by the hope of favors yet to come, stand ready to aid with money and trained political service, we recognize in the eligibility of the President for re-election a most serious danger to that calm, deliberate, and intelligent political action which must characterize a government by the people.

"A true American sentiment recognizes the dignity of labor, and the fact that honor lies in honest toil. Contented labor is an element in national prosperity. Ability to work constitutes the capital and the wages of labor the income of a vast number of our population ; and this interest should be jealously protected. Our workingmen are not asking unreasonable indulgence, but as intelligent and manly citizens they seek the same consideration which those demand who have other interests at stake. They should receive their full share of the care and attention of those who make and execute the laws, to the end that the wants and needs of the employers and the employed shall alike be subserved and the prosperity of the country, the common heritage of both, be advanced. As related to this subject, while we should not discourage the immigration of those who come to acknowledge allegiance to 'our Government, and add to our citizen population, yet, as a means of protection to our workingmen, a different rule should prevail concerning those who, if they come, or are brought to our land, do not intend to become Americans, but will injuriously compete with those justly entitled to our field of labor.

" In a letter accepting the nomination to the office of governor, nearly two years ago, I made the following statement, to which I have steadily adhered :

"'The laboring classes constitute the main part of our population. They should be protected in their efforts peaceably to assert their rights when endangered by aggregated capital, and all statutes on this subject should recognize the care of the State for honest toil, and be framed with a view of improving the condition of the workingmen.'

" A proper regard for the welfare of the workingmen being inseparably connected with the integrity of our institutions, none of our citizens are more interested than they in guarding against any corrupting influences which seek to pervert the beneficent purposes of our Government, and none should be more watchful of the artful machinations of those who allure them to self-inflicted injury.

" In a free country, the curtailment of the absolute rights of the individual should only be such as is essential to the peace and good order of the community. The limit between the proper subjects of government control and those which can be more fittingly left to the moral sense and self-imposed restraint of the citizen should be carefully kept in view. Thus, laws unnecessarily interfering with the habits and customs of any of our people which are not offensive to the moral sentiments of the civilized world, and which are consistent with good citizenship and the public welfare, are unwise and vexatious.

" The commerce of a nation, to a great extent, determines its supremacy. Cheap and easy transportation should therefore be liberally fostered. Within the limits of the Constitution, the general Government should so improve and protect its natural waterways as will enable the producers of the country to reach a profitable market.

" The people pay the wages of the public employés, and they are entitled to the fair and honest work which the money thus paid should command. It is the duty of those intrusted with the management of their affairs to see that such public service is forthcoming. The selection and retention of subordinates in government employment should depend upon their ascertained fitness and the value of their work, and they should be neither expected nor allowed to do questionable party service. The interests of the people will be better protected ; the estimate of public labor and duty will be immensely improved ; public employment will be open to all who can demonstrate their fitness to enter it ; the unseemly scramble for place under the Government, with the consequent importunity which embitters official life, will cease, and the public departments will not be filled with those who conceive it to be their first duty to aid the party to which they owe their places, instead of rendering a patient and honest return to the people.

" I believe that the public temper is such that the voters of the land are prepared to support the party which gives the best promise of administering the Government in the honest, simple, and plain manner which is consistent with its character and purposes. They have learned that mystery and concealment in the management of their affairs cover tricks and betrayal. The statesmanship they require consists in honesty and frugality, a prompt response to the needs of the people, as they arise, and the vigilant protection of all their varied interests.

"If I should be called to the Chief Magistracy of the nation, by the suffrages of my fellow citizens, I will assume the duties of that high office with a solemn determination to dedicate every effort to the country's good, and with an humble reliance upon the favor and support of the Supreme Being, who, I believe, will bless honest human endeavor in the conscientious discharge of public duty."

They were old Jackson Democrats who read with thoughtful care the suggestion of a system of internal improvements under the direction of the Federal Government, but they were willing to wait. They also remembered that General Jackson himself had been strongly in favor of disqualifying any President of the United States for re-election.

Eager politicians of both parties asserted that there were several doubtful States and that the electoral vote of New York might yet be found not absolutely the turning point. It had been counter-balanced by an aggregate of smaller votes in 1876, and had failed to elect Mr. Tilden. It might now be possible to repeat that process upon one side or the other. The best judges, however, studied with care the election returns of the year 1883, and decided that neither Mr. Cleveland nor Mr. Blaine had any hope for important changes elsewhere, and that the former must manage to call out every man who had voted for him for governor in 1882.

With this state of things clearly asserted, if not actually accepted, the campaign assumed a virulently personal nature. The public and private life of each candidate was searched literally by keen detectives. Every error of judgment or of conduct was hunted down and dragged out into unmerciful publicity and partisan rancor, as prosecuting attorney called upon the people as a jury to pass verdicts of utter condemnation of the two distinguished men selected as representatives by the conventions of the great parties. The result was a remarkable illustration of the general capacity of the nation to comprehend and estimate correctly the value of any indictment so presented. The reaction against the tides of abuse seems to have been about equally strong for both Mr. Cleveland and Mr. Blaine. ·The balance of power between the two parties, so well developed prior to the sitting of their national conventions, was in a striking manner transferred to the individual popularity of their candidates. It is not too much to say that there was a nicely equalized amount of very bad mud thrown either way, but it is not needful to preserve any part of it biographically.

The New York State elections of the year 1883 had not been of an exciting nature and had not called out a full vote. Of that which was cast, the Democratic Party could show a majority of over sixteen thousand, and they said : "Grover Cleveland can add a hundred thousand votes to those figures." They were less than correct, for the result largely exceeded that estimate, and yet it was barely sufficient to pull him through.

During the stirring weeks of the canvass Mr. Cleveland studiously avoided furnishing any noteworthy material for the newspaper press reporters. He was not an orator, like his brilliant rival, Mr. Blaine, whose vigorous championship of his party formed so marked a feature of the campaign. The routine business of the governor's office went on as usual, varied only by the continual necessity of attending to enthusiastic political pilgrims. The day of decision came, at last, and when the November polls were closed there was a surprise and a puzzle ready for the American people.

Almost everywhere excepting New York the result was very much what had been looked for. The Republicans had secured one hundred and eighty-two electoral votes, and the Democrats one hundred and eighty-three, but the Empire State, with its thirty-six votes, was in doubt, and only full returns and careful counting could determine the fate of the Presidential election.

The New York Democrats had brought out their last man ; they had apparently lost but moderately by any disaffection ; they had received a large re-enforcement, as in 1882, from the rebellious faction of the Republican Party, and they had piled up an aggregate of five hundred and sixty-three thousand one hundred and fifty-four votes for their leading elector. It was truly a magnificent tribute to Mr. Cleveland, exceeding by twenty-seven thousand eight hundred and thirty-six votes his colossal triumph in 1882. It was a full and complete justification of the wisdom of the convention which nominated him, and yet it was hardly and narrowly sufficient. While a large number of Republicans had

openly voted for Mr. Cleveland, many more had re-
frained from going to the polls, and several thousands had joined the Prohibition Party, which cast
over twenty-five thousand votes. The Greenback
Party, with seventeen thousand, drew about equally
from both of the greater bodies, but it was not so
with the Temperance men. Nevertheless, Mr.
Blaine's foremost elector received, upon a final
count, five hundred and sixty-two thousand and five
ballots, and was only eleven hundred and forty-nine
behind his corresponding competitor. The Republicans had not regained the men they had lost in
1882, yet had brought forward two hundred and
nineteen thousand five hundred and forty-one to
take their places. Where had these all come from?
Some said they were young men just arriving at
the voting age and full of enthusiasm for the historic party. Others said that the tariff and labor
questions had performed the apparent miracle. A
very good explanation as to much the larger part of
it may be found in a story that is told of a traveller
in Illinois just before the Civil War. He was a
Whig, and he said to a gentleman who was of the
same persuasion :

" I wish you would explain one thing. I've been
all over the State, and almost every man I have met
is a Whig. How is it that Illinois always goes
Democratic ?"

" Well," replied his friend, " you ought to be
here on election day. They begin to come in just
after the polls open. You never see them at any
other time. They come from somewhere away out

on the prairie—nobody knows where. They kind o'
rise from the dead on election day. They don't
often come afoot, but every man rides in on a
switch-tailed mare, with a rope halter and no saddle,
and comes along a-whooping, ' Git up, Sal ! Hurrah
for Jackson ! ' He votes the straight Democratic
ticket, and takes a drink—sometimes more'n one—
and rides off, and you won't see him again till the
end of another four years.''

It is so elsewhere, and in New York, away back
among the rural districts and all around among the
haunts of trade, there is an unknowable mass of men
who rarely wake up to an interest in political affairs,
but who can hear the sounds of a national campaign.
They keep still until election day, and then, if they
say anything at all before they vote, it is '' Hurrah
for Abraham Lincoln ! What's his ticket this
time ?'' Mr. Blaine was wisely chosen by the Republican National Convention because of the certainty that he would call out the '' Lincoln Vote.''
Had he been opposed by a Democrat upon whom
the several elements voting for Mr. Cleveland could
not have been concentrated, there would have been
an ample vindication of Mr. Apgar's argument before the Democratic National Convention. It was
too late, after the election, for any Republican to
find fault with the nomination of Mr. Blaine, and
the Mugwump faction, as it continued to be called,
professed itself entirely satisfied with the result.

Governor Cleveland received the first election returns, and endured the few days of apparent uncertainty with undisturbed composure. His support-

ers throughout the country refused to believe that any uncertainty remained, and gave themselves up to a kind of political triumph. It was as if something like a revolution had been accomplished, to the minds of those upon whom no especial responsibility had thereby been imposed. There was, however, much to steady the enthusiasm of the more thoughtful leaders of the Democratic Party, and among these was their chosen chief. The Senate of the United States was still Republican, its party vote standing forty-one to thirty-four, and was likely to furnish a dignified balance wheel to the coming Democratic administration. The old party so long in power had become deeply rooted in all the executive departments, and interference with these roots was hindered by whatever of Civil Service Reform had already been accomplished. There could not now be any such sweeping change of office-holders as had taken place, for instance, upon the accession of Andrew Jackson or of Abraham Lincoln.

The House of Representatives was Democratic by a nominal vote of one hundred and eighty-two to one hundred and forty, but all of the majority votes would not endure too searching analysis with reference to quite a number of possible questions, while the minority was likely to act as a well-disciplined unit. At all events, the executive and legislative branches of the National Government were in excellent condition, considering also the composition of the judiciary, to prevent any perilously rapid changes in the internal affairs of the Republic.

The remainder of the month of November and all of December, 1884, were required for completing the unfinished State business in the hands of the governor. On January 5th, 1885, he sent in his last message to the Legislature. It had been waited for with no little curiosity, for it was expected to contain a review and, perhaps, a glorification of his course as governor, with something in the nature of a foretaste of his Inaugural Address at Washington. When it came, however, it was in these words :

"EXECUTIVE CHAMBER, January 5, 1885.
" *To the Legislature.*
" I hereby resign the office of Governor of the State of New York.
"GROVER CLEVELAND."

Quite a number of witty journalists busied themselves in their next day's prints with experimental inquiries as to the possibility of shortening that message. One man asserted that all he really needed to have said or written was : " Good-by, boys."

The two months following were no more time than was required for preparing to assume the burdens of the national Executive, but an extraordinary number of persons volunteered their advice and assistance. Mr. Cleveland's mail swelled to enormous proportions, and his private secretary was compelled to employ a corps of assistants. The opposition press, with not many marked exceptions, manifested an unexpectedly good spirit under their very trying circumstances, but it was evident that every step taken and every word uttered by the President-elect would be watched and studied with an ability and keenness which a nervous or self-doubtful man might well have dreaded to encounter. Grover Cleveland had no nerves, as he had already proved, and quiet self-reliance was, perhaps, his most marked characteristic. He had finished his great case for the State of New York, and had obtained exceedingly remarkable approval of the manner in which he had managed it. Another and greater case had been placed in his hands, and he was preparing for it, but its nature was not as yet thoroughly defined. In one aspect, it included the old suit of the combined Opposition, mainly consisting of the Democratic Party, *v.* the Republican Party, but there was peril of defeat in making too much of that issue. The first real statesmanship called for from Mr. Cleveland was in the demand upon him that in some way he should appear as " for the People of the United States *v.* Whomsoever-it-may-concern." If he could accomplish that, a sure triumph was before him and before his party, and so he had pointedly assured the committee of the Democratic National Convention, in his oral response accepting the nomination.

For various reasons, a more than ordinary European interest had been taken in the Presidential election of 1884.

In England especially, a marked degree of favor was extended to the party having free-trade tendencies, and English journals now offered vigorously their congratulations upon the triumph of the Democracy. It is true that some of their utterances were eagerly reprinted by Republican Party journals in America, but the intention of the writers was to strengthen the hands of the " Reform President," as, in imitation of his American admirers, they hopefully described Mr. Cleveland.

CHAPTER XVI.

*The Main Question—Old Parties and Oppositions—
New Parties out of Old—Old and New Washing-
ton City—The White House—The Inauguration of
President Cleveland—The Inaugural Address.*

AN outline map, giving the general features of
any country, is likely to be judged as incorrect by
those who have not been accustomed to study the
region as a whole. Dwellers in especially interesting localities may even be indignant that no sign is
given of their favorite river or of their picturesque
range of hills. It is, nevertheless, true that the political history of the United States of America, from
early colonial times till now, adjusts itself perfectly
to the varying phases of one long contest, which is
not ended and which cannot end.

It is the effort to obtain and establish a working
equilibrium between the three great essentials of
our political organism. These are individual freedom, local self-government, and national vigor—the
man, the State, the Union. All questions upon
which parties have been formed and ballots counted
relate to this one long backbone of American politics. Whether the immediate issue has been one of
war or peace, of taxation, of territorial extension,
of internal improvements, of finance, or of slavery,
it has not been and could not be separated from its

proper place in the great conflict. A very natural result of human selfishness and short-sightedness has been the plainly manifest fact that the great mass of the people have been able, from the beginning, to perceive and care for their individual rights and interests first ; secondarily, the supposed rights and interests of their local governments, State or municipal ; thirdly, the righteousness and the importance of the powers vested in the central, federal authority. Part of this very result has been the perception attained concerning the grouped and mutual interests of neighboring States and municipalities. The Civil War of 1861–65 is a sufficient illustration, and indicates the next possible improvement and readjustment of our system of representative self-government.

The indistinctness with which the men of 1776–83 discerned the national idea was manifested in their indifference to the sufferings of Washington's army and their subsequent neglect and refusal to so much as pay the money due to the war-worn Continentals. The outside pressure exercised by Great Britain and other European powers, on the one side, and by the Indian tribes on the other, aided materially in creating the state of mind required for George Washington's apparently unanimous election and re-election, and the parties of the future took form while he held the fragmentary nation together, the respective party chiefs, Alexander Hamilton and Thomas Jefferson, being members of his own Cabinet. As the outside pressure afterward diminished, the Federal Party, representing the idea of central authority, faded away. By the end of four years after the retirement of Washington, the Republican Party, jealously guarding the idea of local self-government, was ready to put Thomas Jefferson into the seat vacated by John Adams. During a quarter of a century, under Jefferson, Madison, and Monroe, the Republican Party retained control, its own factions and the remnant of Federalism answering fairly well the understood public necessity for an active and watchful Opposition. During the administration of John Quincy Adams a long·threatened change came. The old party broke up and its place was taken by the Democratic Party, rallying around Andrew Jackson and ruled by him, but owing much of its discipline and efficiency to the masterly management of Martin Van Buren. The opposition to the new party was fierce enough from the first, but it required time for its combination and organization as the Whig Party. It never served any other distinct purpose than that of modifying and restricting Democratic supremacy, for even questions of tariffs and taxes, of sectional jealousy, of popular ambition for territorial extension, and of the legal right to own slaves, fought as allies of the extreme idea of local self-government, taking form in State rights. Twice only during the period between 1828 and 1860 was a member of the Whig Opposition elected President. In 1840 General Harrison was chosen, only to hold power during one month of 1841, and to be succeeded by John Tyler. It was hardly a break in the long succession. In 1848 General Taylor was chosen, but before his death, in 1850, the great Compromise measures were approaching their adoption, and afterward the administration of President Fillmore did not contain many features to distinguish it from that of the Democratic President Pierce, which followed. During this and the succeeding administration of President Buchanan, there were four organized elements of opposition to the party in power, and this itself was breaking up. The first opponent, in numbers and importance, was the Republican Party, containing many able men, but with no acknowledged chief before its selection of Abraham Lincoln. The second opponent, not in manifest numerical strength but in real importance, was the Secession Party, best represented, even then, by Jefferson Davis. The third opponent, second in numbers, was the Democratic faction led by Stephen A. Douglas. The fourth was a remnant of the old Whig Party, best represented by Millard Fillmore.

The election of Abraham Lincoln came, the Civil War followed, and it is easy to defend the assertion that the old Democratic Party, and each and all of its opponents, disappeared from the political field forever before the close of the year 1861.

There was not an exhalation left of the Whig Party. The Secession Party became the Southern Confederacy. The Republican Party fell very little short of becoming all that remained of the Union and of any hope for the national life. The two wings of the old Democratic Party at the North split into fragments in a manner well illustrated by the subsequent careers of old Democrats like Edwin M. Stanton, Ulysses S. Grant, and John A. Logan.

During the years of the Civil War, the mevitable opposition to the party in power retained the name, but not by any means exclusively the membership, of the Democratic Party. It was kept in very efficient working order, and was ready, when peace came, to receive whatever fragmentary re-enforcements might be developed in the new era. In 1864 it had been able to carry but three States, with twenty-one electoral votes, but in 1868 it controlled eight States, with eighty votes, the ten seceding commonwealths not being represented in the electoral college of either year. In 1872 the Opposition seemed to have lost ground, for although there were now only two States not counted, it could give its candidates but sixty-six votes from seven States.

During the following four years the several elements of the new Democratic Party flowed into it rapidly, and in 1876 it swept seventeen States, with one hundred and eighty-four electoral votes, lacking only one vote of a complete victory. In 1880 seventeen States again declared for the Democracy, but even with five votes added by a divided State, they had but one hundred and fifty-five in all, having lost New York. Perhaps the points most noticeable in these later elections were the extreme compactness and healthful solidity of the two great parties, and the large mass of voters who were acting independently outside of them. The Democratic National Convention nominating Mr. Cleveland, and the Republican National Convention nominating Mr. Blaine, gave their most anxious attention to these points, and governed their action accordingly.

The core of the latter organization consisted of men who had voted for Abraham Lincoln, but the core of the Democratic opposition was made up from all of the several political bodies voting against him. That the old Democratic Party supplied the greater number was doubtless true, but Grover Cleveland knew that he had been elected President of the United States by the ballots of voters who had not been born when George B. McClellan was appointed to the command of the Army of the Potomac. He was now going to Washington, therefore, not as the political successor of James Buchanan, but as the chosen representative of a recently created power, not yet formulated with absolute perfection, and which was, as he again and again forcibly declared, upon its trial before the people. Whether or not his party associates understood the situation, he was in no doubt or darkness whatever. In his speech before the Manhattan Club, in his oral acceptance of the Presidential nomination, and in his carefully worded written response to the Committee of the Chicago Convention, he had stated the plain, unvarnished truth. His party might not like it or might be willing to put it out of sight, but neither he nor they could escape from it.

When, in March, 1861, James Buchanan went away from Washington, he left behind him a queer, ungainly, old-fashioned, straggling village, shortly to become a frontier garrison town, surrounded by long lines of fortifications. During the twenty-four years following his departure, a very remarkable city had been substituted for the old village. The fortifications disappeared soon after the war. Unfinished public buildings were completed, and a number of new and costly structures arose to answer the needs of the increasing volume of national business. The streets and avenues, once existing only upon the elaborate map which had occupied so many of the leisure hours of Thomas Jefferson, were now to a great extent laid out, graded, paved, and lined with residences, hotels, and buildings of a business character. Washington had become also a social as well as a political centre, attracting wealth and fashion from all parts of the country. It had grown into a very respectable representative of the Federal idea, and of the new stability which the national character had assumed.

The political changes which had taken place had added little to the express and manifest power of the President, and the Executive Mansion, the White House, had not lost its original simplicity. Externally it was in excellent repair, and its grounds and shrubbery had been laid out with better taste than formerly, losing the shabby and half-kept look which they had worn in Lincoln's time. Internally the entire building, without any change of plan, had been expensively renewed, making it every way a more commodious and appropriate business office for the Chief Magistrate of the Republic. No art could change it into a comfortable residence.

Rooms had been secured for Mr. Cleveland at the Arlington Hotel, and here his friends pretty successfully defended him from all would-be interviewers during the closing hours of President Arthur's term.

By the courteous invitation of the latter, the President-elect went over to the White House upon the morning of March 4th, 1885, and at noon the outgoing President and his successor were carried in the same carriage to the Capitol. They rode along the avenue between enthusiastic throngs of citizens, a narrow lane for the carriage being kept open by a brilliant military array, contributed by the uniformed militia of several of the nearer States. At the Capitol they were waited for by the exceedingly dignified assembly which is accustomed to attend the solemn occasion of the inauguration of an American President. The Supreme Court, with representatives of other courts ; the Senate and the House of Representatives ; heads of executive departments and officers of high rank in the army and the navy ; representatives of foreign powers ; distinguished men from all parts of the country, by special invitation—all combine to constitute an array of witnesses, which is completed by the thousands of citizens gathered in front of the grand " east front" of the Capitol, at the head of whose flight of steps the temporary platform is erected.

There was, perhaps, but one small incident to distinguish this occasion from either of several of its predecessors. A custom, beginning with George Washington's first taking of the oath in New York, has prepared a table, upon which lies open a large Bible, such as he knelt to kiss. It was not so at the inauguration of President Cleveland. Many long years before, when an ambitious boy went out from his widowed mother's house in the village of Hol-

land Patent, going to find for himself a way in the thronged, hard-working world, he carried with him a little book, not too large to be put into his pocket. It had been his mother's, and it was stamped with her name. It was the Book, and now it was held in the hand of Chief Justice Waite, of the United States Supreme Court, who was to administer the oath of office, as President of the United States, to that very boy, now raised to the chief magistracy of a great nation.

The dignified procession which came out from the Capitol upon the platform assumed its places in silence, the ten thousand citizens before them hushed their tumultuous cheering, and Mr. Cleveland spoke, as follows :

" FELLOW CITIZENS : In the presence of this vast assemblage of my countrymen, I am about to supplement and seal, by the oath which I shall take, the manifestation of the will of a great and free people. In the exercise of their power and right of self-government, they have committed to one of their fellow citizens a supreme and sacred trust ; and he here consecrates himself to their service.

" This impressive ceremony adds little to the solemn sense of responsibility with which I contemplate the duty I owe to all the people of the land ; nothing can relieve me from anxiety lest by any act of mine their interests may suffer, and nothing is needed to strengthen my resolution to engage every faculty and effort in the promotion of their welfare.

" Amid the din of party strife the people's choice was made ; but its attendant circumstances have demonstrated anew the strength and safety of a government by the people. In each succeeding year it more clearly appears that our Democratic principle needs no apology, and that in its fearless and faithful application is to be found the surest guarantee of good government.

" But the best results of the operation of a government wherein every citizen has a share largely depend upon a proper limitation of purely partisan zeal and effort, and a correct appreciation of the time when the heat of the partisan should be merged in the patriotism of the citizen.

" To-day the executive branch of the Government is transferred to new keeping. But this is still the Government of all the people, and it should be none the less an object of their affectionate solicitude. At this hour the animosities of political strife, the bitterness of partisan defeat, and the exultation of partisan triumph, should be supplanted by an ungrudging acquiescence in the popular will, and a sober, conscientious concern for the general weal. Moreover, if, from this hour, we cheerfully and honestly abandon all sectional prejudice and distrust, and determine, with manly confidence in one another, to work out harmoniously the achievements of our national destiny, we shall deserve to realize all the benefits which our happy form of government can bestow.

" On this auspicious occasion we may well renew the pledges of our devotion to the Constitution, which, launched by the founders of the Republic and consecrated by their prayers and patriotic devotion, has for almost a century borne the hopes and the aspirations of a great people, through prosperity and peace, and through the shock of foreign conflicts and the perils of domestic strife and vicissitudes.

" By the Father of his Country our Constitution was commended for adoption as ' the result of a spirit of amity and mutual concession. ' In that same spirit it should be administered, in order to promote the lasting welfare of the country, and to secure the full measure of its priceless benefits to us and to those who will succeed to the blessings of our national life. The large variety of diverse and conflicting interests subject to Federal control, persistently seeking the recognition of their claims, need give us no fear that ' the greatest good to the greatest number ' will fail to be accomplished if, in the halls of national legislation, that spirit of amity and mutual concession shall prevail in which the Constitution had its birth. If this involves the surrender or postponement of private interests and the abandonment of local advantages, compensation will be found in the assurance that thus the common interest is subserved and the general welfare advanced.

" In the discharge of my official duty I shall endeavor to be guided by a just and unstrained construction of the Constitution, a careful observance of the distinction between the powers granted to the Federal Government and those reserved to the State or to the people, and by a cautious appreciation of those functions which, by the Constitution and laws, have been especially assigned to the executive branch of the Government.

" But he who takes the oath to-day to preserve, protect, and defend the Constitution of the United States, only assumes the solemn obligations which every patriotic citizen on the farm, in the workshop, in the busy marts of trade, and everywhere, should share with him. The Constitution which prescribes his oath, my countrymen, is yours ; the Government you have chosen him to administer, for a time, is yours ; the suffrage which executes the will of freemen is yours ; the laws and the entire scheme of our civil rule, from the town meeting to the State capitols and the National Capitol, is yours. Your every voter, as surely as your Chief Magistrate, under the same high sanction, though in a different sphere, exercises a public trust. Nor is this all. Every citizen owes to the country a vigilant watch and close scrutiny of its public servants, and a fair and reasonable estimate of their fidelity and usefulness. Thus is the people's will impressed upon the whole framework of our civil polity—municipal, State, and Federal—and this is the price of our liberty and the inspiration of our faith in the Republic.

" It is the duty of those serving the people in public place to closely limit public expenditures to the actual needs of the Government economically administered, because this bounds the right of the Government to exact tribute from the earnings of labor or the property of the citizen, and because public extravagance begets extravagance among the people. We should never be ashamed of the simplicity and prudential economies which are best suited to the operation of a Republican form of government, and most compatible with the mission of the American people. Those who are selected for a limited time to manage public affairs are still of the people, and may do much by their example to encourage, consistently with the dignity of their official functions, that plain way of life which among their fellow citizens aids integrity and promotes thrift and prosperity.

" The genius of our institutions, the needs of our people in their home life, and the attention which is demanded for the settlement and development of the resources of our vast territory, dictate the scrupulous avoidance of any departure from that foreign policy commended by the history, the traditions, and the prosperity of our

Republic.   It is the policy of independence, favored by our position and defended by our known love of justice and our power.
It is the policy of peace, suitable to our interests.   It is the policy
of neutrality, rejecting any share in foreign broils and ambitions
upon other continents, and repelling their intrusion here.   It is the
policy of Monroe, and Washington, and Jefferson—' Peace, commerce, and honest friendship with all nations ; entangling alliances
with none.'

  " A due regard for the interests and prosperity of all the people
demands that our finances shall be established upon such a sound
and sensible basis as will secure the safety and confidence of business interests and make the wages of labor sure and steady ; that
our system of revenue shall be so adjusted as to relieve the people
of unnecessary taxation, having a due regard to the interests of
capital invested and workingmen employed in American industries,
and preventing the accumulation of a surplus in the Treasury to
tempt extravagance and waste.   Care for the property of the nation
and for the needs of future settlers requires that the public domain
should be protected from purloining schemes and unlawful occupation.

  " The conscience of the people demands that the Indians within
our boundaries shall be fairly and honestly treated as wards of the
Government, and their education and civilization promoted, with
a view to their ultimate citizenship, and that polygamy in the Territories, destructive of the family relation and offensive to the moral
sense of the civilized world, shall be repressed.   The laws should
be rigidly enforced which prohibit the immigration of a servile
class to compete with American labor, with no intention of acquiring citizenship, and bringing with them and retaining habits
and customs repugnant to our civilization.

  " The people demand reform in the administration of the Government, and the application of business principles to public
affairs.   As a means to this end, Civil Service Reform should be
in good faith enforced.   Our citizens have the right to protection
from the incompetence of public employés, who hold their places
solely as the reward of partisan service, and from the corrupting
influence of those who promise and the vicious methods of those
who expect such rewards.   And those who worthily seek public
employment have the right to insist that merit and competency

shall be recognized instead of party subserviency or the surrender of honest political belief.

" In the administration of a government pledged to do equal and exact justice to all men, there should be no pretext for anxiety touching the protection of the freedmen in their rights or their security in the enjoyment of their privileges under the Constitution and its amendments. All discussion as to their fitness for the place accorded to them as American citizens is idle and unprofitable, except as it suggests the necessity for their improvement. The fact that they are citizens entitles them to all the rights due to that relation, and charges them with all its duties, obligations, and responsibilities.

'' These topics, and the constant and ever-varying wants of an active and enterprising population, may well receive the attention and the patriotic endeavor of all who make and execute the Federal law. Our duties are practical, and call for industrious application, an intelligent perception of the claims of public office, and, above all, a firm determination, by united action, to secure to the people of the land the full benefits of the best form of government ever vouchsafed to man. And let us not trust to human effort alone ; but humbly acknowledging the power and goodness of Almighty God, who presides over the destiny of nations, and who has, at all times, been revealed in our country's history, let us invoke His aid and His blessing upon our labors.''

CHAPTER XVII.

Executive Business Offices—A Coat of Arms—The Cabinet—The Commission of General Grant—Office Seekers—A Working President—Death of Vice-President Hendricks—The First Annual Message to Congress.

THE grandly simple ceremonial of the inaugura-tion being ended, the new President re-entered his carriage and drove back through the shouting throngs to the Executive Mansion. Whether or not the vista presented by Pennsylvania Avenue, lined from the Capitol to the White House with cit-izen soldiery and an enthusiastic multitude of his admirers, seemed to Grover Cleveland at all like a dream of swift and most improbable elevation above the quiet place he had occupied only a few months before, his calm, undisturbed, cheerful, yet very business-like demeanor gave no indication. All the critics admitted that he bore himself admirably well, and the Republican press, now become for the time the organs of the Opposition, frankly commended the exceeding prudence of the inaugural address. Some of them said that, with a few improvements and variations, it would have answered equally well for a Republican President. There was nothing Democratic about it, they declared, and his real meaning would not be known until he should send in his first message to Congress, although some things might be learned from his Cabinet nominations.

It was already generally understood that the President's younger sister, Miss Rose Cleveland, was to become the lady of the White House, and that Mr. Daniel S. Lamont was to continue his well-tried and entirely capable services as private secretary, with such assistants as might afterward be named.

The lower story of the White House consists mainly of reception rooms and the state dining room. The upper floor is given to business offices, with the exception of a few rooms reserved for a cramped private residence which is not very private. It was all in readiness to receive its new occupant, and his own rooms were now as near his workshop as ever they had been in the old days of his Buffalo law practice. The work before him now required also that he should retain with him at least one article of faith which he had then declared. Above the bed in the sleeping-room of the suite of apartments over his law offices hung an illuminated allegorical device, representing Life, Duty, and Death. Under this, in letters not legible without attentive examination, was inscribed, "As thy days are, so shall thy strength be." Once, when asked the meaning of it all, Mr. Cleveland replied : "If I have any coat of arms and emblem, it is that. It is a motto I chose years ago, and I devised that form to keep it with me."

The uninterrupted course of public business requires that an incoming President shall speedily send to the Senate the names of his Cabinet. This, therefore, was the first official act of President Cleveland, and all men scrutinized the names with care. A long list of his predecessors had each named his most prominent rival in his own party to be Secretary of State, and the example was followed when Thomas Francis Bayard, of Delaware, was now placed in charge of the foreign affairs of the United States. Equally satisfactory was the selection of Mr. Cleveland's old Albany friend, Daniel Manning, to be Secretary of the Treasury. People outside of Massachusetts knew little about Mr. William C. Endicott, made Secretary of War, but recognized the name better as belonging to old colonial history. William C. Whitney, of New York, was made Secretary of the Navy. Lucius Q. Lamar, of Mississippi, was named Secretary of the Interior, and the fact that he had been an officer in the Confederate Army was mentioned by some men only to arouse a gust of indignant approval. William F. Vilas, of Wisconsin, appointed Postmaster-General, had been an officer in the Union Army, and also Chairman of the Democratic National Convention. Augustus H. Garland, of Arkansas, was appointed Attorney-General, and he, too, had been a Confederate officer. The great fact that the South was unreservedly reinstated in its old place as an integral part of the Union was amply recognized, and even the political enemies of President Cleveland had not expected less of him. The Senate promptly confirmed the nominations, and the Administration was ready to take up the executive business of the nation.

There was something melodramatic and striking in a duty which awaited the return of the President from the Capitol to the White House, and which stood mournfully by while he made out the nominations of his Cabinet officers. The soldier who had earned and worn the highest military fame and rank ever accorded to an American citizen, and who had twice been President of the United States, now in his old age, poor and in debt, was toiling heroically, between the recurring spasms of a surely fatal malady, that he might earn bread for his family. The last act of the Congress which came to a final adjournment at noon of March 4th, 1884, had been to pass a bill placing General Ulysses S. Grant upon the retired list of the army, and the last official act of President Arthur had been the signature of that bill. The War Office made out the commission at once, and it was the first parchment signed by Grover Cleveland as President of the United States.

If the country contains a citizen, otherwise of sound mind but not in favor of the tenure of public offices required by Civil Service Reform and its advocates, there is a possible operation by means of which he might be thoroughly converted to the doctrines in that relation laid down by President Cleveland in his inaugural address and elsewhere. Such an unbeliever might, for experiment, be made President of the United States, with the old office-seeking floodgates thrown wide open. That was first done at the accession of Andrew Jackson, and not even his famous Creek Indian campaign offered a more severe test of his " hickory" toughness of fibre than did the manner in which he endured the assaults of the swarm which poured in upon him.   One Whig statesman asserted that " they came like the Goths and Vandals upon old Rome."   Nothing like it occurred again, of course, until another change in party supremacy ; but there was something more than mere bitterness in the assertion made concerning President Harrison, that " the office seekers worried him into his grave in just four weeks' time."   It was much to the credit of President Tyler that the process of removals and appointments terminated shortly after the executive authority passed to him.

There was another rush of all hungry Whig politicians to Washington when General Taylor was inaugurated, and once more it was asserted that the hearing and decision of their multitudinous claims had much to do with the rapid exhaustion of his vitality.   There were many reasons why the pressure upon President Pierce was less severe, and the next great and complete change of political party rule was postponed until the inauguration of Abraham Lincoln.   The memories of Jackson's day were dwarfed then, for the office seekers packed the lower floor of the White House all day, and a full battalion of them literally camped in the East Room. Appointments, military and civil, formed no small part continually of the burden under which the iron strength of Mr. Lincoln wore away.   Under his successors the evil could not expand to its widest proportions, because all the offices were already in Republican hands, and at last the growing reform of the civil service gradually closed the gates.   They were not securely shut in the spring of 1884, but President Cleveland was not a very encouraging sort of office giver. He was extremely difficult of approach upon such business, and no pressure could make him promise anything. He assisted greatly in perfecting his own deliverance, and the old-time disgrace was not re-enacted. There were official changes, many, and the Opposition journals made the most of them, charging upon the President personally every defect discovered, through all the vast machinery of the departments, in the practical enforcement of the reform principles to which he had declared his devotion. The fact that they found fault might fairly be confronted with the narrow dimensions of such fault as they were able to find. Neither the law nor the methods of its application were as yet perfect, but there had been a vast and plainly manifest improvement.

The old, hard-toiling habits of the Executive Chamber in the State Capitol at Albany were at first transferred, almost in a minute repetition, to the offices of the Executive Mansion at Washington. President Cleveland set himself at work upon a patient and careful study of all the varied features of the vast responsibility placed upon him. "The papers in the case," as prepared for his examination by the heads of departments and their trained subordinates, were all in excellent order and well condensed, or even his habitual diligence would have been insufficient for the task. He had been a working Governor and he now became a working President. Even the legislative branch of the Government was yet to discover how faithfully, during the remaining months of 1885, he prepared himself for dealing intelligently and promptly with the subjects which Congress was afterward likely to put before him. An examination of his first Annual Message, December, 1885, reveals to any practised eye the fact that it grew, paragraph by paragraph, as one after another he reached and grappled with the long list of subjects embraced by it.

While the President went forward steadily with his work, however, a large class of his fellow citizens awoke from a previous misconception of the political situation. The year 1884 had been a time of unusual business depression, and this had been rightly enough connected, in the minds of most men, with the current political canvass and its uncertainties. Of those who suffered from the depression, some had voted one way and some another, in a sort of blind superstition that the election of Mr. Blaine on the one hand, or of Mr. Cleveland on the other, would increase the general volume of business transactions, raise the prices of everything sold, lower the prices of everything bought, make wages higher, rents lower, and bring about good times generally. Mr. Cleveland was elected and inaugurated, and the country was prospering fairly well, but as yet nobody could see that he had done a solitary thing except to mind his business as President. Business and pleasure, toil and rest, night and day, jogged on as before, and the whole land was at peace, and Grover Cleveland was not so much as heard from. There was a universal air of stability returning, instead of the long turmoil of the campaign, and the class of men referred to failed to see that in this fact was brilliantly manifested the genuine conservatism of Republican institutions. Perhaps some of them did begin to grasp the situation, for one intelligent voter is reported as saying : " Never mind, Bill, my boy ; he's nothing but a President, after all, and he can't do much. Just you wait till Congress meets."

One important change took place just before the arrival of that event, for Vice-President Thomas A. Hendricks died, November 25th, 1885. He was a veteran statesman and legislator, an old-time leader of the Democratic Party, and his loss at this juncture left a peculiar condition of affairs. The Senate of the United States was Republican, and its president *pro tempore* was John Sherman, of Ohio, who now became, *ex officio*, Vice-President. He would become President in case of the death of Grover Cleveland, and so the will of the people, declared at the polls in 1884, would be defeated. Men who looked at the robust form of Mr. Cleveland, or grasped his firm, vigorous hand, felt a serene confidence that he would live at least four years more, but the position held by Mr. Sherman had its possibilities, and it emphasized the fact that the old Republican Party had not been altogether driven from power. It still controlled the Senate, and could muster pretty safe majorities in no less than twenty of the States of the Union, with what its captains significantly described as a " good fighting chance" in several more. Never before in the history of the country had two great parties faced each other in precisely such a manner, and there had never before been so very little danger that either would attempt any rash experiments in legislation.   The President's own position called for the wary exercise of the most unwavering prudence, and for the repression of any ambitious impulse which might arise to impress his own will too obviously upon the course of Congressional action.

His first Annual Message, waited for so long and with so deep a public interest, was sent to the Capitol upon December 8th, 1885.   It opened with a brief tribute to the memory of Vice-President Hendricks, and, nearly at its close, the following recommendation was offered :

" The present condition of the law relating to the succession to the Presidency in the event of the death, disability, or removal of both the President and Vice-President is such as to require immediate amendment.   This subject has repeatedly been considered by Congress, but no result has been reached.   The recent lamentable death of the Vice-President, and vacancies at the same time in all other offices the incumbents of which might immediately exercise the functions of the Presidential office, has caused public anxiety, and a just demand that a recurrence of such a condition of affairs should not be permitted."

Proper legal provision was made, and the question of the Presidential succession was removed.

In the second paragraph of the Message the President definitely withdrew from the mistaken idea entertained by too many of his fellow citizens with reference to his part and responsibility in the management of their affairs.   It was an expression of the notable fact that little material for a biographer is offered by the official years in the life of any President of the United States. His individuality has been sometimes almost lost from sight in the vast complication of duties and of consequent actions, in which his share cannot be distinguished from that of men in other departments of the public service. Generals in the field, orators before the people, and leaders in Congress, have seemed to exercise more important functions than those of the national Executive. It has not always been a false appearance. President Cleveland's definition of his position, with reference to the record about to be made, was as follows :

" The Constitution which requires those chosen to legislate for the people to annually meet in the discharge of their solemn trust, also requires the President to give to Congress information of the state of the Union, and recommend to their consideration such measures as he shall deem necessary and expedient. At the threshold of a compliance with these constitutional directions, it is well. for us to bear in mind that our usefulness to the people's interests will be promoted by a constant appreciation of the scope and character of our respective duties as they relate to Federal legislation. While the Executive may recommend such measures as he shall deem expedient, the responsibility for legislative action must and should rest upon those selected by the people to make their laws."

Somewhat more than one fourth part of the long and closely condensed document was devoted to foreign affairs. The relations of the United States with other nations were uniformly friendly and for the greater part entirely satisfactory. Probably the greater public interest was attracted by his manner of dealing with interoceanic canals, involving the Monroe doctrine, and with Chinese diplomatic relations, involving the threatened if not growing evil of Chinese immigration.

The heaped condition of the National Treasury, with its continuing accumulation of useless silver dollars, was depicted in figures with which all men were familiar, but with which no Congressional majority had yet found courage and wisdom to deal. Enormous imports and exports, unmeasured internal trade, and almost measureless production and consumption, in what has become the richest country on the earth, have made even the huge volume of the national debt and the swollen millions of the revenue seem of less importance than formerly. The public mind is hardly agitated over an item of a hundred millions or so, equal to the entire private fortune of either of several of its richest men. There was much, however, of the shrewdness of the " counsel for the people" in the manner in which the leading question resultant from the figures was handled :

" The fact that our revenues are in excess of the actual needs of an economical administration of the Government, justifies a reduction in the amount exacted from the people for its support. Our Government is but the means established by the will of a free people, by which certain principles are applied which they have adopted for their benefit and protection ; and it is never better administered and its true spirit is never better observed than when the people's taxation for its support is scrupulously limited to the actual necessity of expenditure, and distributed according to a just and equitable plan.

" The proposition with which we have to deal is the reduction of the revenue received by the Government, and indirectly paid by the people from custom duties. The question of free trade is not involved, nor is there now any occasion for the general discussion of the wisdom or expediency of a protective system.

" Justice and fairness dictate that in any modification of our present laws relating to revenue, the industries and interests which have been encouraged by such laws, and in which our citizens

have large investments, should not be ruthlessly injured or destroyed. We should also deal with the subject in such manner as
to protect the interests of American labor, which is the capital of
our workingmen ; its stability and proper remuneration furnish
the most justifiable pretext for a protective policy.

" Within these limitations a certain reduction should be made in
our customs revenue. The amount of such reduction having been
determined, the inquiry follows, Where can it best be remitted,
and what articles can best be released from duty, in the interest of
our citizens ?

" I think the reduction should be made in the revenue derived
from a tax upon the imported necessaries of life. We thus directly
lessen the cost of living in every family of the land, and release to
the people in every humble home a larger measure of the rewards
of frugal industry."

The silver coinage question was examined at great
length and in a manner which met the entire approval of the best financiers of all parties.

Army and navy matters, the affairs of the national
police, were presented in a way which proved that
they had been in no manner neglected, the related
subject of pensions receiving caustic references which
were a sure promise of veto messages yet to come.
The army required legislation as to minor details,
but previous utterances of the President, while yet
only Governor of New York, had shown that he was
even angrily aroused concerning the condition of
the navy, as well as of American commercial shipping interests generally. Whether as to ships of
war or ships of peace, the Stars and Stripes had been
all but forgotten upon the high seas. The message
lost its dry and business-like tone at this place, and
acquired a wholesome ring, as it declared :

" All must admit the importance of an effective navy to a nation
like ours, having such an extended sea coast to protect. And yet

we have not a single vessel of war that could keep the seas against
a first-class vessel of any important power. Such a condition
ought not longer to continue. The nation that cannot resist ag-
gression is constantly exposed to it. Its foreign policy is of necessity weak, and its negotiations are conducted with disadvantage,
because it is not in condition to enforce the terms dictated by its
sense of right and justice.

" Inspired, as I am, by the hope, shared by all patriotic citizens,
that the day is not very far distant when our navy will be such as
befits our standing among the nations of the earth, and rejoiced at
every step that leads in the direction of such a consummation, I
deem it my duty to especially direct the attention of Congress to
the close of the report of the Secretary of the Navy, in which the
humiliating weakness of the present organization of his department is exhibited, and the startling abuses and waste of its present
methods are exposed. The conviction is forced upon us with the
certainty of mathematical demonstration, that before we proceed
further in the restoration of a navy we need a thoroughly reorgan-
ized Navy Department. The fact that within seventeen years
more than seventy-five millions of dollars have been spent in the
construction, repair, equipment, and armament of vessels, and the
further fact that, instead of an effective and creditable fleet, we
have only the discontent and apprehension of a nation undefended
by war vessels, added to the disclosures now made, do not permit
us to doubt that every attempt to revive our navy has thus far, for
the most part, been misdirected, and all our efforts in that direction
have been little better than blind gropings, and expensive, aimless
follies.

" Unquestionably if we are content with the maintenance of a
Navy Department simply as a shabby ornament to the Government, a constant watchfulness may prevent some of the scandal
and abuse which have found their way into our present organization, and its incurable waste may be reduced to the minimum.
But if we desire to build ships for present usefulness instead of
naval reminders of the days that are past, we must have a department organized for the work, supplied with all the talent and ingenuity our country affords, prepared to take advantage of the
experience of other nations, systematized so that all effort shall
unite and lead in one direction, and fully imbued with the conviction that war vessels, though new, are useless unless they combine

all that the ingenuity of man has up to this day brought forth relating to their construction.

"I earnestly commend the portion of the Secretary's report devoted to this subject to the attention of Congress, in the hope that
his suggestions touching the reorganization of his department may
be adopted as the first step toward the reconstruction of our navy."

The Republican Opposition was afterward enabled
to point some pretty sharp arrows with its criticisms
upon the administrative efforts made in the direction
indicated, and the reform in the navy of the United
States was of slow advancement, in spite of the official zeal with which it was undertaken.   The zeal
was an excellent thing, nevertheless, and the efforts
were by no means unfruitful.   The obstacles in the
way were largely such as would have been swept out
of existence by the sound of a hostile gun in American waters, and it may be that there is no other
sufficient stimulus to the national pride.   The people seem to be indifferent to the mere cash losses
consequent upon leaving the ocean carrying trade,
with all its shipbuilding, in the hands of other nations.

The Post Office Department and the National
Judiciary offered each important subjects for legislation.   When the Department of the Interior was
reached, there was again evidence that something
more than a sense of official duty had been at work.

"The most intricate and difficult subject in charge of this department is the treatment and management of the Indians.   I am
satisfied that some progress may be noted in their condition as a
result of a prudent administration of the present laws and regulations for their control.

"But it is submitted that there is lack of a fixed purpose or policy on this subject, which should be supplied. It is useless to dilate upon the wrongs of the Indians, and as useless to indulge in the heartless belief that because their wrongs are revenged in their own atrocious manner, therefore they should be exterminated.

" They are within the care of our Government, and their rights are, or should be, protected from invasion by the most solemn obligations. They are properly enough called the wards of the Government ; and it should be borne in mind that this guardian- ship involves, on our part, efforts for the improvement of their condition and the enforcement of their rights. There seems to be general concurrence in the proposition that the ultimate object of their treatment should be their civilization and citizenship. Fitted by these to keep pace in the march of progress with the advanced civilization about them, they will readily assimilate with the mass of our population, assuming the responsibilities and receiving the protection incident to this condition.

" The difficulty appears to be in the selection of the means to be at present employed toward the attainment of this result.

" Our Indian population, exclusive of those in Alaska, is reported as numbering two hundred and sixty thousand, nearly all being located on lands set apart for their use and occupation, aggregat- ing over one hundred and thirty-four millions of acres. These lands are included in the boundaries of one hundred and seventy-one reservations of different dimensions, scattered in twenty-one States and Territories, presenting great variations in climate and in the kind and quality of their soils. Among the Indians upon these several reservations there exist the most marked differences in natural traits and disposition and in their progress toward civiliza- tion. While some are lazy, vicious, and stupid, others are indus- trious, peaceful, and intelligent ; while a portion of them are self- supporting and independent, and have so far advanced in civiliza- tion that they make their own laws, administered through officers of their own choice, and educate their children in schools of their own establishment and maintenance, others still retain, in squalor and dependence, almost the savagery of their natural state.

" In dealing with this question, the desires manifested by the Indians should not be ignored. Here, again, we find a great diversity. With some the tribal relation is cherished with the utmost tenacity, while its hold upon others is considerably re- laxed ; the love of home is strong with all, and yet there are those

whose attachment to a particular locality is by no means unyield-
ing ; the ownership of their lands in severalty is much desired by
some, while by others, and sometimes among the most civilized,
such a distribution would be bitterly opposed.

" The variation of their wants, growing out of and connected
with the character of their several locations, should be regarded.
Some are upon reservations most fit for grazing, but without flocks
or herds ; and some, on arable land, have no agricultural imple-
ments ; while some of the reservations are double the size necessary to maintain the number of Indians now upon them, in a few
cases, perhaps, they should be enlarged.

" Add to all this the difference in the administration of the
agencies. While the same duties are devolved upon all, the disposition of the agents, and the manner of their contact with the Indians, have much to do with their condition and welfare. The agent
who perfunctorily performs his duty and slothfully neglects all
opportunity to advance their moral and physical improvement, and
fails to inspire them with a desire for better things, will accomplish
nothing in the direction of their civilization ; while he who feels
the burden of an important trust, and has an interest in his work,
will, by consistent example, firm yet considerate treatment, and
well-directed aid and encouragement, constantly lead those under
his charge toward the light of their enfranchisement.

" The history of all the progress which has been made in the
civilization of the Indian, I think will disclose the fact that the beginning has been religious teaching, followed by or accompanying
secular education. While the self-sacrificing and pious men and
women who have aided in this good work by their independent
endeavor have for their reward the beneficent results of their labor
and the consciousness of Christian duty well performed, their valuable services should be fully acknowleged by all who, under the
law, are charged with the control and management of our Indian
wards."

General and specific information and recommendations were added, and the President had evidently
relieved his conscience concerning his duty to the
red men.

The condition and management of the public lands,

the railway grants of them, the frauds and extravagances of the past and the prudences demanded in
the present were duly set forth, but the Message did
not again arise above the dry level of a legal argument until it reached the besmirched boundaries of
the hapless Territory of Utah. After saying that
during the later history of that region the laws of
the United States had been measurably better enforced than formerly, the Message went on :

" The Utah Commissioners express the opinion, based upon
such information as they are able to obtain, that but few polygamous marriages have taken place in the Territory during the last
year. They further report that while there cannot be found upon
the registration lists of voters the name of a man actually guilty of
polygamy, and while none of that class are holding office, yet at
the last election in the Territory all the officers elected, except in
one county, were men who, though not actually living in the practice of polygamy, subscribe to the doctrine of polygamous marriages as a divine revelation and a law unto all, higher and more
binding upon the conscience than any human law, local or national. Thus is the strange spectacle presented of a community
protected by a republican form of government, to which they owe
allegiance, sustaining by their suffrages a principle and a belief
which set at naught that obligation of absolute obedience to the
law of the land, which lies at the foundation of republican institutions.

" The strength, the perpetuity, and the destiny of the nation
rest upon our homes, established by the law of God, guarded by
parental care, regulated by parental authority, and sanctified by
parental love.

" These are not the homes of polygamy.

" The mothers of our land, who rule the nation as they mould
the characters and guide the actions of their sons, live according to
God's holy ordinances, and each, secure and happy in the exclusive love of the father of her children, sheds the warm light of true
womanhood, unperverted and unpolluted, upon all within her pure
and wholesome family circle.

" These are not the cheerless, crushed, and unwomanly mothers of polygamy.

" The fathers of our families are the best citizens of the Republic. Wife and children are the sources of patriotism, and conjugal and parental affection beget devotion to the country. The man who, undefiled with plural marriage, is surrounded in his single home with his wife and children, has a stake in the country which inspires him with respect for its laws and courage for its defence.

" These are not the fathers of polygamous families.

" There is no feature of this practice, or the system which sanctions it, which is not opposed to all that is of value in our institutions.

" There should be no relaxation in the firm but just execution of the law now in operation, and I should be glad to approve such further discreet legislation as will rid the country of this blot upon its fair fame.

" Since the people upholding polygamy in our Territories are re-enforced by immigration from other lands, I recommend that a law be passed to prevent the importation of Mormons into the country."

The paragraphs with reference to the subject of Civil Service Reform added nothing of special importance to the President's previous utterances in the same relation, but were a very fair statement of the measurable progress already made.

The needs of the Congressional library were presented, and the affairs of the District of Columbia were not forgotten. The Message concluded as follows :

" In conclusion, I commend to the wise care and thoughtful attention of Congress the needs, the welfare, and the aspirations of an intelligent and generous nation. To subordinate these to the narrow advantages of partisanship or the accomplishment of selfish aims is to violate the people's trust and betray the people's interests. But an individual sense of responsibility on the part of each of us, and a stern determination to perform our duty well, must give us place among those who have added in their day and generation to the glory and prosperity of our beloved land."

A more thoroughly business-like, conservative, and unsensational document had never been transmitted to Congress by a President of the United States. If Grover Cleveland had been in office during nine years, instead of only during nine months, there could not have been a more utter absence of any sense of newness or awkwardness. He seemed to feel entirely at home, and to take up the affairs of the nation, with reference to other nations, even, very much as he had taken up the affairs of the city of Buffalo. Unseen at first, but more keenly perceived and openly acknowledged afterward, was this peculiar element of the strength of his individual character and position. He all but compelled men to take him as a matter of course, unless their partisan relations and purposes brought them into opposition. It was an equally inevitable result that all opposition should find its place unreservedly and unalterably, time being given for its development and adjustment. Nothing but the occurrence of some great and unexpected occasion could arouse any fervor of mere enthusiasm for or against such an embodiment of fixed and unimpassioned purposes.

The Message was sifted carefully by the Opposition press, but even the Republican journals praised it, and Congress, in both Houses, settled down to its huge volume of legislative work.

CHAPTER XVIII.

The Political Situation—The Chinese Question—The Labor Commission—The Butter Bill—The Social Season—A Wedding at the White House—The Home at Oak View.

NEITHER the details of Congressional legislation nor the correspondent action of the President have any place in a biography, except in so far as they offer some illustration of individual character. The first Message of President Cleveland sufficiently set forth the political fact that he had no great revolution to propose or to lead. The United States did not offer any field for startling innovations, and Mr. Cleveland was not an inventive genius of startling statesmanship. As between the two great political parties, the margin of numerical strength was too narrow to encourage hysterical experiments. Outside of them was a large popular vote, controllable by neither, a sort of unknown sea in which all sorts of social theorists were cruising around upon more or less adventurous voyages of discovery. If anything worth having should be found by these explorers, it would surely be seized and occupied by some responsible power, just as all the geographical western world had been, or just as the work of the old abolition extremists had been absorbed by the Republican Party and by the course of events.

It soon became evident that the President was as yet making no special effort to impress himself upon current legislation.   He gave, however, a very careful and toilsome attention to his constitutional duty of examining before signature whatever bills were sent to him.

No other class of legislative work presented him with such a continuous and varied series of opportunities for expressing his opinion, as did the long procession of enactments conferring or increasing pensions.   Veto followed veto, each accompanied by its own compact explanation, and each explanation sufficient to satisfy any Congressman that he should not have voted for that particular draft upon the Treasury.   Some of the vetoes, in all their seriousness, had a sound of fun in them, so grotesquely improper or so manifestly fraudulent were the pensions granted.   In due course of time the number of these vetoes grew to what the grocers call a gross, with a baker's dozen or so to spare, and it may well be that the list could have been honestly increased.

If there had been some critics who were disposed to attribute the President's repeated utterances upon the Chinese question to mere race prejudice, or to a demagoguish fishing for popularity among the recently imported part of our voting population, he removed that false impression by the matter and manner of a special message, March 2d, 1886.   This message was accompanied by full copies of diplomatic correspondence between the United States and China, and with tabulated statements of the number, nature, and pecuniary amount of claims and counter-claims existing between the two countries. It appeared that Americans in China had fared badly enough, and that Chinese in America had been generally well treated, except in specified cases as little within the control of our Government as were the independent acts of Chinese pirates in their own seas. The President quoted liberally from his previous Annual Message, and added, speaking of the most serious cause of Chinese complaint :

"The facts, which so far are not controverted or affected by any exculpatory or mitigating testimony, show the murder of a number of Chinese subjects in September last at Rock Springs, the wounding of many others, and the spoliation of the property of all when the unhappy survivors had been driven from their habitations. There is no allegation that the victims, by any lawless or disorderly act on their part, contributed to bring about a collision. On the contrary, it appears that the law-abiding disposition of these people, who were sojourners in our midst under the sanction of hospitality and express treaty obligations, was made the pretext for the attack upon them. This outrage upon law and treaty engagements was committed by a lawless mob. None of the aggressors, happily for the national good fame, appear by the reports to have been citizens of the United States. They were aliens, engaged in that remote district as mining laborers, who became excited against the Chinese laborers, as it would seem, because of their refusal to join them in a strike to secure higher wages. The oppression of Chinese subjects by their rivals in the competition for labor does not differ in violence and illegality from that applied to other classes of native or alien labor. All are equally under the protection of law, and equally entitled to enjoy the benefits of assured public order.

"Were there no treaty in existence referring to the rights of Chinese subjects, did they come hither as all other strangers who voluntarily resort to this land of freedom, of self-government, and of laws, here peaceably to win their bread and to live their lives, there can be no question that they would be entitled still to the

same measure of protection from violence and the same free forum
for the redress of their grievances as any other aliens."

With reference to the future politics of the United
States, a much more important, although extremely
conservative message, was sent to Congress upon
April. 22d, 1886. It proposed that the existing Labor Bureau should be increased to a Board of Commissioners, with powers of arbitration, capable of further increase and extension. Among other things,
he said :

" I am satisfied, however, that something may be done under
Federal authority to prevent the disturbances which so often arise
from disputes between employers and the employed, and which at
times seriously threaten the business interests of the country ; and
in my opinion the proper theory upon which to proceed is that of
voluntary arbitration as the means of settling these difficulties.

" But I suggest that, instead of arbitrators chosen in the heat of
conflicting claims, and after each dispute shall arise, for the purpose of determining the same, there be created a Commission of
Labor, consisting of three members, who shall be regular officers
of the Government, charged among other duties with the consideration and settlement, when possible, of all controversies between
labor and capital."

President Cleveland's toilsome experiences as executive editor and State critic for the Albany Legislature were forcibly suggested, August 2d, 1886,
by the message with which he accompanied his
approval of what was called the Butter Bill. It pur-
ported to be " An act defining butter, also imposing
a tax upon and regulating the manufacture, sale,
importation, and exportation of oleomargerine."
There had been fun in Congress over that bill, and
the President was not alone in questioning the constitutionality of some of its provisions. He could

not, as at Albany, have it mended before signing, so he signed it and asked to have it mended afterward.

With the return of Congress for the Winter session of 1885–86, the regular social season of the capital also began, but the story of the bachelor's hall at the Governor's House in Albany was not to be repeated. It was not the first time in American history that the White House had been occupied by a wifeless President. Thomas Jefferson, for instance, had been compelled to appeal to Mrs. Madison and her sister to aid him in dispensing his liberal hospitalities. Andrew Jackson had been provided for by Mr. and Mrs. Donelson. James Buchanan had been entirely satisfied with the social success attained by his dashing niece, Miss Harriet Lane. President Cleveland turned over that entire branch of his executive responsibilities to his sister, Miss Rose Cleveland, and Washington society declared itself satisfied. There were those, indeed, who quoted the remark of Uncle Lewis F. Allen, and declared that "she inherited the brains of the family," but they may have been ultra-protectionists. The season, social and legislative, went on to an end much more smoothly than had been anticipated. The crowds who attended public receptions at the White House came away with almost invariably pleasant reminiscences of their burly, hearty Chief Magistrate. It was exceedingly agreeable to any poor man or woman to be greeted so well, for even Grover Cleveland's enemies were fair enough to confess that he made a point of honor, so to

speak, of his dealings with Abraham Lincoln's
" plain people." Lincoln himself was hardly more
fond of children.

Possibly—for some things are beyond ready reading—Mr. Cleveland's kindly way toward the very
young had something to do with another change
which drew nearer and nearer through all the months
of that Winter and Spring. When, in July, 1875,
his former law partner and intimate personal friend,
Oscar Folsom, of Buffalo, was so suddenly and sadly
removed from the bright career seemingly before
him, he left a widow and a daughter. The latter
was then a school girl of about eleven years of age—
a very pretty, bright, vivacious little lady, and she
grew up with a strong liking for the exceedingly kind
and smiling gentleman who had been so warm a
friend to her father. The family property was also
said to owe much to the intelligent care he had bestowed upon its management, and her mother, Mrs.
Folsom, was upon terms of close intimacy with Mr.
Cleveland's sisters. The bright girlhood expanded
into a brighter womanhood, and nobody knows or
has any business to know when or how one form of
liking ripened into another. At last, however,
everybody did know, or said they knew, that there
would one day be a wedding at the White House,
and that the bride would be Miss Frances Folsom.

Rumor was right for once. There had never been
a wedding in the quaint old dwelling of the Presidents, but at last the day was set for one, and grand
preparations were made by a host of interested people. The newspaper reporters, in particular, worked

hard, and the artists who cut wooden portraits for illustrative purposes.

The wedding took place at the Executive Mansion, June 2d, 1886, with the roses in full bloom, and the occasion passed brilliantly, without one untoward incident. The entire nation joined in hearty expressions of good will, and, for a few days, there seemed to be no party lines in existence. There is a vast deal of genuine, kindly human nature among the American people, and they intensely approve of weddings.

The bridegroom and bride, with a merry party of friends, made a wedding trip to a picturesque summer resort called Deer Park, among the Maryland mountains. For a few days only, however, could the President just then be spared from his pressing official duties, and on June 8th he was once more in Washington. Even in his return, however, he had accomplished an important reform. During an entire generation it had been sufficiently well understood that the White House was imperfectly suited to the uses of a family residence. It had been little more than endurable, and plan after plan had been proposed for the selection of a more retired locality, and the construction of such a dwelling as the good taste and self-respect of a great people might induce them to provide for their chosen Chief Magistrate. Every such suggestion had been choked to death, however, by the more or less malicious employment of the word "palace," and nothing definite had been done. Grover Cleveland was not the man to wait for the action of other people. He looked around Washington while he was getting ready to be married, found a house that suited him, struck a bargain for it, and bought it in May, 1886. "Oak View," as it is called, is a part of the old Greene estate. The house is somewhat old fashioned, but well built, of stone. The ground floor contains reception rooms, dining room, library, kitchen, and so forth, the sleeping rooms being all in the second story. There are about twenty-eight acres of land, of good quality, part under cultivation. The garden and out buildings are good. There are noble oaks and other shade trees, and the view from the commanding ridge upon which the house stands warrants and explains its name. It is a very pleasant place, especially for a summer residence to which a hard-worked President may escape from the mere business office into which the White House was in this manner wisely turned ; but there is no suggestion of a palace—nothing but ordinary common sense reaching out after such every-day comfort as belongs to any citizen. There is a morning and evening drive to and from the White House of about four miles, through Georgetown and along the Tenallytown road. It is a pleasant highway, and even the newspaper reporters have never succeeded in breaking through the guarded retirement provided for the President's family at the Oak View end of the morning and evening drive.

In that first summer of their married life, Mr. and Mrs. Cleveland did not remain long at Oak View. As soon as the business of the nation permitted, on August 16th, they left Washington for the North.

A month was spent among the Adirondacks, where the President could indulge to the uttermost his life-long fondness for fishing and hunting. There were brief visits to other places, with everywhere an enthusiastic heartiness of popular welcome. The greeting given at Harvard University included the honorary degree of Doctor of Laws, conferred with much more zeal and heartiness than had attended the memorable occasion when Andrew Jackson received a similar honor.

The scholarly reasons for its bestowal in the present instance were eloquently expressed by James Russell Lowell.

That was early in November, and shortly afterward the President and his young wife were once more at home in the substantial stone cottage on the Tenallytown road, north of Washington.

CHAPTER XIX.

The New Management of Social Affairs—The Oppo-
sition—The Dependent Pension Bill—The Texas
Aid Bill—Second Annual Message—An Island
Queen—A Centennial Year—Summer Vacation—
Tours West, and South—Annual Message to the
Fiftieth Congress—The Mills Bill.

THE society side of life at the White House,
when the new season opened, was found to have undergone a change. There was something of a change
perceptible also in the manner and methods of the
transaction of executive business. While the public
receptions were more brilliant and enjoyable than
before, it was understood that the President was not
permitted to give quite so many hours of each day to
unremitting toil. His old work-a-day habits were
strong upon him and could not be altogether broken
up, but there was not so much need for hard study.
He had very thoroughly mastered the great case in
his hands, so far as it was in his hands, shrewdly
marking the limits of his possible control and responsibility. There was need for prudence, since
there was no feature of the political situation more
noteworthy than the activity and capacity displayed,
in and out of Congress, by the compact and perfectly organized Republican Opposition. No de-

A RECEPTION AT THE WHITE HOUSE.

fect, real or apparent, in the enforcement of the Civil Service Reform measures ; no error or delay of any sort in the conduct of the executive departments ; no bad generalship on the part of the Democratic majority in Congress ; not even manifestations of the President's well-understood desire to heal any remaining irritation in the Southern section of the country, escaped the most searching analysis and the most caustic commentary. Hardly during the Mexican War, when a Whig Opposition in Congress superintended President Polk's management of armies led by Whig generals, had there been a more incisive treatment of every step taken, or not taken, by the Administration. Long before the close of 1887 it was plainly manifest that both parties were preparing for the Presidential campaign of 1888. The course taken by the Republican leaders and press could have but one result, for it steadily took away from the party in nominal power any supposable right to name its own representative, and the very persistency and steadiness of the President's action from day to day unified and sealed the process.

The stream of pension act vetoes flowed on, in a succession of smaller and larger ripples, until, on February 11th, 1887, all minor messages of this sort were forgotten in the stir occasioned by the President's reasons for returning unsigned what was known as the Dependent Pension Bill. The Message began :

" I herewith return without my approval House bill No. 10,457, entitled ' An act for the relief of dependent parents and honorably

242   GROVER CLEVELAND.

discharged soldiers and sailors who are now disabled and dependent upon their own labor for support.'

" This is the first general bill that has been sanctioned by the
Congress since the close of the late Civil War, permitting a pension
to the soldiers and sailors who served in that war upon the ground
of service and present disability alone, and in the entire absence of
any injuries received by the casualties or incidents of such service."

The history of United States pension legislation
was briefly but pointedly reviewed ; the operative
and legal defects of the bill were set forth at length,
and the Message concluded with a paragraph which
did honor to the President's fidelity to his trust :

" I adhere to the sentiments thus heretofore expressed. But the
evil threatened by this bill is in my opinion such that, charged
with a great responsibility in behalf of the people, I cannot do
otherwise than to bring to the consideration of this measure my
best efforts of thought and judgment, and perform my constitutional duty in relation thereto, regardless of all consequences, except such as appear to me to be related to the best and highest interests of the country."

Perhaps another and equally important declaration
that President Cleveland was as far as ever from any
willingness to sacrifice constitutional law to personal
or party popularity was given February 16th, 1887,
in his veto of the act to enable the Commissioner
of Agriculture to make a special distribution of seeds
in the drought-stricken counties of Texas.   He was
sorry for all who suffered, but he said :

" I can find no warrant for such an appropriation in the Constitution ; and I do not believe that the power and duty of the General Government ought to be extended to the relief of individual
suffering which is in no manner properly related to the public service or benefit. A prevalent tendency to disregard the limited
mission of this power and duty should, I think, be steadfastly
resisted, to the end that the lesson should be constantly enforced

that though the people support the Government, the Government should not support the people."

It was an utter repudiation of the paternal idea of human government, which from time to time comes creeping in to effect some kind of administrative compromise with the opposite idea expressed by American institutions.

The Message sent by the President to Congress at the opening of the second session of the Forty-ninth Congress, December 6th, 1886, was very full and elaborate, but it was strictly supplementary to his first Annual Message to the same body in 1885. Its individual features, however interesting, do not require quotation. As a whole, however, it suggested to those who read it a second time the truth that there had somehow been an advance, a growth, during the twelve months, and that the writer of this Message had obtained a better grasp of the subjects with which he was dealing.

Among the minor vetoes which from time to time came drifting in upon the table of either House of Congress, were a number preventing the establishment, here and there, of ports of entry, and the erection of public buildings which did not, in the President's view of requisite economies, appear to be warranted by any business requirement. Perhaps one way of disposing of a small and troublesome local demand was to pass its bill and send it to the White House for execution by the former Sheriff of Erie County.

Among the varied foreign affairs in which President Cleveland had manifested especial interest from the beginning were the relations of the United States to Hawaii. They were closely connected with the great subject of American commerce, and its future prosperity upon the Pacific Ocean. He had requested the especial attention of Congress to the existing state and apparent promise of this important interest.

In May, 1887, Queen Kapiolani, of Hawaii, visited the United States, and Mrs. Cleveland was the first lady of the White House to receive there, as a guest, an actual crowned ruler of any country, large or small. She afterward returned the call of the Hawaiian queen at her hotel, and paid every needed attention to the dusky representative of the ancient race of islanders. Miss Harriet Lane, in her day, had received the Prince of Wales, but he had been only a very young Englishman, sent out by his mother to see the world, and had not been a crowned head at all.

The Summer and Autumn of 1887 were employed largely in what bore a semblance of a prolonged vacation from the toils of office, but it had been clearly perceived by other Presidents that a public use might be served in a laborious tour of the country. Mr. Cleveland himself had seen but little of it outside of the State of New York prior to the year 1887.

It was a year of general prosperity, and there were several marks by which it became notable in the chronology of the United States, as well as in the life of Grover Cleveland.

In May the President discharged acceptably the duties assigned to him at the unveiling of the memorial statue of President Garfield, at Washington. Later still there was international importance in his presence and participation in the grand ceremonial attending the unveiling of the Bartholdi statue of Liberty Enlightening the World, in New York Harbor. July found him at the old homestead in Holland Patent, now, since his mother's death, the home of his sister Rose. He had visited it when mayor and when governor. The old doorway through which he went out to seek his fortune, with nothing in his pocket but a borrowed twenty-five dollars and his mother's Bible, had thickly clustering memories around it for the mind and heart of the busy statesman and party leader. Clinton and other places known to his earlier days were also visited, and then there were weeks of rest at Marion, on the Massachusetts sea coast.

The year 1887 was the centennial year of the Constitution of the United States, and the citizens of Philadelphia invited all Americans to join with them in a suitable commemoration of that marvellous triumph of far-seeing statesmanship. The middle of September, therefore, found the President in that city. The 16th, upon which, as the first citizen of the Republic, he reviewed the great procession gathered in honor of national law and liberty, was a sort of climax in the remarkable career of Grover Cleveland. There was something noteworthy by all in the fact that, at the end of a hundred years, the guarded working of the Constitution found all the executive power which it conferred and limited entrusted by the people to the son of a village pas-

tor.   His immediate predecessor, Arthur, had been
also the son of a rural minister, and just before him
had been Garfield, himself a preacher and teacher.
Not from the great wealth and the influential family connections had the searching eyes of parties and
popular majorities picked out their ruling men.

President Cleveland spent a few days in Washington after the centennial celebration, but on September
tember 30th he began another tour westward, vis-
iting Indianapolis, St. Louis, Chicago, Milwaukee,
Madison, St. Paul, Minneapolis, Omaha, Kansas
City, Memphis, Nashville, Montgomery in Alabama,
Atlanta, and intermediate places, returning to Washington about the middle of October.   The people
of many States had seen and heard the President
whom they had elected, and everywhere they had
welcomed him with tumultuous cordiality.   His tour
had been in some respects much more like that of
Andrew Jackson than like the almost uncriticised
pilgrimage of James Monroe, for the Opposition
press was busy all the while, and not altogether
good naturedly.   During the following Winter, in
February and March, 1888, a Southern trip was
made as far as Jacksonville, Fla., and return, with
everywhere enthusiastic receptions.

The Fiftieth Congress of the United States assembled and organized for business in the first week
of December, 1887, and notified the President that
it was ready to receive any communication which
he might deem it his duty to make.   His Message,
sent accordingly to the Senate and House of Representatives, bore date December 6th, and might al-

most equally well have been described as a message
to the Democratic and Republican parties, outlining
to both of them the political battlefield selected by
Field Marshal Grover Cleveland for the great Presidential battle of 1888. There was hardly any resemblance between this Annual Message and those
which had been sent to the Forty-ninth Congress
from the same hand, and there were not lacking a
score or so of sharp-tongued Republican orators who
expressed what they called their pleasure at the
manner in which the President was calling his Democratic majority to account for not having done its
duty. Some of them even went farther than that,
but they were wrong, for the President was thoroughly in earnest. If his own party had indeed
been derelict, he was the last man to hesitate in
any utterance calculated to bring it up to the
line.

The entire mass of miscellaneous public business,
at home and abroad, was put out of sight, and the
Message dealt with one subject only. That it did
so was a master stroke of political wisdom, and in
the manner of the act there came out prominently the
individual characteristics which account for every step
of the swift successes thus far obtained by Grover
Cleveland. He appeared as the chosen and official
counsel and advocate of the people, for the removal
of an evil which he proceeded to define. To do this
he was fully entitled, under the Constitution, and
his position was to this extent unassailable. A
wrong state of things existed, as all men knew, and
he described it forcibly.

" You are confronted at the threshold of your legislative duties with a condition of the national finances which imperatively demands immediate and careful consideration.

" The amount of money annually exacted, through the operation of present laws, from the industries and necessities of the people, largely exceeds the sum necessary to meet the expenses of the Government.

" When we consider that the theory of our institutions guarantees to every citizen the full enjoyment of all the fruits of his industry and enterprise, with only such deduction as may be his share toward the careful and economical maintenance of the Government which protects him, it is plain that the exaction of more than this is indefensible extortion, and a culpable betrayal of American fairness and justice. This wrong inflicted upon those who bear the burden of national taxation, like other wrongs, multiplies a brood of evil consequences. The public treasury, which should only exist as a conduit conveying the people's tribute to its legitimate objects of expenditure, becomes a hoarding place for money needlessly withdrawn from trade and the people's use, thus crippling our national energies, suspending our country's development, preventing investment in productive enterprise, threatening financial disturbance, and inviting schemes of public plunder."

The Message proceeded to give Treasury facts and figures, stating that no sufficient measures of relief from current and threatening evils were within the scope of any lawful authority possessed by the Executive. The defects of several proposed or supposable measures were also presented, and this part of the important paper concluded as follows :

" I have deemed it my duty to thus bring to the knowledge of my countrymen, as well as to the attention of their representatives charged with the responsibility of legislative relief, the gravity of our financial situation. The failure of the Congress heretofore to provide against the dangers which it was quite evident the very nature of the difficulty must necessarily produce, caused a condition of financial distress and apprehension since your last adjournment, which taxed to the utmost all the authority and expedients within executive control ; and these appear now to be exhausted. If disaster results from the continued inaction of Congress, the responsibility must rest where it belongs."

" The failure of the Congress," composed as it was of intelligent and patriotic men, had not been caused by any disposition to neglect its duties. One large part of its membership did not believe a Treasury surplus to be the great evil which it appeared to the President and to some other men. Another considerable cohort averred that the present system, nominally taxing four thousand articles of import and a few luxuries raised and manufactured at home, as whiskey and tobacco, did not really tax anybody in a perceptible or burdensome manner. Yet another argued that any known evil now existing was of minor importance compared to such as might be created by " tinkering the tariff." There were those who wanted free trade or nothing. There were quite a number who did not at all know what they wanted, and up to that hour there had been no leader capable of rallying and cementing a majority for a bold and determined forward movement. Precisely the required leader upon one side had now come, having a ready-made majority, and he had spoken, and it might be of less or more importance that in concentrating his own forces he also indicated to the Opposition its own inevitable rallying point. His attempt to discuss the questions of the tariff and the revenue without relation to those of protection and free trade was, of course, a failure. If he indeed succeeded in separating them in his own mind, he could not separate them in the minds of

other men.   In paragraph after paragraph he en-
ergetically fought over the old fight which has been
from the beginning.   He said, for instance :

" But our present tariff laws, the vicious, inequitable, and illogi-
cal source of unnecessary taxation, ought to be at once revised and
amended.   These laws, as their primary and plain effect, raise the
price to consumers of all articles imported and subject to duty, by
precisely the sum paid for such duties.   Thus the amount of the
duty measures the tax paid by those who purchase for use these
imported articles.   Many of these things, however, are raised or
manufactured in our own country, and the duties now levied upon
foreign goods and products are called protection to these home
manufactures, because they render it possible for those of our people who are manufacturers, to make these taxed articles and sell
them for a price equal to that demanded for the imported goods
that have paid customs duty.   So it happens that while comparatively a few use the imported articles, millions of our people, who
never use and never saw any of the foreign products, purchase and
use things of the same kind made in this country, and pay therefor
nearly or quite the same enhanced price which the duty adds to
the imported articles.   Those who buy imports pay the duty
charged thereon into the public treasury, but the great majority of
our citizens, who buy domestic articles of the same class, pay a
sum at least approximately equal to this duty to the home manu-
facturer.   This reference to the operation of our tariff laws is not
made by way of instruction, but in order that we may be constantly reminded of the manner in which they impose a burden
upon those who consume domestic products as well as those who
consume imported articles, and thus create a tax upon all our
people."

After a further and more detailed discussion of
the general subject, he added :

" Our progress toward a wise conclusion will not be improved
by dwelling upon the theories of protection and free trade.   This
savors too much of bandying epithets.   It is a *condition* which
confronts us—not a theory.   Relief from this condition may involve a slight reduction of the advantages which we award our

home productions, but the entire withdrawal of such advantages should not be contemplated. The question of free trade is absolutely irrelevant ; and the persistent claim made in certain quarters that all efforts to relieve the people from unjust and unnecessary taxation are schemes of so-called free traders, is mischievous and far removed from any consideration for the public good.''

Almost in conclusion, rather than at the beginning of the Message, the absence of any presentation of other national affairs was referred to :

"The Constitution provides that the President ' shall, from time to time, give to the Congress information of the state of the Union.' It has been the custom of the Executive, in compliance with this provision, to annually exhibit to the Congress, at the opening of its session, the general condition of the country, and to detail, with some particularity, the operations of the different executive departments. It would be especially agreeable to follow this course at the present time, and to call attention to the valuable accomplishments of these departments during the last fiscal year. But I am so much impressed with the paramount importance of the subject to which this communication has thus far been devoted, that I shall forego the addition of any other topic, and only urge upon your immediate consideration the 'state of the Union' as shown in the present condition of our treasury and our general fiscal situation, upon which every element of our safety and prosperity depends.''

The Message created a profound sensation in Congress, and was read with interest throughout the country. Republican journalists pulled it in pieces, divided it, and were even honestly gratified that it had been written and sent precisely in that manner. Not at first was it so plain as it soon grew to be that President Cleveland had "forced the fighting." Men might disagree with him as to the nature and extent of the evil, and they might altogether dissent from his ideas of a possible remedy, but there the disagreement in a manner ended, for all men of all parties were compelled to perceive that something practical must be done.   Just behind that perception loomed up another, that the President asked the country whether or not it would trust the Democratic Party, led by him, as a potential Committee of Ways and Means in the matter of all financial remedies and their application.

The Democratic majority in the House of Representatives at once accepted the situation, and moved into line under the direction of its leader.   The President's Message was duly referred to the Committee of Ways and Means, and, during the four months following, a bill was constructed in accordance with his recommendations.   The Mills Bill, taking its name from the chairman of the committee, "A bill to reduce taxation and simplify the laws in relation to the collection of the revenue," was but the declared policy of the President, carefully elaborated in the form of practical legislation. Behind it the Democratic Party became a unit, and against it the Republican Opposition arrayed itself with a distinctness which was well expressed in the language of the report presented by the minority of the Committee of Ways and Means at the same time with the report of the majority and the bill itself, as follows :

" The bill is a radical reversal of the tariff policy of the country which for the most part has prevailed since the foundation of the Government, and under which we have made industrial and agricultural progress without a parallel in the world's history.   If enacted into law it will disturb every branch of business, retard manufacturing and agricultural prosperity, and seriously impair our industrial independence. It undertakes to revise our entire revenue system ; substantially all of the tariff schedules are affected ; both classification and rates are changed. Specific duties are in many cases changed to ad valorem, which all experience has shown is productive of frauds and undervaluations. It does not correct the irregularities of the present tariff, it only aggravates them. It introduces uncertainties in interpretation, which will embarrass its administration, promote contention and litigation, and give to the customs officers a latitude of construction which will produce endless controversy and confusion. It is marked with a sectionalism which every patriotic citizen must deplore.''

CHAPTER XX.

An Undisputed Leadership—The Democratic National
Convention—Grover Cleveland Renominated for
President by Acclamation—Allen G. Thurman for
Vice-President—The National Republican Conven-
tion—Harrison and Morton.

THERE had been changes in the Cabinet of President Cleveland, in the Senate, and in the House of
Representatives. Able men of his party were rising
to prominence and almost to fame, and there were
yet remaining many of the old leaders whose names
were part of the political history of the country.
Nevertheless there was hardly a voice of dissent to
the continually reiterated assertion, made by journals of every shade of party affiliation, that his nomination for a second term was inevitable. There had
been no change which removed the political necessity so pointedly presented to the Chicago Democratic National Convention of 1884, while his every
public act since taking the oath of office had added
to the solid strength of his individual position. Not
since the day of Andrew Jackson's second nomination had one American citizen so completely embodied and represented his party. It was a matter
of course that upon him should be concentrated
every possible criticism and assault of the Opposition.

The Mills Tariff Bill, reported in April, was but an explanatory preface of the platform to be adopted by the National Democratic Convention, and this had been summoned to meet in St. Louis on June 5th, 1888.

The intervening weeks passed rapidly, and the delegates came together according to the summons, but only as a species of grand, national ratification meeting. Every State and Territory was represented, and it was not altogether an easy task to bring so enthusiastic an assemblage to order for the formal transaction of its business. All preliminaries were completed by half past ten o'clock of June 6th. After that there were speeches made, resolutions offered, motions by the dozen and amendments by the score, but all these were of small importance. The real business of the day, the usual call of States breaking down—after the voice of New York had been conceded the first utterance and had been heard —consisted of the nomination of Grover Cleveland, by acclamation. There was no useless and tiresome balloting, for there was no possible competition. It was as if the convention of 1884, after an adjournment of four years, had reassembled to congratulate itself upon the wisdom and success of the action which it then had taken. Something to that effect was expressed in the first paragraph of the platform, which also contained a full adoption of the President's Message to the Fiftieth Congress and of the Mills Tariff Bill. It read :

" The Democratic Party of the United States, in national convention assembled, renews the pledge of its fidelity to Democratic faith, and reaffirms the platform adopted by its representatives in the convention of 1884, and endorses the views expressed by President Cleveland in his last Annual Message to Congress as the correct interpretation of that platform upon the question of tariff reduction, and also endorses the effort of our Democratic representatives in Congress to secure a reduction of excessive taxation."

The third section of the platform was as follows :

" The Democratic Party welcomes an exacting scrutiny of the administration of the executive power which four years ago was committed to its trust in the election of Grover Cleveland for President of the United States, and it challenges the most searching inquiry concerning its fidelity and devotion to the pledges which then invited the suffrages of the people. During a most critical period of our financial affairs, resulting from overtaxation, the anomalous condition of our currency and a public debt unmatured, it has, by the adoption of a wise and conservative course, not only averted a disaster, but greatly promoted the prosperity of the people."

Whatever else was added in assertion of legislative attainments or in criticisms of the past and present course of the Republican Party, these two " planks " and the nomination itself constituted the platform upon which the party was prepared to go before the people. Its political history prior to 1884 was well represented by the nomination of the veteran statesman, Allen G. Thurman, of Ohio, for Vice-President. The convention adjourned, having fully and satisfactorily accomplished its duty, but it had not placed any new or unexpected problem before the keen eyes of its watchful antagonist. Every Republican in the land had been prepared for precisely this result, and most of the editorial comments had been carefully written out beforehand. The campaign had been going on for a long time, hardly lacking the element of party platforms and opposing candidates. In fact, so far as current discussion went, that had been sufficiently supplied. The issue in 1888 was so manifestly the same as in 1884, now more clearly presented and personified, that the situation at last created seemed to demand, for its perfection, the renomination of Mr. Blaine. Even after that gentleman had very positively declared his aversion to becoming again a candidate, there were indications of a combative disposition to name him also by acclamation. He was travelling in Europe, however, and every word which came from him assured his party that it must choose some other leader. The Republican National Convention had been summoned to meet at Chicago on June 19th, 1888, as if this also were an adjourned gathering of the delegates of 1884. To a remarkably large number it did consist of the same men, as resolute as ever, and prepared to deal thoughtfully and coolly with the problem which Grover Cleveland had put before them. Indeed, the air of deliberation which prevailed when the convention met and organized for business was in marked contrast with the stormy enthusiasm which had prevailed at St. Louis. The platform adopted was in full accord with the Republican platform of 1884, and with the report of the minority of the Committee of Ways and Means against the Mills Tariff Bill. It discredited every Democratic claim to executive or legislative reform or advancement, and it took an entirely opposition view of President Cleveland's administration.

. The platform having been adopted, the conven-

tion proceeded to ballot for a candidate, and here
again there was the same spirit of thoughtful inquiry.
There were rivalries between old party leaders, as
usual, but there was a noteworthy absence of discord
on the eve of such a struggle as was evidently before them.   Ballot after ballot was taken without
reaching a result, and on Saturday, June 23d, the
convention adjourned until Monday, to give its
members an opportunity to go to meeting and think
the matter over.   On Monday they met again, and
nominated General Benjamin Harrison, of Indiana,
for President, and Levi P. Morton, of New York,
for Vice-President.

One curious uncertainty as yet seemed to hover
over the political battlefield.   When, on June 6th,
Private Secretary Lamont carried to President Cleveland the telegram announcing the result at St. Louis,
it is said that he found him in his library, examining
some text-books designed for use in the schools for
little Indians, upon the Western reservations.   The
President turned for a moment from his collection
of school literature, glanced at the telegram, nodded,
turned back again, and made no sign.   He had not
heard any news truly, and twenty days more went
by without any other American hearing what he proposed doing with reference to the nomination.   All
the while his own friends and most of his enemies
took his acceptance for granted, the latter adding, in
print, italicized quotations of all his public declarations concerning the advisability of limiting United
States Presidents each to a single term in office.
The Republicans, therefore, had nominated Harri-

son and Morton without feeling sure that, after all, the Democratic ticket would be Cleveland and Thurman. They were not longer kept in suspense, for it was almost as if the party in power had waited for their action before putting the finishing touch upon its own. At two o'clock in the afternoon of June 26th, the day following the adjournment of the National Republican Convention, the committee appointed by the National Democratic Convention arrived at the Executive Mansion to present to President Cleveland the formal announcement of his renomination. The committee consisted of Hon. Patrick Collins, of Massachusetts, and delegates from thirty-four States and eight Territories. They were received in the spacious East Room, and were accompanied by a number of gentlemen of distinction and representatives of the press. The President was attended by the members of his Cabinet and by personal friends. He seemed in excellent health and spirits, but wore the air of guarded reserve which had latterly been more and more noticed by all who approached him.

The Chairman of the Committee discharged, as follows, the duty assigned to him :

" SIR : The delegates to the National Democratic Convention, representing every State and Territory of our Union, having assembled in the city of St. Louis on June 5th, for the purpose of nominating candidates for the offices of President and Vice-President of the United States, it has become the honorable and pleasing duty of this committee to formally announce to you that without a ballot you were by acclamation chosen as the standard bearer of the Democratic Party for the Chief Executiveship of this country at the election to be held in November next.

" Great as is such a distinction under any circumstances, it is the more flattering and profound when it is remembered that you have been selected as your own successor to an office the duties of which, always onerous, have been rendered of an extraordinarily sensitive, difficult, and delicate nature, because of a change of political parties and methods after twenty-four years of uninter- rupted domination.   This exaltation is, if possible, added to by the fact that the declaration of principles—based upon your last Annual Message to the Congress of the United States, relative to a tariff reduction and a diminution of the expenses of the Government —throws down the direct and defiant challenge for an exacting scrutiny of the administration of the executive power, which four years ago was committed in its trust to the election of Grover Cleveland, President of the United States, and for the most search- ing inquiry concerning its fidelity and devotion to the pledges which then invited the suffrages of the people.

" An engrossed copy of that platform, adopted without a dis- senting voice, is herewith tendered to you.

" In conveying, sir, to you the responsible trust which has been confided to them, this committee beg, individually and collectively, to express the great pleasure which they have felt at the results attending the National Convention of the Democratic Party, and to offer to you their best wishes for official and personal success and happiness."

Mr. Thomas S. Pettit, one of the secretaries of the convention, stepped forward and delivered the engrossed copy of the platform, and President Cleve- land very deliberately and emphatically responded :

" I cannot but be profoundly impressed when I see about me the messengers of the National Democracy, bearing its summons to duty.   The political party to which I owe allegiance both honors and commands me.   It places in my hand its proud standard, and bids me bear it high at the front, in a battle which it wages, bravely, because conscious of right, confidently, because its trust is in the people, and soberly, because it comprehends the obliga- tions which success imposes.

" The message which you bring awakens within me the liveliest sense of personal gratitude and satisfaction, and the honor which you tender me is in itself so great that there might well be no room for any other sentiment. And yet I cannot rid myself of grave and serious thoughts when I remember that party supremacy is not alone involved in the conflict which presses upon us, but that we struggle to secure and save the cherished institutions, the welfare and happiness of a nation of freemen.

"Familiarity with the great office which I hold has but added to my apprehension of its sacred character and the consecration demanded of him who assumes its immense responsibilities. It is the repository of the people's will and power. Within its vision should be the protection and welfare of the humblest citizen, and with quick ear it should catch from the remotest corner of the land the plea of the people for justice and for right. For the sake of the people, he who holds this office of theirs should resist every encroachment upon its legitimate functions, and for the sake of the integrity and usefulness of the office, it should be kept near to the people and be administered in full sympathy with their wants and needs.

"This occasion reminds me most vividly of the scene when, four years ago, I received a message from my party similar to that which you now deliver. With all that has passed since that day, I can truly say that the feeling of awe with which I heard the summons then is intensified many fold when it is repeated now.

"Four years ago I knew that our Chief Executive office, if not carefully guarded, might drift little by little away from the people to whom it belonged, and become a perversion of all it ought to be ; but I did not know how much its moorings had already been loosened. I knew four years ago how well devised were the principles of true Democracy for the successful operation of a government by the people and for the people ; but I did not know how absolutely necessary their application then was for the restoration to the people of their safety and prosperity. I knew then that abuses and extravagances had crept into the management of public affairs ; but I did not know their numerous forms, nor the tenacity of their grasp. I knew then something of the bitterness of partisan obstruction ; but I did not know how bitter, how reckless, and how shameless it could be. I knew, too, that the American people were patriotic and just, but I did not know how grandly they loved their country, nor how noble and generous they were.

" I shall not dwell upon the acts and the policy of the Administration now drawing to its close. Its record is open to every citizen of the land. And yet I will not be denied the privilege of asserting at this time that in the exercise of the functions of the high
trust confided to me, I have yielded obedience only to the Constitution and the solemn obligation of my oath of office. I have done
those things which, in the light of the understanding God has given
me, seemed most conducive to the welfare of my countrymen and
the promotion of good government. I would not if I could, for
myself nor for you, avoid a single consequence of a fair interpretation of my course.

" It but remains for me to say to you, and through you to the
Democracy of the nation, that I accept the nomination with which
they have honored me, and that I will in due time signify such
acceptance in the usual formal manner."

The political business in their hands being completed, the members of the committee were invited
into the Blue Room, to be received by Mrs. Cleveland, Mrs. Lamont, Mrs. Hoyt, the President's sister, Mrs. William Cleveland, his brother's wife, Mrs.
Endicott, and other ladies.

When the similar committee of the National Democratic Convention of 1884 announced to Governor
Cleveland, in the Executive Mansion at Albany, his
first nomination to the Presidency, his oral response
had been regarded as incomplete. The country
waited with more than a little curiosity for the full
text of his formal letter of acceptance, imagining
that it might contain fresh matter of importance.
It was hardly so in 1888. When the thoughtfully
measured sentences of his reply to the address of
Chairman Collins were printed in the journals of
both parties, and read by all Americans who knew
how to read, there was an universal feeling that lit-

tle or nothing could be added. The parties and their nominations and their record were before the nation for judgment, with a thoroughness of presentation, on either side, which had never been surpassed in the political history of the United States.

The Lives of the Presidents

— OF THE —

UNITED STATES.

A new series of importance, which will be completed in about ten volumes.

By WILLIAM O. STODDARD,

Author of " The Life of Abraham Lincoln," " Dab Kinzer," " Esau Hardery," etc., etc.

Written so as to interest all readers, especially young people, and designed to be strictly accurate and valuable, and to give the results of the latest research.

The intention is to make it the STANDARD series of its class.

Each volume, 12mo, from new type on good paper, with illustrations. Bound uniformly in red cloth, with attractive design in black and gold on covers, showing portraits of Washington, Lincoln, Grant, and Garfield. Each volume, $1.25.

1. George Washington.

2. John Adams and Thomas Jefferson.

3. James Madison, James Monroe, and John Quincy Adams.

4. Andrew Jackson and Martin Van Buren.

*5. Ulysses S. Grant.

*Other volumes in preparation. The *Life of Grant* is published out of its chronological order because of the present great interest in the subject.

Any of these books can be had of your bookseller, or will be sent, postpaid, on receipt of advertised price, by the publisher.

FREDERICK A. STOKES,

SUCCESSOR TO WHITE, STOKES, & ALLEN,

182 FIFTH AVENUE, NEW YORK.

www.ingramcontent.com/pod-product-compliance
Lightning Source LLC
Chambersburg PA
CBHW021054030726
47496CB00006B/1834